KRISTY DIXON

THE
AMETHYST
CROWN

Book Cover by Miblart

Edited by Whitney Morsillo

1st edition 2023

978-1-960841-12-4 ebook

978-1-960841-13-1 paperback

978-1-960841-14-8 hardback

http://www.kristydixonbooks.com

For Glenn and Julie Dixon

Chapter 1

Mucking out stalls in a smelly barn was not a job for a princess. Dree knew this because her mother told her. She didn't specifically say, "Mucking out stalls," but she would have if she ever would have suspected her daughter of doing it someday. Dree pushed a light brown curl behind her ear as she sighed. She wasn't sure she counted as a princess anymore.

She shoveled the last of the stinking mess into a wheelbarrow and leaned her shovel against the stall. It didn't look as good as when the stable hands did it, but what did they expect? She was here working as a maid, not a stable boy. For being majestic creatures, alicorns sure weren't clean. Dree took a handkerchief from her pocket and wiped her brow. Any job that caused a person to sweat was not for a princess. Sweat was unbecoming. More motherly advice.

"I'll get the wheelbarrow for you," Dree's friend Sen said, coming up from behind.

Dree jumped. "Can't you walk louder? You almost gave me a heart attack!"

Sen didn't say anything, he just pushed his black curly bangs from his eyes and grabbed the wheelbarrow. Dree shook her head. She shouldn't snap at him. He was the only friend she had. Without him, she didn't know where she would be. She might have been forced to go home and take the consequences of running away.

"Sorry I snapped," she said, catching up to him.

"No problem."

"I'm just so mad! I made one little mistake, and Vetta has me out with the stable hands."

"And are you so much better than the stable hands?" a deep voice said from behind them. She spun around to see Mace, the *king* of the stable hands, standing there with his arms folded across his chest. His brown hair was damp with sweat and his eyes judged her.

Sen sighed and dropped the handles of the wheelbarrow. Dree frowned. He probably thought he was going to have to defend her again. It seemed to be his calling in life. Sen had built up a lot of muscle working here, but he had nothing on Mace.

"I didn't say I was better," Dree said, crossing her own arms and glaring up at the tall, annoying man. "I'm just saying that it isn't my job, and I shouldn't have to do it."

"You really shouldn't have to do it," he said. "Now, I have to get one of my boys to go in and do it right."

"It looks fine," she argued, wishing she could kick him in the shins with her smelly boot. He had been a pain in her side since she took this job. Nothing she did was right in his eyes. As a maid and a stable master, their paths rarely crossed, but when they did, it was never pleasant.

"Fine, but not good," Mace said.

Dree ground her teeth. "Maybe you should tell Vetta not to send me out to do your job."

Mace nodded. "I will. It would help if you stopped incurring her wrath."

"She searches for reasons to punish me."

Mace rolled his eyes. "Sure she does. Just make sure you aren't in my stables again."

"Come on, Dree," Sen said, motioning forward with his head. He started pushing the wheelbarrow again, and she followed, dragging her feet against the weeds to wipe the muck from her boots.

"Why is he always so mean?" she asked.

"Don't know," Sen said. "You shouldn't argue with him. He enjoys confrontations, so it doesn't get you anywhere."

He was probably right. She couldn't think of one conversation she'd had with the man that hadn't been an argument.

"Sometimes I just want to break down and tell everyone that I'm Princess Lesandri and they have to do what I say. I'd start by having Vetta lick the muck off my boots and then find something equally distasteful for Mace."

"You wouldn't," Sen said, stopping to dump the manure from the wheelbarrow onto the edge of the wheat field. "You're just having a bad day."

Dree studied him. He had changed so much in the two years she had known him. When they first met, she thought of him as short, but now, he towered above her. His dark hair was getting longer and curled a little on top, and he had filled out from all the work he did at this place. Vetta put him in charge of all the fields, even though he was young. In such a high position, he could spend his time bossing people around and not doing any grunt work, but that wasn't his way. He worked harder than anyone here.

"Do you ever wish you had stayed on Earth with your family?" she asked. Sen had taken her to Mexico for a short time to visit his family but neither one of them had felt like they belonged there. Sen was born into this world, but his father was from Earth.

"No. Visiting is fine, but I don't like that place. I feel like Earth is almost the same as Basura except there is no magic, the air is dirty, and they don't have fun things like dragons and alicorns. I guess they have television and cars, but I'd prefer a unicorn. My brothers all like it there, and I'm happy for them."

"You have a nice family. If mine had been like yours, I wouldn't have run off. I don't know why you stay here with me. You could do so much more with your life."

"It's good, honest work. I don't know why you stay here," he said, raising his eyebrow. "Our friends could help you get a job that is much more fulfilling. I know you hate it here."

"*Your* friends," Dree said, gazing over the wheat field. "You and your friends saved the world. Everyone in the world knows your name. All I did was get in the way. You can have any job you want, but you stay here to make sure I don't get into trouble."

"They're your friends too."

"No. They tolerate me. They all thought I was weak and useless. I couldn't even—" She stopped. No use bringing up her former betrothed. Once the law changed and arranged marriages were abolished, he dropped her without a second thought. She knew she wasn't being fair. She had spent years despising the arrangement. Why blame him for feeling the same way?

"There are much better places we could work," Sen said.

"Yes, but my father would never search for me here."

"Do you want to spend the rest of your life working for Vetta? You should think about it." Sen turned and walked away.

The rest of her life. She didn't want to spend the rest of her life here. Dree hated it here. She hated living in a castle as well. Maybe she wasn't a content person. She followed Sen at a distance. Living in a castle wasn't bad, it was just boring. Her parents didn't let her do anything, but not because they cared about her. She was an embarrassment to them. It wasn't easy to be born without magic.

She had magic now, thanks to Sen and his friends. They had changed the world. When an evil organization had tried to take over and caused an entire continent to be blanketed in darkness, Sen and his friends had performed some ancient magic called the silver eclipse. They fixed the weather and unintentionally gave everyone in the world magic.

When Dree was younger, her parents kept her from people so she wouldn't embarrass them. Her older brother was their perfect child. Her parents arranged her marriage with the governor's son of a far off land because they assumed nobody would agree to marriage with a princess that had no magic.

Dree ran away to get away from the marriage and somehow ended up in the company of none other than her future husband and his friends. Now that the law had changed, he was no longer tied to her. It hurt at first when he ditched her so fast, but she had come to terms with it.

Dree sighed. Sen was right. This wasn't the life she wanted. "Sen?" she called, running behind him. "Sendo, wait!" He turned and watched her. "Do you think there is somewhere else we can go where my father won't find me?"

Sen raised an eyebrow, which she took as surprise. Sen wasn't big on showing emotion. She always felt victorious if she got him to smile or frown. "You really want to go somewhere else?"

"I think so. You're right. Going back home would be better than staying here."

"We could leave the Northern Kingdom. Your father is more likely to hunt for you in your own country. Why don't you let me think about it for a few days?"

"Alright."

They walked up to the main house in silence. It was a beautiful two-story home. Dree loved the wrap-around porch. It went around the entire house. She daydreamed about sitting on the porch swing reading. Of course, that wasn't allowed. Before they reached the door, it flew open and Vetta poked her blonde fuzzy head out.

"Dree, inside!" she barked. "I will have a word in the parlor." She smiled and batted her eyes at Sen. "Hello, Sen. The fields are looking marvelous. The king's eye will be on us for sure this year. You're doing a wonderful job."

Dree dropped her boots by the door and brushed past the woman, trying to hide her disgust. Vetta always tried to flirt with Sen and Mace. She wasn't old, but she was too old for them, in her opinion. She had to be pushing thirty-five. As a wealthy widow that was still young, she felt it was her duty to flaunt herself in front of everyone. Dree made her way to the parlor to wait. She could hear Vetta attempting to flirt with Sen. *Good luck with that.* Sen was good at keeping quiet.

The parlor made Dree want to puke. It was covered in more pink lace than was sane. Every pillow had at least three rows of the stuff. Even the sofa had pink lacy ruffles running in rows down the length of it. The curtains matched the sofa, and the carpet was pink. Dree shook her head. Three years ago, she would have loved it. She was a princess, after all, but it was her goal to hate everything Vetta liked.

Vetta floated into the room, her long pink dress dragging behind her. She sat in a ruffly pink chair, and Dree stood in front of her, waiting.

"I hope you've learned your lesson?" Vetta asked, running her hand over the arm of the chair.

"Yes, ma'am," Dree said, looking down at her stockings, trying to appear humble.

"Good. There is another issue we need to address," she said, smiling like a hyena. "I don't like it when you flirt with the workers."

Dree's eyes jerked up in surprise. "I don't flirt with anyone."

"Please, Dree," she sighed dramatically. "I saw you just now from the window, talking to Sen."

"Yes, talking. Sen is my friend."

"I don't like it," she said, still grinning. Her eyes were hard and cold. "Stay away from Mace as well. I don't want you distracting him from his work."

"I stay away from him as much as I can. I can't tolerate that man."

"Please," she laughed. "No woman on Basura would avoid Mace or Sen. Those men are gorgeous and would capture anyone's attention. I realize it's hard for all the maids. You all have to work and live around me, and it must be difficult to live without comparing yourself to me." She fluffed her sleeve.

Vetta was something else. Dree had never compared herself to the woman. Vetta was fancy with her frilly dresses and too much makeup, but she wasn't a natural beauty. Dree knew it was vanity, and she tried to keep it in check, but she knew she was pretty. People had always admired her light brown curls and flawless skin. She wondered if that was the real reason Vetta hated her.

Dree was smart enough to understand that appearances didn't matter. If they did, then Tal might have stayed and honored their marriage arrangement. Plenty of other couples had honored theirs, even with the changing of the law. Why was she even thinking about this? It would have been easier if Tal had been ugly and unpleasant, but he had an adorable crooked grin, and his brown hair was what he called an organized mess. She'd found him attractive against her will. After she got to know him, she came to like him. He thought she was weak and silly. He had been right—she was back then. Two years could change a person, though. Sen taught her how to cook and clean, even how to use a crossbow.

"Are you even listening to me?" Vetta asked, narrowing her eyes. She wasn't, but she nodded. "You may leave," she hissed.

Dree bowed her head as little as she could without incurring Vetta's wrath and left the room. She stormed outside and grabbed her dirty boots, shoving them back on. The sun was going down, but she wasn't tired. She walked down to a small creek that ran through Vetta's property and sat at its edge.

What was she doing? She was wasting her time in this place. If she returned home, she would be of service to her kingdom. At least, she would if her father ever forgave her for running away. She'd left a note, but the gossip in the kingdom said that she had been kidnapped and there was a reward for her return.

Dree wrapped her arms around her legs and pulled her knees into herself. She heard someone come up to the side of her and sit, but she didn't turn. It wasn't unusual for

Sen to find her here. He would sit and let her complain. He rarely responded, but it was nice of him to listen.

"Do you remember when we met?" she asked him, as she stared into the water. "You put me in a headlock and had a knife to my throat."

"I don't remember that at all," said Mace's deep voice. He laughed when Dree jumped to her feet and put her hand to her startled heart. "Who did you think I was?" he asked, running a hand through his dark brown hair.

"What are you doing here?" she demanded, glaring down at him. "I thought you were Sen!"

"Well, that's interesting," he said, throwing a rock into the water. "Sen put a knife to your throat? You have to watch out for the quiet ones."

"What are you doing here?"

"Sen gave me a lecture," Mace admitted. "He told me I better apologize and stop being mean to you."

"And everyone listens to Sen because he was one of the chosen ones."

"Something like that. The members of The Silver Eclipse did a great service to the world. They deserve respect. So, why did he have a knife at your throat?"

She sat back down and threw her own rock. "Probably because I had a crossbow pointed at his friends."

Mace's eyes sparkled. "That would do it."

Dree threw her arms in the air. "I was alone in the forest. I didn't know who to trust."

"Well, that makes sense."

"You've apologized. You may leave now."

He leaned toward her. "I didn't actually apologize. I just said Sen told me to."

Dree rolled her eyes. "Fine. You can still leave."

"I don't mean to be negative all the time," he said, tossing another rock. "I know all the maids fear me."

She held back a rude snort. The maids were not scared of him. Most of them were half in love with him, and Dree couldn't understand it. He was handsome to be sure, but he was rude to everyone who wasn't one of his workers.

"So, why are you so rude?"

"No idea. I just hate it here, I guess."

"Hate it? You get paid more than most people here, and Vetta thinks you're the greatest thing to happen to the place."

"Vetta's a pain in the backside. She thinks everyone should throw themselves at her feet because she's on good terms with the king."

"I doubt the king even knows who she is," Dree said. "He doesn't concern himself with people beneath himself, even if they bring in a nice set of crops every year."

"From what I've heard, King Miadd is a lot better than his father was."

Dree tapped the side of her head. "Not better, smarter."

"What do you mean?"

"King Rihen was a tyrant," she explained. "He over taxed the people until they revolted. My father saw—" Heat crawled up her neck at the slip of tongue. "Um, my father said that King Miadd recognized his father's flaws, so he didn't tax the people the same way. It wasn't that he was better, or more compassionate. The people accepted him because he wasn't as oppressive as the previous king."

"I don't understand kings and their need for power. They could do so much good, and most of them don't."

She glanced sideways at him. "What would you do as king?"

"A lot more than Miadd. I'll be twenty next month. That opens a lot of doors. I plan on traveling to the other continent and trying to start a political life. You can't run for governor until you're thirty, so I have ten years to get ready."

"You want to be a governor?" That was odd. She didn't know this man at all, apparently. "I think you have to be native to the area."

"The governor of Akkron has a member of her council from this continent. Things are changing all the time."

Dree didn't respond to that. She knew Governor Zera personally. She was a good leader and a kind person, and she was doing great things. Great things like abolishing marriage laws...

"I didn't take you as a politician."

"I can make a difference. If I wasn't opposed to King Miadd, I would try to get on his council," he said, making a small ball of light appear in his hand. He tossed it from one hand to the other.

Dree stood. Even though she could do magic now, she usually didn't, and she didn't like when other people did, either. She guessed she was still bitter about how people treated her when they knew she couldn't do it. She did occasionally make an orb of light, but that was because she was scared of the dark. It was the only magic she let Sen teach her.

"I should go. Vetta told me not to talk to you."

He raised his brow. "Why?"

Dree grinned mischievously. "I suppose it's because she wants all of your attention."

He let out a long breath. "I need to get out of here." He let his light go out and pushed his shaggy brown hair out of his eyes. Dree wondered if long bangs were the new style, or if Mace and Sen were just behind on their haircuts.

"I will try to be nicer," he said.

Dree tilted her head. "I'll believe that when I see it."

It was a lie. The next time Dree passed Mace, he mumbled something at her and retreated in the other direction. Fine by her. She had more important things to think about. Sen was still trying to figure out where they should go. He wanted to make sure it was a place they would like, and he needed to find it without asking his friends for help. It would be easier if they did, but she didn't want to see Tal again.

A week crawled by, and Dree told herself to be patient. Now that she had decided she wanted to leave, everyday felt like a week. Vetta had her scrubbing along the corners of the wall and the floor, and her back was not happy. Vetta had nothing better to do today than to follow her around, pointing out places she could do better.

"I shouldn't be surprised at your lack of attention to detail," Vetta said, peering down at her. "You realize I only keep you on as a favor to Sen."

Dree's knees were aching. She crawled around the room, trying her best to ignore Vetta's annoying prattle.

"Oh, look. You missed a spot," Vetta said, stepping on Dree's hand. "Oops," she said, twisting her foot before getting off. "Sorry about that."

Dree held in a yelp and sat up, holding her throbbing hand. How did Vetta keep any of her employees? The woman was a monster.

"Don't stop on my account," Vetta said with a smile.

Dree was done. She wasn't taking this woman any longer. Sen was just going to have to figure something out spur of the moment because she was finished. She opened her mouth to tell Vetta everything she had wanted to say for two years, but before she could speak, Mace came bursting into the room.

"Mace, what is it?" Vetta asked, hurrying to his side.

Dree stood and wondered about the disheveled appearance of the stable master.

"I was in town," he said, breathing deeply. He ran a hand through his already mussed hair. "It's the king."

"The king is here?" Vetta asked, clapping her hands.

"No, he's dead."

"Dead?" Dree asked, dropping her rag.

Mace glanced at her, then back at Vetta. "He was out in the forest running a drill with his guards. There was an ambush, and the king went down. The men responsible were killed, but that doesn't change the outcome."

"My goodness," Vetta said, pulling out a fan and waving it frantically at herself. "Has Prince Raz taken the throne?"

Dree swallowed hard. Raz would be a worse king than her father. Possibly worse than her grandfather.

Mace's eyes dimmed. "No. The crowned prince was killed as well."

A chill traveled from Dree's head to her toes and she rubbed the goosebumps on her arms. She put a hand to her middle as a sick feeling settled in her stomach and she prayed she wouldn't throw up.

"Oh dear. What will this mean for my crops? Who will approve of them?" Vetta moaned, pressing her hands to her cheeks.

Dree laughed to keep from crying. "*That* is your worry? You are the most ridiculous woman I've ever met. Your crops won't go to waste."

Vetta bent down and slapped her across the face. Dree's head bumped the wall, but she barely noticed. "You will not talk to me that way!"

Mace took a step toward her, then shook his head. "The captain of the king's guard thinks he'll be able to find Princess Lesandri," Mace said, drawing the attention away from her. "He's a skilled tracker and the King's Council has decided that the princess will marry him before she takes the throne."

Dree's eyebrows rose, and she forgot about her stinging cheek. "Wait, marry who?"

"The captain of the guard. I guess it makes sense, since the king is always a mighty warrior. He won't be made king, though, only a prince. That man shouldn't have power. He's corrupt on so many levels."

"Marry Captain Lenzo?" Dree laughed. Captain Lenzo was sixty if he was a day and more like her father than she could tolerate. People whispered he was practicing to become a sorcerer. She laughed more. What was wrong with her? Tears ran down her face as she hid her face in her hands. She was laughing and crying at the same time. What a wonderful ruler she would make. She couldn't even control herself.

"Have you gone mad?" Vetta asked, kicking her leg.

Dree laughed harder.

"Are you alright?" Mace asked from somewhere near her.

She nodded and tried to get control of herself.

"I'm not sure we should put our kingdom in the hands of an irresponsible runaway princess," Mace said. "We need someone confident."

"Runaway?" Vetta asked. "I thought she was abducted. I'm sure that is what we were told."

"I doubt it. They didn't try hard enough to find her."

"You don't know the situation," Dree said, wiping her eyes.

"A princess will be a lot easier for me to deal with," Vetta said, tapping her chin. "It could be beneficial to me. She's probably weak minded or she wouldn't have run away. I'm going to have to think on this. I bet I can get her to triple prices on wheat if I come up with a good enough story."

"She'll see through that," Dree said, walking toward the door. She held her head high and ignored Vetta babbling behind her.

Chapter 2

"Sen!" Dree yelled, as she ran toward the fields. "Sendo, where are you?" A bunch of farmhands glanced up at her. She must look frazzled from her crazy little laughing episode. "Sen!"

"Right here," he said, coming up behind her. He used his sleeve to wipe sweat from his face. "What's wrong?"

Dree grabbed him and pulled him away from the others. As soon as she was sure they wouldn't be overheard, she stopped. "My father and brother were killed," she spat out.

He put a hand on Dree's shoulder and patted it awkwardly a few times. For Sen, that was like giving someone a bearhug. "I'm sorry. Are you okay?"

"I'm fine. I can't remember my father ever saying a kind thing to me. Raz was the same. That isn't my worry."

"You'll be queen."

Her lip trembled. "Yes. I never expected something like this. I don't want to be queen."

Sen looked into her eyes. "Think of all the good you can do."

"Yes, and I will do it, but I can't marry Captain Lenzo."

He tilted his head and studied her. "Why would you marry him?"

"That is what the King's Council decided. I can't command them until after I'm crowned."

"What can we do?" Sen asked, rubbing the dark stubble on his chin.

She gazed down at the ground. "I have to marry someone else before I go back."

Dree glanced up to see Sen's eyes widen in surprise. If she hadn't been so agitated, she would have been proud of herself for taking him by surprise.

"Marry who?" he asked.

Dree looked at him with pleading eyes.

He shifted from one foot to the other. "No. Dree, I can't."

She grabbed his upper arm with both hands and looked up at him. "Why not? It wouldn't have to change anything between us."

"I'm not old enough to get married. I'm only eighteen."

"So am I."

He pulled away from her and looked up at the blue sky. "I know, but—I just don't think I can."

"You followed me across the world and spent two years in this place just to help me, and now you can't do this?"

"This is different."

Dree sighed. In her mind, he had agreed without hesitation. "Why?"

"There are lots of things you don't know about me, Dree." He stared at the ground. She was making him show all sorts of emotions today. "It's silly, but I want to fall in love someday. My parents had a great marriage, and I want that."

"We wouldn't have to get married. It could just be a marriage contract." After the arranged marriage laws had been abolished, there was a marriage law made. Two people could get a marriage contract, and it was almost as good as being married. It was officiated by a priest, and it couldn't be broken, except by the couple. Even Lenzo wouldn't be able to break it, and she could become queen without being married, so long as the contract was official.

"That's almost the same," Sen said.

"Fine," Dree said, pacing across the weeds. "But I have to have a marriage contract before I go back. If Captain Lenzo has decided to find me, he will, and I will never marry him."

"How about Mace?" Sen suggested.

Dree stopped in her tracks. "Mace? He's the rudest person on the farm besides Vetta."

"I admit he has some issues, but he's the best one I can think of."

"Anyone would be better."

"Not anyone around here," Sen said, shrugging. "He's strong, and he has a good mind. I've talked to him about politics, and the guy knows what he's talking about. He might be moody, but he wants to do big things."

She crossed her arms. "So, he wants power."

"No, he wants to help people. He has some good ideas. I actually enjoy talking to him. He also said he refuses to get married. I guess he had a bad relationship and doesn't want to try again. He's perfect."

"That doesn't sound perfect," she said, wringing her hands.

"If he doesn't want to get married, you wouldn't need to worry about trying to fall in love or anything. It would be a business arrangement. He would have the power to make some good changes, and you would get someone to work with. He is competent."

"Ugh." Dree rubbed circles into the side of her head with her fingers. She could feel the veins throbbing. "Is that really my best option?"

"It's the best I can come up with."

"There isn't enough time to plan. I feel like Captain Lenzo is going to show up any second."

"Then, you better go talk to Mace."

She let out a slow breath. This was not how she had expected this day to go.

Dree stood nervously outside the bunkhouse and pushed a brown ringlet behind her ear. She rubbed her hand over her green dress and fussed with the sleeve. Stalling wasn't the answer, and she'd been stalling for an hour. She had already changed into a clean dress. No use proposing in a dirty one. *Proposing.* Not only that, but to a man she didn't even like, and who didn't like her. Who would have guessed?

She couldn't believe Sen had turned her down. Somehow, that hurt more than finding out about her father and brother. There had never been anything romantic between them, but he was the only person she had ever really cared about. He was also the only person who had ever seemed to care about what happened to her. She raised her hand to knock.

"What are you doing here?" came Mace's voice from behind her. She spun around. His arms were crossed, and he didn't look happy.

She swallowed. "I need to talk to you. In private."

He raised his brow. "Alright," he said. "Let's walk down to the creek."

They walked in silence. Butterflies were playing octaball in her stomach. How was she going to say this? When they got to the creek, Mace plopped down in the dirt and waited. Dree took her time settling onto the ground, arranging her dress to allow her to sit comfortably.

"Vetta is furious with you," he said, as she fussed with a loose thread on her dress.

"I don't care. I'm done with this place."

"I thought you might be. I can't believe you let that witch slap you."

"Hitting her back wouldn't have helped, though I was tempted."

"So was I." He stared into her eyes. "Why don't you spit out what you want to say? You look like you might puke or pass out or something."

"I need a favor," Dree said, biting her lip.

"From me?" he asked, gesturing at himself.

She nodded. "A big favor. The biggest one I've ever asked of anyone."

His eyebrow rose. "I'm intrigued. Ask away. You can't surprise me."

"I think I can," she said, focusing on her hands. She gazed up into his green eyes and blurted it out. "I need you to enter into a marriage contract with me."

Mace opened his mouth and then closed it. "I don't understand."

"I need a marriage contract. Immediately."

"Why?" he asked. He shifted, and she was sure he was going to run.

"Captain Lenzo can't be allowed to control the kingdom. I know how you feel about me, and I know how you feel about Princess Lesandri."

"Do you?" he asked, running a hand through his hair. "Wait—" He studied Dree, and his eyes narrowed.

"I am Princess Lesandri."

Mace studied her for a moment longer. "Wow. You really are, aren't you?"

Dree nodded and forced her hands to stay still in her lap. "I need to have a marriage contract before Captain Lenzo finds me. If I already have one, he can't marry me."

"This is crazy," he said, gazing up at the clear sky. "Why me? Why not Sen?"

"Sen's my best friend. You don't marry your best friend."

Mace grinned. "He said, 'no,' huh?"

She ignored him. "I need someone who will help me succeed. You can do that. I would appreciate your advice and help. I'm not asking for any type of relationship from you, except as my partner in running the kingdom. You don't need to worry that I'm a silly girl trying to fall in love. I'm practical," Dree lied. She wanted to fall in love someday, but it would not happen now.

"This is a lot to think about."

"There isn't time to think. Captain Lenzo could show up any second and then I'll be trapped."

Mace's eyes danced. "Some things make a lot more sense. You're a princess. That's why you didn't know how to do anything when you first came here."

"I don't know why I bothered," Dree muttered, getting to her feet. She turned, ready to stomp away. She'd never heard of a princess that was rejected by three men, and two in one day, for that matter. Why hadn't Sen agreed?

"Stop," Mace said, grabbing her shoulder. "I'll do it."

"Really?"

"I can't let Lenzo have any more power than he already does. That would be detrimental to the kingdom."

She nodded. "Good. We agree on something at least. Now, let's hurry before we change our minds."

After the fastest marriage contract ceremony on the planet, Mace helped Dree climb onto his alicorn. He mounted behind her and headed to Vetta's house to collect their things. It felt strange. They were bound.

"Did you see the priest's face when you told him your name?" Mace asked, as the black alicorn trotted down the paved street. "He definitely recognized it."

"Yes. We're going to need to hurry before word gets around."

"Even if he hadn't recognized it, he would have thought it was strange the way you insisted on it being fast, with no kissing. Are you that scared of kissing me? I'm not a bad kisser."

Dree smiled. She wished she could see his face. "How do you know? Do you kiss yourself often?"

"I've never had a complaint."

Dree rolled her eyes. "Maybe they were just too polite to tell you."

"Do I need to prove it to you?"

"Nope," she blurted out. "That is not part of the arrangement."

He chuckled. She tried to push away her wish that it was Sen who was bound to her. The alicorn turned onto a dirt road leading to Vetta's house. They rode the rest of the way in silence. When they reached the house, Vetta came storming out before they could dismount.

"Where have you been?" she demanded. "I've had the entire house waiting on you." Dree looked at Mace and he shrugged as he lowered her to the ground. "Follow me, both of you." They followed her into the parlor. Vetta had crammed everyone who worked there into the ruffle filled room. Dree knew what this meant. This was the way Vetta fired people. She claimed the humiliation was a good way to help a person do a better job in their next position.

Dree smiled. This could be fun. "I suppose I'm fired?"

Vetta frowned. "I have not given you permission to speak."

Dree raised her eyebrow and smiled at her. She tried to feel angry, but she was so happy to be leaving. She willed her eyes to stop sparkling. "Actually, you are the one that doesn't have permission to speak."

"Are you mocking me?" Vetta asked, her face red with anger.

Dree's smile widened.

Vetta raised her hand to strike, but before she could move, Mace caught her wrist.

"Don't touch my fiancé," he said.

"Your what?" Vetta sputtered, ripping her arm away from him.

"You heard me," Mace said. "You don't need to fire us. We quit. So does Sen."

Sen nodded.

"What?" Vetta exploded. "How could this happen? Where do you think you're going to go? I won't give you a recommendation! You better rethink this whole thing right now, Mace!"

"We don't need a recommendation," Dree said. "It might be you who needs one."

"What are you talking about?"

"It's a great offense to strike royalty. You might need someone to speak for you, to keep you out of prison."

"Prison? What are you talking about?" Vetta fumed. "I swear, Dree, I will make you regret this."

"You may call me Princess Lesandri or Your Majesty," Dree said. She felt pompous saying it, but it was worth it to see the look on Vetta's face. Her eyes bugged out, and she was as red as a tomato.

"That can't be possible," she sputtered.

"It's true," Sen said, making his way through the crowd.

"We will gather our things and leave immediately," Dree said. "Anyone here who would like a new position is welcome to join us at the castle in a month's time.

A sea of shocked faces stared at her.

"I'll be expecting a letter of apology before the month is up," she said to Vetta.

The woman's eyes narrowed, but she nodded.

"Do you have anything more you want to say?"

Vetta shook her head.

"I'm going to go grab my stuff and give some of the others instructions," Sen said to Dree. "Vetta has one of the most prosperous farms in the kingdom. We don't want to lose her crops."

Dree nodded. "Meet us out front in ten minutes."

He nodded and scampered off.

"I can't believe you're going to leave me in a lurch like this, Mace," Vetta said, finding her voice. "Who will take care of the stables?"

"Most of the boys can do it. The stables will be fine," Mace said. "I'm going to run to the bunkhouse and get my things. Ten minutes?" he asked, glancing at Dree.

She nodded and headed for the room she shared with the other maids. Grabbing a bag, she shoved all of her things into it. She didn't have much. When she ran away, all she took was a crossbow.

"Your Majesty? Princess?"

"Yes?" Dree turned to see a maid named Halla standing in the doorway. The girl fiddled with her hands and didn't meet her gaze. Halla had always been quiet. Her black hair was pulled back into a tight bun with small curls escaping around the edges.

"Did you mean what you said about letting people join you?" she asked quietly.

"Yes. I need a month to figure some things out, and then you are welcome to come. Should I watch for you?" Dree asked, latching her bag.

"Yes," Halla said with a small smile. "Thank you." She wiped the sweat from her smooth cheek. The girl was nervous. Dree didn't know her well because Halla kept mostly to herself. She was a hard worker and never caused any problems. She was probably seventeen or eighteen, and if Dree remembered correctly, she had been here about a year.

"You might want to think about it," Dree said, slinging her bag over her shoulder. "Working at a castle can be hard."

"It can't be worse than it is here," Halla said, shuddering.

Dree frowned. She thought the only person Vetta had a grudge against these days was her. "Does Vetta treat you poorly?"

Halla looked at the floor and shifted from one foot to the other. "Not much worse than she treats anyone she sees as a threat."

"I'm surprised the woman even hires pretty girls," Dree said. "She is the jealous type."

"I'm not pretty," Halla said. "She has other reasons for hating me."

Dree raised her eyebrow. Halla didn't think she was pretty? The girl was beautiful. She must possess the modesty Dree was lacking. "Oh?" Dree asked.

Halla only nodded in response.

"Alright. I'll watch for you in a month."

"Thank you," Halla said with the first genuine smile Dree had ever seen from her. It slipped away fast. "I'll be there—if Vetta lets me go."

"Don't ask for permission. She doesn't own you."

Halla nodded again, but she didn't seem convinced.

"If you don't show up in a month and a half, I'll have someone come for you."

"Halla!" Vetta screamed up the stairs. "Where are you?"

"Thank you," Halla said before disappearing out the door. She peeked back. "You're going to be a great queen."

Dree sighed. She hoped Halla was right.

"I don't understand why we aren't teleporting," Mace said, as the three of them rode unicorns down a wide dirt path.

Dree ran her hand over her unicorn's white mane. "Teleporting is for lazy people."

"Are you sure you aren't just trying to prolong getting to your castle?"

"Dree isn't a fan of magic," Sen said.

"What? Why?" Mace asked with a frown. "Magic makes so many things easier."

"Easier isn't always better," Dree said, ignoring his irritated tone. "Teleporting was a lost skill until the last few years. You survived before then."

Mace rolled his eyes. "Yeah, and ever since I learned to do it, it's saved me a lot of time. Did you even bother to learn how? I mean, Sen told me I couldn't teach it to anyone else, but I thought he would teach you."

"I don't need to know how. I don't understand why Sen taught you."

"If you're going to try to convince her, it's a losing battle," Sen said, watching ahead. "Believe me, I've tried."

"So, you don't do any magic?"

Dree glanced sideways at him. "I make light. That's all."

"Why is that acceptable and the other things aren't?"

Dree's mouth formed a tight line. She knew her logic wasn't sound, so trying to explain it to someone else wouldn't be beneficial.

Sen's mouth twitched in what might be something close to a smile. He had been trying to get her to learn magic for two years. He probably thought he had an ally in Mace now.

"When people summon things, they do it so they don't have to get off their chair and walk up the stairs. Teleporting happens because people don't want to travel. We are going to turn into lazy people if we use magic too much. Light isn't something you need to not be lazy. It's just something that's necessary." She knew it was a pathetic argument.

"She's scared of the dark," Sen said.

Mace laughed, and Dree shot him the dirtiest look she could manage.

"Don't tell him my secrets," Dree said.

He grinned. "I'm going to find them out eventually."

"Eventually isn't now, and you don't need to know them all at once."

Mace glanced at her and tilted his head. "Can you at least tell me why you ran away? It's not normal for a princess to run away and become a maid. When a princess goes missing, it seems like there would be a huge manhunt. All I ever heard was a weak attempt at offering a reward."

Dree sighed. He might as well know. "I was born without magic."

"And that's why you hate it?"

She shrugged. "My parents were embarrassed and tried to keep it from the people. They arranged a marriage between me and the son of a governor on the other continent. I got tired of the way they treated me, so I ran away."

"And decided to be a maid?"

"I figured they wouldn't find me, although if they wanted to find me, they could have. Captain Lenzo can sniff out anyone."

"How did you end up with Sen?"

"Sen and his friends needed some water from our well."

"Right, for the silver eclipse?"

"Yes." The silver eclipse was the magic Sen and his friends had summoned to fix the world. It was also the event that caused everyone in the world to have magic. "My father wouldn't give them the water, so I found them and gave it to them. They let me stay with them until they saved the world."

Sen nodded. "You should have seen her back then. She didn't know how to do anything. She tried to sneak up on us with a crossbow that she didn't know how to use."

"Ah," Mace said. "Which led to you having a knife at her throat."

"Yep. She was pretty clueless back then. She believed in the boogeyman and every other scary thing her parents could come up with to keep her afraid and obedient."

"I wasn't that bad," Dree muttered. She knew it was a lie. She had been sixteen and still believed goblins were spying on her to make sure she did her schoolwork. "Besides, I've learned a lot in the last two years."

Mace looked skeptical. "Just not a lot of magic."

"I don't need magic. Sen taught me to use my crossbow, and he taught me to fight. I'm alright at defending myself."

Sen nodded. "It's true. She's gotten pretty good."

"Self-defense is important," Mace said thoughtfully. "But what if I decided to knock you over with magic? Magic is always going to win because you don't have to make contact."

Dree's mouth formed a tight line. That was exactly what Sen kept telling her. Maybe she was being silly. Perhaps she should learn basic magic. Learning it didn't mean she had to use it regularly.

Mace drummed his fingers against his unicorn's reins. "You need to learn some magic. It's good to possess the ability, and you wouldn't have to use it unless you need it."

Dree peered over at him. Could he read her mind? No. Mind reading wasn't a thing. People could communicate telepathically, but most people avoided it. It was a sure way to make a person sick.

"I'll think about it," she said.

"As queen, it's a smart thing to have an advantage," he said. "What if someone means you harm? You could teleport away and save yourself."

"I suppose," Dree said. He was right. Sen had been right for years. She sighed. She was going to have to learn magic and how to rule a kingdom at the same time.

Chapter 3

Sen spread his bedroll over a patch of hard packed dirt and sat on it. Mace was still annoyed they weren't teleporting to the castle, but Sen didn't care. Being here or there didn't make a big difference to him. He had spent the last two years trying to help Dree, and if she wasn't in a hurry to get home, then he wasn't, either.

He watched Mace throw down his bedroll and tend to the unicorns and wondered if he had made the right decision when he convinced Dree to choose Mace. Mace wasn't always pleasant, but Sen believed he had a good heart. Sen was more of an observer than anything else, and he had noticed that even though Mace talked tough, he was one of the first people to secretly help someone.

Dree sat on her bedroll and pulled off her boots. She rubbed her stockinged foot and grimaced. She spent little time in boots. Vetta demanded the maids work without shoes so they wouldn't make the house dirty. Her braid was a mess, and she kept yawning.

Sen wondered if he would have a place in Dree's kingdom. It didn't take much to keep him happy. Good food and a little competition were all he needed. He hadn't had much in the way of competitions since he started following Dree around. It might be good to go his own way soon.

Now that Dree had Mace, she wouldn't need him. They had become good friends, but it all started as a service project for Sen. He had never met anyone as clueless as Dree, and he felt like it would be a benefit to her to teach her some life skills. She tried hard, and she learned fast. There were still a lot of simple things she didn't understand how to do, but she had come miles from where she was when she met him.

Who was Sen fooling? He was an idiot. He could have any job in the world because of his help with the silver eclipse, and he had stayed two years with Dree. A guy didn't do that for no reason. He was completely, one hundred percent, in love with her. He had been for almost as long as he had known her.

"You look exhausted," Mace said to Dree, as he crawled under his blanket. "You could be home in your own bed right now if you weren't so stubborn."

"That doesn't mean I would be any less exhausted," Dree said, rubbing her other foot. "I'm not sure I want to face my mother. She's going to have a lot to say to me when I return."

"But you're going to be the new queen, right? Doesn't that mean you outrank her?"

"In some ways," she said. "But can you really outrank your mother?"

"So, we're sleeping on the ground because you're scared of your mother, not because you don't want to teleport?"

"Maybe both," she said. "I haven't let Sen teleport me anywhere in ages. You can ask him."

Sen nodded. "It's true." Dree hadn't liked magic when he first met her, but she seemed more and more against it as time went on.

Dree looked pointedly at Mace. "If it was up to me, no one would have magic."

Sen climbed out of his bedroll and crawled over to hers. "Let me see your foot."

Dree peered up at him with a horrified expression on her face. "No, why?"

"Just let me look at it. Do you have blisters?" He touched her foot, and she pulled away.

"It's just sore. It's fine." She pulled her foot closer to herself. "These boots have always been tight."

"Fine," he said, going back to his space. Arguing with her never got him anywhere.

Mace rolled over. "You need to get over the magic thing. Think of all the time you're wasting doing things the hard way."

"Think of how lazy everyone is going to get now that everyone can do magic. It will not happen to me." She pulled herself under her blanket and laid down.

Sen leaned back and got comfortable. He didn't mind sleeping on the ground. He yawned. "Do you suppose any of Vetta's staff will take you up on the offer to come work at the castle?" He had the feeling most of them might.

"At least one will," Dree said. "I talked to Halla before we left, and she's planning on coming."

Mace's head turned abruptly toward her. "Halla? She's coming?"

"Yes. I guess Vetta treats her as badly as she treated me."

"Vetta doesn't like competition," Mace said. "She treats all the pretty girls like garbage."

"Interesting," was all Sen could manage. His mind had turned into a mess he couldn't sort out. It was almost full dark now.

In less than five minutes, he could hear Mace breathing deeply and Dree hadn't moved. They were most likely asleep.

Sen never had trouble sleeping, but he was wide awake. What kind of guy refused to marry the girl he was in love with? Even worse, he had pushed her into a contract with Mace. He should have taken time to think. He had day-dreamed about Dree falling for him. After two years of hoping something would happen, he realized Dree would never see him as more than a friend.

When she told him about needing to get married, he had only thought about how hard it would be to mar-ry someone he loved and not have them love him back. He'd thought it would be too painful. Now that the de-cision had been made, he realized how wrong he was. He should've jumped at the opportunity. Once Dree was set-tled, he was going to leave. He couldn't watch her fall in love with Mace.

Dree's eyes popped open. What was that sound? She shivered and pulled her blanket up under her chin. It was probably nothing. Even if it was, Mace was sleeping on one side of her and Sen on the other. If there was anything out there, it would get them first. She was too scared to feel guilty for having that thought. The sound came again.

"Sen?" she whispered. "Sendo, wake up!"

"What's wrong?" Sen asked, bringing up an orb of light.

"No light!" Dree said. He let it go out. "I heard something. Over there." She pointed into a clump of trees.

Sen came up on his elbow and turned to the place she pointed. "I don't hear anything. It was probably a dream."

"No, I heard it twice," she said.

"It's probably an animal. Go back to sleep."

Her eyes scanned the dark shadows. "What if it's a mean animal?"

Sen sighed and sat up. He pulled up a dim light and placed it near him as he pulled on his boots.

"What's going on?" Mace asked.

"I'm going to check the trees," Sen said, getting to his feet. "I have to make sure the boogeyman isn't hiding in there."

"Oh, alright," Mace said, rolling over.

"Aren't you even worried?" she whispered to Mace.

"No."

Sen walked into the trees, and Dree listened hard. She hoped he didn't get eaten or something. She counted in her head. When she got to one hundred and thirty-four, Sen came clomping back.

"There's nothing there," he said, kicking off his boots. "It was probably just a squirrel or something."

"Thanks for checking."

"Sure," he said, going back to bed.

Dree was wide awake now. She was still scared of whatever was out there. Maybe her aversion to magic was ridiculous. She could be in a nice, soft bed right now. Mace probably thought he was going to have to spend the rest of his life checking for the boogeyman. Dree knew it didn't exist, but she only found that out two years ago.

She still couldn't believe Sen touched her sock. It had been inside her sweaty boot all day. Her foot probably smelled horrible, and her sock had been damp. She didn't want him to think she was disgusting. Not that it mattered. He hadn't wanted to marry her before the gross sock touched his hand.

It wasn't as dark as when they had gone to sleep. Morning must be coming. Dree heard another sound in the opposite direction of the first one and closed her eyes, trying to block it out.

"We have you surrounded!" a deep voice yelled. Dree sat up and looked around frantically. Sen and Mace were on their feet. Mace was holding a sword, and Sen had a knife. Several men in armor stepped out of the trees and walked carefully toward them. They all carried swords, and there were at least ten of them. Dree recognized them as her father's guards.

"Stand down!" she commanded, as she got to her feet. "What is the meaning of this?"

Captain Lenzo stepped forward. "Princess Lesandri," he said, bowing. "We've come to take you home. We will save you from these scoundrels," he said, motioning toward Sen and Mace.

"I do not need to be saved from them," she said, glaring at the tall, bearded man. "They are escorting me to the castle."

"No need," Captain Lenzo said. "We will take you from here."

"They are returning with me."

He ran a hand over his brown beard and studied Sen and Mace. "Are these the men who abducted you two years ago?"

"No one abducted me," she said, holding her head high. She would not appear weak in front of him. "I left of my own accord. My parents knew this, and I suspect you do as well."

"We were told you were kidnapped," he said. He looked older than the last time she saw him. Gray streaks ran through his beard and hair.

Dree crossed her arms. "If you thought I was kidnapped, you would have searched for me. Look how fast you found me when you wanted to."

Lenzo's eyes narrowed. "Who are these men that accompany you? We must make sure they are harmless."

"This is Sendo," she said, motioning to him. "He is from Boztoll. And this is Mace," she said, suddenly not knowing what to say.

"We have a marriage contract," Mace said, looking Lenzo in the eyes.

Dree wasn't sure which one of them appeared more threatening at the moment.

"What?" Lenzo asked, his teeth grinding together.

Dree wanted to smile, but she kept her mouth in a tight line. It didn't bother her at all to foil Lenzo's plans. A marriage contract could not be dissolved by him and so he would never get her or the kingdom.

"We will return to the castle on our own," she said.

"The King's Council will not be happy," Lenzo finally said. "They would not choose the likes of him as your husband."

"I'm sure they wouldn't," Dree said. "But a contract is a contract, and there isn't anything they can do about it."

Lenzo gave her a smile that didn't reach his eyes. "That is a matter of opinion." He motioned to his men, and they all disappeared as quickly as they had come.

"We need to get back to the castle," Dree said, pulling on her boots. "Get the unicorns, and we can teleport. I want to get back before they do, or at least at their heels. I don't want Lenzo to have time to plan anything."

"A marriage contract can't be broken," Mace said, grabbing his boots. "You don't have to worry."

"I am worried," Dree admitted. "I might have made a mistake when I roped you into this."

Mace shrugged. "I made my choice."

"Lenzo has no morals. I never stopped to think. I would still have to marry him if he kills you." She shivered at the thought.

"He won't kill me."

"He didn't get to be Captain of the Guard for being weak. He's a great warrior." Dree chewed on her lip. "Maybe you should go into hiding."

"I'm not going into hiding," he said, hanging his sword on one unicorn. "I'm not scared of Lenzo."

"You will have to be careful," Sen said. "You can't trust a man like him."

"I'll be careful, but I'm not hiding from him. I'm pretty good at magic, and I'm great at sword fighting."

"So is he," Dree said, "and he's had a lot more experience than you. He's been the captain for as long as you've been alive."

Sen nodded. "And I beat you at swords every time we spar."

"Don't worry. It'll be fine."

"I wonder if Lenzo can teleport," she said, biting her lip.

"Who knows?" Mace muttered, leading the unicorn closer. "I wouldn't be surprised either way. The only reason anyone at Vetta's can do it is because Sen taught them."

"It seems like something that would spread fast, but I only taught you," Sen said. "Two years ago, there were only a handful of people that knew how to do it, and a lot of them were arrested. I'm not sure whether my friends have taught it to others. It only takes one person to teach it and it could be everywhere."

"I haven't tried it," Dree said. "Can you take all three of us and the unicorns?" she asked Sen.

He nodded. "Sure. I can take anything I'm touching."

"I'm good at it as well," Mace said.

"Sen should take all of us. He knows where the castle is, and it would be good if we all stuck together."

Mace glanced around the castle and held back a sigh. All he had seen was the entryway, a hall, and the throne room, and it seemed like an uncomfortable place to spend the rest of his life. The gray stone walls were dull and considering how thick the walls were, it was chilly. The rooms were too big to feel cozy, but then, what was he expecting? It was a castle. Colorful tapestries hung on the walls, but they weren't enough to produce a homey feel. He didn't know why he cared. He hadn't lived in a place he would call homey in over seven years.

The outside of the castle was impressive, he would give it that. It boasted six turrets with spires and several balconies. The grounds were almost completely surrounded by picturesque gardens. Mace could only imagine how many people it would take for their upkeep.

Guards had been lined up in front of the drawbridge. Mace had been slightly disappointed to find there wasn't a moat. The drawbridge just opened onto hard packed dirt.

A set of guards outside the castle had taken their unicorns and led them away. They all seemed surprised Dree had returned so quickly. Mace assumed that meant Lenzo and his men couldn't teleport. He hoped it took them a long time to return.

"It's so strange to be back," Dree said, running her hand over the gold plated throne. At least, Mace assumed it was gold plated. It was too big to be made entirely of gold.

A woman came bursting into the room. "Lesandri!" she said, spreading her arms and walking toward her. This had to be the queen. She was probably around forty and had Dree's curly brown hair. Her long green dress billowed behind her and gave Mace the impression of a peacock.

"Hello, Mother," Dree said, as the woman gave her a quick stiff hug.

"Is that all you have to say?" the woman asked. "After two years? No apology or anything? Who are these people with you?"

"This is Sen," she said, gesturing to Sen as he nodded. "And this is Mace. We have a marriage contract. Sen and Mace, this is my mother, Queen Navina."

"Excuse me?" the Queen said, her eyes narrowed. "Marriage contract?"

"Yes," Dree said.

Navina turned and studied Mace. He did his best to stand tall and not cower. It took a lot to intimidate him, but this woman knew how to glare.

The queen ground her teeth with an audible crack. "Lesandri, I cannot believe the lengths you will go through to defy us."

"What do you mean?"

"First, you run off, and now, you come back with him. I know you well enough. I bet you heard the news of your father and brother, and you knew the counsel would have a husband picked out for you. You probably grabbed the first man you saw and bribed him into a contract."

"That isn't true," Dree said, crossing her arms. "I've known Mace for two years." Mace didn't add that they had only spoken a few times in those two years, and none of their conversations were what could be called pleasant.

"We heard about Governor Briggs's son. As soon as Akkron got rid of arranged marriages, he moved on fast enough. We heard rumors you were with him for a time. It's pretty sad you couldn't secure him yourself. You should have known that the council would want you to be with someone like Captain Lenzo."

Mace shook his head. Queen Navina hadn't seen her daughter in two years and this was the reunion?

"I would never marry him," Dree said, lifting her chin slightly.

"This is going to cause so many problems."

"He's closer to *your* age. You could marry him."

Navina narrowed her eyes. "I don't appreciate your attitude."

"Noted," Dree said, shrugging. "Why concern yourself with these things? You aren't the queen anymore. You should probably think about what you are going to do now."

"Please, Lesandri," she said, putting a hand to her forehead. "You are no more fit to be a queen than that man is to be married to a queen. You need me."

"You made me dependent on you," Dree said. "But that was then. I've learned a lot since I left here. You can't scare me with stories of goblins and trolls anymore. Now, if you will excuse us, we have a lot to attend to."

Navina's mouth hung open as she watched her daughter leave the room. Sen and Mace followed behind her. They moved down the hallway at top speed, and then she stopped abruptly and turned to them.

"I've never been good at storming off," she said. "My hands are shaking."

"I always thought you were pretty good at storming off actually," Mace said, trying not to smile.

"Well, you bring it out in me. What do we do now? My mother is more right than I want to admit. I wasn't raised to be a queen. I was raised to not embarrass my parents."

"We'll figure it out," he said, and Sen nodded in agreement.

"We need to change out of these clothes," Dree said. "Nobody is going to take us seriously if we aren't well dressed."

The next morning, Mace frowned at himself in the mirror. He looked ridiculous. A servant had led him to a large bedroom and brought him a change of clothing. The blue tunic he was wearing was embellished around the bottom and the sleeves. He had never worn anything like it, and it felt wrong. The trousers weren't bad, but the tunic was ridiculous. Almost as ridiculous as his room.

The bed had a wooden frame with four tall wooden posts. Intricately carved birds and leaves adorned the posts. A canopy was draped over the bed and had made him feel claustrophobic throughout the night. A large fireplace sat in the middle of one wall and above it was the most hideous painting Mace had ever seen. It was either a man that looked like a boar, or a boar pretending to be a man.

Mace spun around as he heard a small snort behind him. Sen stood in the doorway with his arms crossed. He wasn't smiling, but there was humor in his eyes.

"What are you scoffing at?" he asked.

"Nothing," Sen said, entering the room and closing the door.

"Good because you look just as ridiculous."

Sen glanced down at his green tunic. "Yeah, but I don't care what I look like. You seem ready to bite someone."

Mace pulled at the sleeve. "It's going to take some getting used to."

Sen sat on the large, overstuffed bed. "I want to warn you about Dree."

"Isn't it a little late for that?" he asked, crossing his arms over his chest.

"I don't mean to warn you away from her. Dree is gullible. When I met her, she believed in every mythical scary thing you can imagine. Her parents kept her scared so she wouldn't act out. They also didn't teach her to do many useful things."

"Yeah, I remember when she first came to Vetta's. Vetta never would have hired her if you weren't part of the deal."

"She tries to compensate for feeling helpless by being defiant. I've noticed the more defiant she is, the more unsure she is. She leaps into things sometimes just to prove she isn't scared."

"I've seen her jump into things, but I didn't think she was scared of anything."

"I've been trying to help her. I taught her what she needed to know so she could work for Vetta. She can use a crossbow now and do some self-defense. Every time she brings up something crazy, I tell her whether or not it's true. She's gotten a lot better, but with the amount of work Vetta had her doing, I haven't had a lot of time with her."

Mace leaned against the wall and looked at Sen thoughtfully. "Just out of curiosity, why didn't she force you into her marriage contract? You're famous. You would be a much better candidate than me."

Sen shifted on the bed. "She asked me, but I couldn't do it."

"Why?"

"It's hard to explain. I've spent the last two years taking care of Dree. Eventually, I need to be my own person."

"Did you tell her to ask me? She doesn't like me."

"I suggested you."

"I'm sure she was ecstatic."

Sen's mouth turned up slightly. "She was against it, but she saw the sense in it. You'll be able to help her a lot more than anyone else I know. You understand your politics, and you have good intentions."

Mace nodded. He had always wanted a political career. This would give him more opportunities than he had ever dreamed of. Perhaps more than he wanted. "I feel guilty for agreeing to it," he admitted. "It's like I'm using her to get what I want."

"She knows that. And she's using you. It probably doesn't count as using if you are both aware of it. It's more like you are benefiting from each other."

That was what Mace kept telling himself. He hoped it was true. He didn't want to be a prince, though. That was more responsibility than he wanted. He would prefer to be on a council or spend time as a governor. It would give him a chance to make a change, but not tie him in for life.

"If you change your mind, I'm willing to break the contract," Mace said, watching Sen closely. "You could still be with her."

Sen looked up quickly and then away. Mace wasn't buying Sen's excuses for not marrying Dree. He'd seen the way he watched her and the way he always jumped to her aid. He still couldn't understand why he hadn't jumped at the chance to be with her.

A hard pounding sounded on the door, and then it burst open. Dree came into the room with a worried expression on her face. Mace watched Sen out of the corner of his eye as he studied her. She was wearing a long, elegant dress, and her hair was pulled back with a few soft curls falling to the sides. A small diamond studded tiara rested on her head. She looked like a princess for the first time. Sen was difficult to read, but there was something in his eyes—

"Captain Lenzo and his men are back. He wants to meet with you in an hour."

"With me?" Mace motioned at himself.

"Yes," she said, running her hand over her dress. "Are you sure you shouldn't go into hiding? I don't trust him."

"I will not hide."

"I'll feel so guilty if anything happens to you."

"Don't let the embroidery on his shirt fool you," Sen said. "He's tougher than he seems."

"Thanks a lot," Mace said, shaking his head.

"I know he's tough," Dree said. "But Lenzo is a trained warrior, and it's whispered he's a wizard or sorcerer. I'm not sure what I should do. I don't want him to remain the captain of the guard, but I'm scared to let him go."

"Don't do anything yet," Mace said. "We can observe him more before we make any decisions."

"I want you to be careful. Try not to get in his way," Dree said, wringing her hands.

"Where does he want to meet?"

"In the courtyard."

Mace nodded. "Alright."

Dree bit her lip. "You don't have to meet him. We can come up with an excuse."

"No, I might as well get it over with." There was no reason to put off the inevitable.

Chapter 4

Lenzo glared at the two pirates in front of him. A worse excuse for criminals he had never seen. Captain Ernesto was a large man with an enormous hat that boasted one large feather. The other pirate was a smaller man with an eyepatch.

"Do we have a deal?" Lenzo asked the pirates, as they both fidgeted.

"So, we take the crown and destroy it, and then you pay us?" asked Captain Ernesto.

"Do you think you can handle it?"

"Aye."

"I don't like it," said the other man. "We aren't that type of pirates."

Lenzo raised his brow. "Yes, I've heard. You are more into juvenile pranks than piracy."

The pirate kicked at a stone on the ground. "It keeps people off our backs."

"No one will respect you as a pirate unless you do something more impressive."

The pirate captain scratched his chin. "I do want to be thought of as a legitimate pirate."

"This will do it," Lenzo assured the man. "The amethyst crown is the most guarded artifact in the Northern Kingdom. If people believe you were able to steal it, they will take you seriously."

The shorter one crossed his arms. "If it's so well guarded, how are you going to get it?"

"Quiet, Oscar," said the captain. "I'm trying to make a deal here."

"I already have the crown. I'm offering you a lot of money," Lenzo said, holding up a bag of gold. "More than you've ever seen."

The captain licked his lips, and Oscar frowned.

"Do you want to go down in history as the pirates who occasionally played a joke on people, or the pirates who stole the amethyst crown?"

"We'll do it," the captain said, his eyes on the gold.

"No, Ernesto," Oscar begged. "If we do this, the entire kingdom will be after us. Who cares if you have money if you lose your head?"

Lenzo didn't have time for this. "I will marry the princess in the near future. I will make sure no harm comes to you."

"It's a deal," Ernesto said, grabbing Lenzo's hand. He shook it vigorously. Lenzo resisted the urge to wipe it on his pant leg. Pirates were disgusting creatures.

"One other thing," Lenzo said, motioning to someone in the distance. A young blond man with intense eyes walked toward them carrying a wooden box. "This is Garin. He will go with you to make sure you don't take off with the crown or fail to destroy it. You will sail to Mermaid's Demise and throw the crown into the whirlpool."

"That changes everything," Oscar said. "Right, Ernesto? It's suicide to go near Mermaid's Demise. No ships that sail there ever return. I think he wants us to get sucked in so that we destroy the crown and he doesn't have to pay us."

"Hush, Oscar," Ernesto scolded. "We don't have to go into the whirlpool."

Oscar wrung his hands and his eyes pleaded with his leader. "No ship is going to sail right into it. They obviously get sucked in. We shouldn't do it. No amount of money is worth being dead over."

"You don't have to come," Captain Ernesto said. He looked eagerly up at Lenzo. "Where is the crown?"

Lenzo took the wooden box from Garin and handed it to the man. "Guard it well. I will only pay when Garin tells me you threw it into the whirlpool."

Ernesto nodded and motioned for Garin to follow him. Garin nodded at Lenzo and stomped after him. Oscar looked torn before he trotted off behind them. He might look like the weak link in that duo, but he was smarter than his captain. If the captain could see through his own greed, he might avoid the misfortune that was sure to drag him down.

Lenzo smiled. Those pirates were a bigger joke than he had given them credit for. He was fairly certain Garin wouldn't let them throw the crown into the whirlpool. Garin was loyal to Lenzo because he was well paid. The crown was worth more than Garin would be able to resist. The man was greedy.

If the pirates weren't sucked into the whirlpool, it was likely Garin would steal the crown and never be heard from again. He was corrupt, but careful. Whatever happened, it would delay Princess Lesandri becoming queen long enough to dispose of her fiancé. It would be unfortunate to lose Garin, but it was a price Lenzo would pay.

Lenzo made his way toward the bakery and entered like the king he would soon be. He rubbed a hand over his beard and smiled at the woman behind the counter. It had been a productive morning, and he deserved a sweet roll.

Dree walked swiftly across the large courtyard, glad to see that it was empty. Most of the courtyard was covered in neatly trimmed grass, but there was one large tree in the corner, and she assumed that was the place Lenzo would stand to talk to Mace. The courtyard was in the back of the castle, and was surrounded by a twenty-foot stone wall. The back door to the castle opened into it and was the only way in or out. It was hot, and the tree was the only shade.

She made sure her cloak was fastened, and she pulled the hood over her head.

Gazing up into the high branches, she nodded resolutely. She had never climbed a tree before, but how hard could it be? Children did it all the time. She took a quick glance around to make sure nobody had entered the courtyard, then started up the tree. This was a breeze. Dree smiled. It was actually fun. She climbed higher until she felt like the branches might be getting thinner, and she made herself comfortable, sitting on a sturdy branch.

She hoped they would stand under the tree. Dree trusted Mace, but she wanted to hear what Lenzo said for herself. Britches would have been more practical. She adjusted her dress and made sure the cape covered as much as possible. The pink on her dress might stand out if someone looked up.

She was so high! Her parents never let her do things like climb trees. It appeared she was a natural. She waited for about ten minutes before she saw Mace and Sen enter the courtyard. They walked over to the tree and waited. Her hands felt sweaty, and she tried to breathe normally. She wasn't sure what she would do if they saw her. Lenzo was only a minute behind them. He still wore his armor and his sword.

Mace stood up straight but didn't appear intimidated. "What do you want?"

Lenzo's eyebrow rose. "What do I want? I will not begin on that."

"Why am I here?" Mace asked, rolling his eyes.

Lenzo poked Mace in the chest with his finger. "That's what I've been wondering. You don't belong here."

Mace refused to take a step back. "Maybe not, but I'm here."

"Yes, and that's a problem. I have no doubt Princess Lesandri heard of her father's and brother's deaths and forced you to agree to marry her. She made a mistake in that act of defiance."

Sen tilted his head. "Defiance? She's the one that's going to be queen. She gets to make the decisions."

Dree smiled. It was nice to know he still had her back.

"She isn't starting out well," Lenzo said, rubbing the hilt of his sword. "She should have chosen someone that was more capable."

"I'm plenty capable," Mace said, crossing his arms.

"You're barely old enough to have a marriage contract. When a queen rules, her husband is in control of the army. What is your experience?"

"I don't have to account to you."

"You are unacceptable, and I won't let the kingdom fall because the princess would choose to marry looks over capability."

"Are you saying I'm pretty?" Mace asked, grinning. "I mean, I get it a lot, but not from anyone as accomplished as the captain of the guard."

Dree smiled and shifted on her branch.

Lenzo didn't seem amused. "You have two choices," he said through clenched teeth. "Allow me to guide you, or you can disappear. You and your friend."

Sen's eyes gleamed. Obviously, Lenzo didn't know how fast Sen could whip out a knife.

"Hm," Mace said, unconcerned. "I'll have to think about it."

Lenzo glared at him, then turned and stormed away. Mace saluted at his back.

"We probably shouldn't tell Dree about this," Mace told Sen. "She'll try to get me to go into hiding again."

"Probably," Sen agreed. "It might not be a bad idea, though. If you hide until after Dree is crowned, Lenzo couldn't do anything. It wouldn't benefit him to get rid of you after because she won't have to listen to the council."

"I'm not hiding, and I need a nap," he said with a sigh. "I'll stay here in the shade and meet up with you later." Mace sat down next to the tree and laid down with his hands behind his head.

"I'll stay here," Sen said, cutting a branch off the tree. He was lucky her mother didn't see him do that. She loved this tree. He sat on the ground and started making cuts to the branch.

Dree frowned. How many knives did Sen have on him? She'd never even seen that one before.

There was no way she could stay up here for an entire nap and whittling session. She was already uncomfortable. After five minutes, Mace seemed to be breathing deeply. Dree carefully started down the tree. Down was harder than up, though. She was finding it difficult to navigate. Her dress and cloak kept blowing around, blocking the branches beneath her.

She was going to have to go down the backside to avoid Sen seeing her. The chances of getting down without him noticing were slim. Perhaps if she had worn britches...

"Are you going to ask for help?" Mace asked after a few minutes. His eyes were still closed.

Dree frowned and glared down at him. "You knew I was here?"

Sen peered up at her and put his knife away. "We were watching the courtyard to make sure Lenzo didn't try anything. We saw you climb up."

"Why didn't you say something?"

Mace opened his eyes. "Because we made a bet about how long you would stay up there if we didn't leave."

Sen stood. "And I won," he said, starting up the tree. "Mace thought you would be stubborn and stay up there until we left. I gave you less than ten minutes."

Dree took another step down. "Do you think Lenzo saw me?"

"No," Sen said, reaching her. "I don't think he would have ignored you if he had. Take off your cloak and throw it down. It's boiling. Why are you wearing it?"

"I wanted to blend in," she said, stabilizing herself before she tossed her cloak.

"So, are you going to spy every time I talk to someone?" Mace asked.

"No," she said, taking a step down. It was easier without the cloak. "I just wanted to hear what he was going to say."

"Don't step there," Sen commanded. "Step on the branch to your left."

Dree rolled her eyes, but obeyed. "I think I can climb down a tree."

He shrugged. "Alright." He grabbed a branch and swung to the grass.

"Show off," she muttered, as she made her way slowly down. She felt a lot better when her feet touched the ground.

"Never climbed a tree before?" Mace asked.

"No."

"I'm just glad you didn't fall on our heads."

Dree giggled as she pictured herself falling on Captain Lenzo's head. "I don't know how I would have explained that."

Mace grinned and offered her his arm, shaking his head when she hesitated. "I won't bite you. We need people to assume we like each other."

Dree took his arm and sighed. She wished Mace did like her, at least a little. She also wished Sen had agreed to marry her, so what was the point of wishing? It wasn't going to happen.

Mace glanced sideways at her as they began walking. "I'm not distasteful to everyone, you know. You heard Captain Lenzo. He thinks I'm pretty."

"I think you're pretty," Sen said, tagging along behind them. "Pretty ridiculous."

Mace laughed. "It's true."

"Lesandri!" Navina called from the castle door.

Dree let go of Mace and spun around. "What is it, Mother?"

Navina charged toward them with a determined look on her face. "While you are out here wasting time, the kingdom is in peril!"

"In peril?" Dree asked, raising her eyebrow.

"The amethyst crown has been stolen," she said, her eyes wide with fear.

Dree put a hand to her chest. "Stolen? How? It's the most guarded thing in the kingdom!"

"We don't know how. Captain Lenzo will handle things, but you know how important that crown is! Without it, everything might fall apart!"

"When did it go missing? It couldn't have gotten far."

"None of it makes any sense," Navina said, wringing her hands. "It is watched night and day. The guards never left their posts, and they saw nothing. It can't have been gone for more than a day."

"It could get pretty far in a day," Mace said. "Especially if someone could teleport or ride an alicorn. What's so special about it?"

"This isn't your concern," Navina said, frowning at him.

"It's more his concern than yours," Dree said.

Navina's eyes narrowed. "Fine. I'll stop worrying and leave it to the three of you. I'm not the one that will suffer if it isn't found." She turned and stomped away.

"What's the amethyst crown?" Mace asked.

"It's a symbol of the kingdom. It's been around for generations. Nobody knows where it came from. It hasn't been worn in over two hundred years because there hasn't been a ruling queen on the throne in that long. I can't be crowned without it. It's tradition." Dree was trying to hide her panic as she blabbed on. "It's supposed to have magical powers that help rule the kingdom."

"So, without it, you won't be queen?"

She tapped her lip. "Well, I still will be, but it makes things complicated."

Mace held up two fingers. "So, you can't be queen without the crown and without being married? Anything else?"

"No, that's all. I don't think they will actually make us get married before I'm crowned. The contract is enough."

"I say we search Lenzo and his room. He's my guess."

Sen shook his head. "I doubt he would be careless enough to hide it in his room."

Mace shrugged. "What do we do, then?"

Dree sighed. "I do not know. I am open to suggestions."

Sen's eyebrows came together. "Once people learn about your crown, it might start a panic. People get worked up about things like this."

"Lovely," Dree said, rubbing her temples. "We must find it before that happens."

"I'll go find out the word in the city," Sen said. "I'm good at getting information."

"We are not leaving this to the likes of you!" Captain Lenzo said, striding up behind them. "The guard will take care of this, not children."

"Sen is capable," Dree said to the man.

Lenzo placed his hands at his hips. "Oh, and what fantastic feats has he accomplished?"

"Really?" Dree asked. "Amazing. Someone who hasn't heard of you," she said, cocking her head at Sen. She stared back at the guard. "Sen was one of the five who saved Basura two years ago."

Captain Lenzo looked at Sen with surprise. "You are a member of The Silver Eclipse?"

"I was," he said, shrugging. Sen hated recognition.

"He also named the world," Dree bragged.

"Well, that was technically my dad."

Sen's father had called the world Basura, and so Sen and his brothers called it the same, not realizing it meant garbage in their father's native language.

"I suppose you could be of some use," Lenzo said. "I'll give you instructions."

"I don't need instructions. I'll be back with something. Don't worry."

"There is a rumor about pirates," Lenzo said, rubbing his beard. "Some claim they saw some around the city. Are you ready for that?"

"Pirates?" Dree asked, rolling her eyes. "We aren't children. There's no such thing. I'm not as gullible as I used to be."

Sen stepped close to her and whispered, "There are pirates."

"What? Really? Well, why haven't I heard of them? My mother used every other thing to scare me. She never mentioned pirates."

"You haven't been around," the captain said with narrowed eyes. "I suppose there are many things you do not know." He turned and walked away.

"Why would pirates be here?" Dree asked. "We aren't a port city. We aren't close to any water, in fact."

"I've heard of them," Mace said. "They haven't been around for long, and they haven't caused a lot of trouble. It seems like it's been harmless pranks, for the most part."

"Pranks?" Dree asked. "From pirates?"

"Yeah," Sen added. "It's been strange. That's why no one has gone after them too vigorously."

"What kind of pranks?"

"All I remember is something about breaking into a public building at night and rubbing butter all over the place. They were all things like that. They stole some things as well, but nothing big enough to cause a panic."

Mace nodded. "They released a bunch of pigs into a library in Grenta. They almost got caught that time because they stayed to watch."

"Are they teenagers?" Dree wondered.

Sen shook his head. "No, that's the weird thing. They've been described as middle-aged men. I'm going to go ask around. I'll catch up later."

Dree watched Sen dash down the hallway. *Pirates*. She looked at Mace. "If they were only pulling pranks, they must have changed their objectives if they stole the crown. It wouldn't be an easy thing to steal. Lots of attempts have been made over the years, and all ended poorly for the perpetrators."

"What do you want me to do?" Mace asked, raising his eyebrow.

Dree felt panicked. She did not know what to do in this situation and it made her feel sick. She might be a princess, but she hadn't been raised to be a queen. Dree didn't want Mace to know how useless she really was.

"How much authority do you possess right now?" he asked, ignoring his first question. "It sounds like the council has some power. And what about your mother?"

"My mother has no authority over anything anymore. I can make all decisions, but the council gets the last say in anything important until I'm crowned. After I'm crowned, they can counsel me, but mine is the final say."

"Will they take advantage of the power while they have it?" he asked, cocking his head as he studied her.

"I'm not sure. They might, to some degree, but I assume they won't want to get on my bad side. As soon as I'm queen, I can replace them if I desire."

Mace sighed. "Should we talk to them?"

Dree let out a slow breath. She hated the thought of standing in front of the council, but it was probably best. "I suppose so. We should wait for Sen to get back so he can come as well. That way, he can report on anything he finds."

Sen held in a yawn as he listened to the council argue back and forth. The room was split. Some believed the guards should go after the pirates, and others thought it was pointless. They had listened for a minute to what Dree had to say but quickly cut her off and were now ignoring her. Dree had quickly faded into the background and wasn't trying to call attention to herself.

The surrounding city was all abuzz about the pirates. From what was being said, Sen felt justified in thinking the pirates were more like overgrown children than true villains. They had stolen a few things, but nothing they took was as high profile as the amethyst crown. The crown was heavily guarded, and the pirates only took things that were easy to snatch.

"This is a waste of time," he whispered to Dree and Mace. "Let's get out of here."

They left the room without any of the council paying attention.

"Your council is a mess," Mace told Dree, as they closed the door and made their way down the hall. "As soon as you're crowned, you should replace at least part of them, starting with the head."

Dree chewed her lip. "I agree, but the thought of doing it makes me nervous."

"You're going to need to step up a little harder," Sen said. "When we were in there, the council was in control. You need to hold control. I'm not saying people need to fear you, but they need to know who holds the reins." Sen felt guilty when he saw Dree's face fall. He knew she was doing the best she could, but she was going to have to learn to hold her ground.

"We need to do something fast," Mace said. "The longer we wait, the further the crown will get. If it was pirates, and they took it to sea, we probably have no chance of finding it. The ocean is vast and there aren't a lot of ships built well enough to take it on."

Mace was probably right about that. Long ago, there had been great fleets of ships that belonged the continents. There had been peace between the continents for so long that the fleets were eventually unnecessary, and now, most people only sailed small boats that could go from island to island. If the pirates had a ship that was strong and seaworthy, it would be close to impossible to find them in the enormous ocean.

"It sounds like the pirates aren't in the city anymore," Sen said. "From what I heard, they have a ship docked in Grenta, so I'm assuming that's where they're headed. How far is that?"

"Grenta is a two-day ride," Dree said, stopping when the hall split. "Do you suppose the pirates can teleport?"

Sen thought for a moment. "I doubt it. Teleporting hasn't caught on like it would have if people were teaching it heavily. The only person I've taught is Mace. I don't know about the rest of my friends, but I don't imagine they are teaching it to people, either."

"Can we teleport there, then?" she asked. "We could get there first and surprise them."

"I suppose we could," Sen said. "I have my doubts about blaming them. From what I hear, they seem too under-qualified to pull it off."

"I still think we should be looking closer at Captain Lenzo," Mace said. "He has the most to gain from slowing down your coronation. It gives him more time to figure out how to get rid of me."

"But if we teleport, we can be fast," Dree said. "We could go search for the pirate ship and wait for the pirates. We can be back in two days."

"That gives Lenzo two days to start something," Mace said, shaking his head. "I don't like it."

"I can go after the pirates, and you two can stay here," Sen said.

"No, I want to go," Dree said. "The thought of waiting around here makes me nervous."

"More nervous than chasing pirates?" Sen asked.

"Yes. Staying here is like waiting for something bad to happen. I need to become the person people listen to around here, but I need to get some of my thoughts together first. It will be good for me to do something."

"I'll stay here and keep watch on Lenzo," Mace said. "You two can go after the pirates."

Sen crossed his arms and frowned. "I'm not sure we should leave you alone. You're the one Lenzo is going to go after if he's determined to marry Dree. If we leave, you are defenseless."

"I can handle myself," Mace said. "Do I have any authority?" he asked, looking at Dree. "Will anyone listen to me?"

"Yes," Dree said. "Everyone should obey you, except the council."

"Then, I'll be fine. I can probably even intimidate the council if they realize you might get rid of some of them when you're crowned."

"Why can't I get people to listen to me?" Dree mumbled.

Sen shrugged. "As soon as the council disagreed with you, you became quiet. You can't let them push you around. You must be the boss, and you need to let them know it."

"That's true," Mace agreed, rubbing his chin. "You never seemed intimidated by Vetta. I could always tell you were holding back your temper with her. As soon as the council ignored you, you faded into the background."

Dree kicked at the rug. "That's what they taught me to do growing up. Being back at the castle brings back those memories."

"When do you want to go?" Sen asked. It wasn't the time to dwell on the past.

"It should probably be soon," she said. "I don't want to spend time sailing around searching for them."

"Me either," Sen said. "If they sail before we get there, we have little to no chance of finding them."

"You two go," Mace said. "I'll keep Lenzo in line."

Dree snorted. "I don't think anyone can get that man to do anything he doesn't want to."

"I'm sure you're right. I'll keep an eye on him, though."

"There you are," Navina said, walking swiftly toward Dree. "I should have realized that just because you finally made your way home, that didn't mean you were going to be visible. Where have you been?"

Dree rolled her eyes. "We were talking to the council."

Navina tossed her hair over her shoulder. "I suppose that is something."

"I'm not helpless, Mother."

Fire burned in Navina's eyes. "And yet you do not know how to rule a kingdom."

"I don't," Dree admitted. "But that is your and Father's fault, not mine. I'm going to learn."

"You can't blame us for your shortcomings."

"When I met Dree, she still thought there was a monster under her bed," Sen said, trying not to let too much disgust show. He probably didn't need to try. People always teased him about not showing emotion, but when it came to Dree, he was overprotective.

"Sometimes it is important to tell children things to keep them inline," Navina said, glaring at him.

"She was sixteen."

"Yes, and very obedient."

"Until she ran away. For two years."

Navina's eyes narrowed. "I don't need parenting advice from you."

"Mother, let's go talk in private," Dree said, taking her mother's arm and walking her away. "Sen, I'll meet you out front in fifteen minutes."

"I'll be there."

Mace sighed. "I hope the former queen isn't planning on staying around forever."

Sen couldn't agree more. "Yeah, she's a bit much. Maybe she'll mellow once she gets used to not being queen."

"I've heard you talk more today than in the last two years."

Sen nodded. "And it's exhausting. Socializing zaps my energy. I feel like I need a nap."

Mace laughed. "It sounds like you're hunting pirates in fifteen minutes, so I don't think you're going to get one."

"That's alright. Dree doesn't make me tired. Just everyone else."

"Mmhmm," Mace said, giving him a look Sen couldn't interpret.

"Chasing pirates sounds exciting as well. So long as they don't want to have a conversation."

"I'm still curious about you and Dree and the knife," Mace said with a grin.

"Which time?" Sen asked, flipping out a knife.

Mace raised his brows. "Whoa, that was fast. There's more than one story about you two and a knife?"

"Yep. The first time, she pulled a crossbow on me and my friends. The second time, she followed us, and I didn't know it was her."

"Well, I guess it shows she's brave."

"Yeah, just not always careful."

Mace tilted his head and looked at Sen. "I thought you taught her to use a crossbow."

Sen smirked. "I did. She didn't know how to use it when she pulled it on us. We were lucky she didn't accidentally shoot us. She didn't even have the safety on. She wasn't really a threat, even with the crossbow. The five of us had magic, and she didn't."

"But you used a knife? Not magic?"

Sen shrugged. "We didn't know she didn't have magic. I mean, we all thought she didn't, because she had the crossbow and all, but we couldn't be sure. She was so focused on trying to sound confident that I easily snuck around behind her."

"I hope she's learned to be more careful."

"A little."

"I don't want to spend the rest of my life keeping her out of trouble."

Sen nodded, but he didn't agree. He would love to spend the rest of his life watching out for her.

Chapter 5

Halla flattened herself against the side of the house and peeked around the corner. Vetta was standing, talking with a soldier. Halla pulled her head back and listened.

"I don't understand why you're here, but I'm listening," Vetta was saying.

"I realize how important your farm is to the Northern Kingdom. I'm not sure Princess Lesandri does," the man said. "The princess was supposed to marry me. If she had, I would have taken care of things. The princess doesn't seem to follow protocol well."

Vetta sniffed. "I'm not surprised. She worked here for two years, and it was almost impossible to get good results from her. I only kept her here as a favor."

"I need you to tell me everything you can about the princess's time here, as well as about the two young men she left with. If you cooperate with me, when I marry the princess, your farm will be rewarded and the talk of the kingdom. I'll make sure of it."

"Of course," Vetta purred. "Why don't we go inside where we can talk over tea?"

Halla's eyes widened, and she tiptoed to the other side of the house. If that man was planning on marrying Dree, that meant he was planning on getting rid of Mace. Would Vetta really want that? Vetta had drooled over Mace and Sen in an aggravating manner. Still, Vetta liked power, and she loved her farm.

Halla hurried into the house and ran up to her room. She'd planned on traveling to the castle in a month, but she needed to go now. If she didn't warn Mace, he might end up dead. That was the only way that soldier could break a marriage contract. She shoved her things into a bag as quickly as she could.

How was she going to get to the castle? She'd never been anywhere near it, and she hadn't done a lot of impulsive things in her life. Halla had been raised by her mother on a small farm, and when her mother passed away, she'd been forced to come here and work for her half-sister, Vetta. She hadn't expected Vetta to welcome her with open arms, but she'd been shocked at the hostility of the woman.

The sisters had never met until Halla's mother passed. Her father had died years earlier and had never been a great father. After Vetta's mother died, her father had left Vetta to run the farm. Even though it wasn't Halla's fault, Vetta blamed Halla and her mother for her father's absence.

No one had guessed the two were sisters. There was an obvious resemblance in the shape of their mouths, but nobody saw it past their complexions. Vetta was pale and avoided the sun at all costs. Halla's mother was from the Southern Kingdom and boasted beautiful brown skin and thick black hair. People told Halla she looked like her mother, but she didn't see it. Her mother had been a flawless beauty.

Adventures were not things that Halla sought. The thought of traveling to the unknown castle made her stomach turn, but she had to do it for Mace. She had never actually talked to him, and he scared her a little, but something about him made her heart beat out of control.

Even if he didn't, she couldn't let an innocent person get hurt. She would go to the castle, warn him, and hope they still let her work there even though she came early. There was no way Vetta would let her come back if she left.

Grenta was a busy port town with people hurrying in all directions. Dree wasn't used to seeing so many people doing so many things. She'd also never been shoved around so much. As soon as Sen teleported them to this place, she had been bumped and pushed all over the street. Sen had finally grabbed her arm and pushed their way to the port.

"Why is everyone in such a hurry?" she asked, wondering how Sen had gotten so good at navigating crowds.

"It's morning, so people are going to work," Sen said, leading her toward the ocean.

"I don't understand why they are so pushy."

"I guess we might have gotten through better if you wore your tiara, but that would defeat the purpose of going unnoticed. I still think your dress is too fancy."

Dree glanced down at her dark blue dress. "I threw away all of the clothing from Vetta's and you didn't give me enough time to find something more practical."

Sen was wearing one of his old tunics and had a sword at his waist. He preferred a knife, but if they had a confrontation with the pirates, he wanted to be prepared.

She glared at a man as he pushed past her. "I hope we beat the pirates here. If they have already left, I have little hope of us catching them."

"There isn't much chance they know how to teleport," Sen said. "We left fast enough. We probably beat them. We might be waiting for them a lot longer than we want."

Dree's eyes widened as they rounded a corner, and the ocean came into view. "I always forget how impressive the ocean is. I've only seen it a couple times, and that was years ago."

"I would bet that's the ship we want," Sen said, pointing at a medium-sized ship. It was flying a black flag with a skull and crossbones.

Dree ran a hand through her curls as she studied the ship. "How can we be sure? I thought it would be bigger."

"Well, for one thing, it's the only ship here. Then, there's the flag."

She squinted up at the flag. "That's a pirate flag?"

Sen nodded. "Don't you remember that pirate movie we watched when we were on Earth? It had flags like that."

Dree shrugged. When they spent time on Earth, Sen's family had been obsessed with a thing called a television. Dree hadn't seen the appeal. It was an amazing invention, but most of the things they watched scared her. She remembered a pirate movie, but she hadn't paid a lot of attention because it terrified her. It seemed so real.

Sen led her closer to the ship. "Basura and Earth have had a lot of crossovers during the years, but I am surprised they have the same flag."

"I've studied a lot of history, and there was never anything about real pirates."

"It's not surprising. Since it's been peaceful between the continents for so many years, there aren't many boats on the waters. What is a pirate really going to do? With no ships to raid, it's pointless."

"They aren't very careful," Dree said, spotting a ramp going up to the ship. "Anyone can go up there. Even if they didn't steal the crown, we need to put a stop to this. We wouldn't want others to start causing problems because we aren't proactive."

Sen tilted his head and studied the vessel. "Should we go up?"

"I guess. We can surprise them when they board."

"We don't know how many of them there are. There might be some still up there, come to think of it."

Dree hesitated. She didn't stop to think about how many pirates there were. "I bet there are some up there. It would be silly to leave the ship unprotected."

"They aren't the smartest group from what I hear."

Dree cupped her hands around her mouth and yelled, "Hello on board!"

Sen rolled his eyes. "Come on, Dree. That's not how you sneak."

She frowned. "But wouldn't it be better to know if anyone's there?"

"Perhaps, but we'd lose any element of surprise."

"Nobody's coming."

"I'll go up. You stay here until I check."

Dree nodded and moved off to the side. No one was paying her any attention, but it might be better to not stand staring at the ship. She tried not to fidget as she waited. The sun was heating things up, and she wished she had worn a cooler dress. Sen had tried to get her to wear a tunic and britches, but that was a style Dree wasn't ready to embrace. Most women wore britches, but she was a princess. Even when she worked for Vetta, she wore a dress most days.

Dree crossed her arms and stared up at the ship. Why was it taking so long? If there were pirates on board and they had Sen, what could she do? Sen was great at sneaking and fighting. If he got captured, there was no chance for her.

She waited a few more minutes and then tiptoed up the ramp, making sure her boots made as little noise as possible. Her heart pounded as she reached the top. She stepped onto the clean deck and looked around. There was no sign of Sen—or anyone else.

Dree chewed her lip and wondered what to do next. She took a few steps forward and gasped as the ground started to sink. Her boots were slowly lowering into the wooden deck like they would in quicksand. She tried to lift her foot, but it was stuck.

"Sen!" she called, as she kept trying to free herself. Her boots had completely disappeared, and she was up to her knees. What kind of magic was this? She'd never heard of sinking floors. The wooden planks rippled like water as she continued to sink. Why hadn't she learned any magic?

There was a way to speak telepathically to a person in their mind, but Dree had never tried it. It made people sick, so it wasn't a popular type of magic. She knew you had to know the person's location to get a message to them, and you had to concentrate on them and whisper. It was hard to focus when you were up to your waist and sinking fast.

She tried to concentrate on Mace at the palace. "Help!" she whispered, louder than she meant. She closed her mouth and eyes as she sank all the way beneath the deck. She screamed as she fell and slammed into the floor.

"Are you alright?" Sen asked, helping her to her feet.

"Fine," she said, squinting into the dimly lit space. Sen was holding an orb of light, but it was still hard to see after being in the sun.

"I hoped you would go for help instead of coming up," Sen said.

"I was worried. You were taking so long. Where are we?"

"A small cell," Sen said, holding up his light to illuminate the space. Dree studied the bars and sighed. The area was only about ten feet both ways.

"Can't you teleport us out?"

Sen shook his head. "Nope. I tried. They must've made the bars of something that stops that. I can still do other magic, but nothing I've tried has been helpful."

"I tried to send a message to Mace as I was falling, but I don't know if he got it."

"I sent out a couple of messages as I was sinking, but no one answered."

"So, what do we do?"

"I'm not sure."

Dree crossed her arms and jiggled her leg. She wasn't used to Sen not knowing what to do. He always had a way out.

"Can't you use a fireball to burn through the floor?" He was one of the few people that could do that.

Sen raised his eyebrow. "Do you want to be stuck in a ship that's on fire? Even if I made a hole in the floor, water would come in and we would drown."

"Right," Dree said, looking around for a solution. "Can you pick the lock?"

"Maybe," he said, pulling out a small knife. "Can you hold up a light?"

Dree pulled up an orb of light and was happy she at least knew how to do that. When they got out of this, she was learning basic magic. Sen reached around the bars and stuck his knife into the lock. Dree came in closer and held the light near him.

"It's no use," he said, pulling his knife out. "I think we're stuck here until someone comes."

Dree sank down onto the floor. "What are the chances they let us go?"

"I don't know," he said, sitting next to her. "I'm hoping someone heard my call and just didn't have time to answer."

"Can we send a message to someone else?"

Sen shook his head. "I'm worried it's another thing that doesn't work down here. I tried to send one to you and tell you not to come on board."

She blew out a breath. "I obviously didn't get that one."

"I sent one to a friend as I was falling. I hope he got it."

"What if the pirates don't come back for a long time? We could freeze or starve. I knew we should've worn cloaks."

"We would have stood out too much. If we were on the other continent, nobody would think twice, but people only seem to wear capes and cloaks here when it's cold. We won't freeze anyway. Nights are still warm. I can try to summon some food, but if we can't teleport, I doubt I can summon."

Dree couldn't remember the exact art of summoning, but she knew you couldn't take something from anywhere. You had to know the exact location of the thing you wanted to summon and people put protection spells on their homes so that criminals couldn't steal things.

"The only food I know of is at the castle, and the castle has a lot of protection put on it."

"We can think about it later," Sen said. "We shouldn't be hungry for a while."

Dree sat up straight. "Did you hear that?" she whispered. Someone was walking above. "Do we yell for help or try to stay quiet?"

Sen stood and stared at the ceiling, but Dree couldn't read his expression. "I'm not sure."

More footsteps followed, and Dree took a deep breath, trying to still her pounding heart.

"It sounds like there are a lot of them," she said, standing. She wanted to grab his arm, but Sen wasn't a touchy person. It would probably make him uncomfortable. "We can probably talk our way out of this. If I have to, I can tell them who I am."

"No," Sen said. "They're pirates. If they find out who you are, what's to stop them from ransoming you? We save that as a last option. Don't worry, we'll figure this out."

Dree felt better. Sen always made things better. "I don't know what I would do without you. I should put you on my council once I'm queen."

Sen glanced at her and then away. "I'm not going to stick around once you're crowned. It's time for me to figure out where I belong."

Dree felt her stomach drop. She'd never imagined Sen leaving. He'd been with her through everything. How could she be queen without him? Now wasn't the time to dwell on it, though. One problem at a time.

"The ship is moving," Sen said. "I thought they would check down here first."

"We can't get taken out to the ocean!" she exclaimed. "We have no chance out there."

"If we can get out of the cell, we can teleport. It won't matter how far out in the ocean we are. Someone's coming down the stairs."

Dree's eyes jerked toward the stairs, and she grabbed Sen's hand. She was relieved when he didn't pull away. A tall, middle-aged man in a tunic came bounding down the stairs. The pirate hat with a large feather was the only thing that marked him as a pirate. He was carrying a lantern, which he almost dropped when he saw the two of them.

The man blinked a few times and then yelled up the stairs, "Prisoners!" More footsteps on the stairs, and another man appeared. He had a matching pirate hat minus the feather, and he wore an eye patch. He was also wearing a regular tunic.

"Who are you?" the first man growled, as he squinted at them.

Dree had let her light go out, so the only light source was the pirate's lantern.

"No one of consequence," Sen said. "We just wanted to see the ship, and we fell in."

"Likely story," the first man said.

"Look at them," the shorter man with the eye patch said. "They're only kids. We should dock again and throw them off."

"I'm not docking. There were people on our trail."

"We can swim back," Sen said. Dree cringed. She didn't know how to swim. It would be humiliating if Sen had to tow her to shore.

"No," the first man said. "Just because they're young doesn't mean they're innocent."

"Come on, Ernesto. We'll have more people after us if we take them."

Ernesto scratched at the black stubble on his chin. "If you sneak onto a pirate ship, you probably don't tell people. No one will suspect they're with us."

"But what will we do with them?"

"We'll leave them here for now. Put a band on their wrists and then we'll meet up top to discuss it."

The shorter man sighed. "Fine, but I think this is a mistake." He grabbed something and came near the bars. "Put out your hand."

Dree shared a look with Sen. He shrugged.

"I said, put out your hand. I'm not gonna hurt you."

"Hurry up, Oscar," Ernesto said.

Oscar reached through the bars and grabbed Dree's hand. She resisted pulling away as he put something that appeared to be a metal bracelet on her wrist. It clicked into place, and he released her. He motioned for Sen's hand and put one on him.

"I'll leave the lantern," Ernesto said, placing it on a table a few feet away from the cell. "You won't be able to do any magic with those cuffs on. And hand me that sword."

Dree's heart fell. If Sen couldn't do magic, they were stuck. Sen handed the man his sword, and they watched the two men disappear up the stairs.

She gazed around their prison. "Now what? Maybe I can squeeze through the bars?"

Sen sat on the floor. "I doubt it. I don't think we're getting out of here without help. At least it's clean."

Dree sighed. Was Sen giving up? He was always the one with a solution. She studied the bars. They weren't as close together as they should be. Sen was probably right, though. Even if she could squeeze through, there was a ship full of pirates up above. Still, if they got out now, they weren't far from shore. The longer they stayed, the less chance they had of getting rescued.

"What are you doing?" Sen asked when Dree put her head up to the bars.

"I bet I can get through."

"Don't. You'll get stuck."

Dree put her head on the bars and pushed it through. "I can do it."

"Even if you can, I can't, and you'll just be stuck out there."

She pushed part of her shoulder through and realized she couldn't make it. "Blast. I thought I could fit." She pulled her shoulder back in and then tried her head. It wouldn't go back. But it had to fit. She just put it in, and she was sure it hadn't grown. Sen was quiet behind her. She could guess he was staring at her with his stoic expression, wondering why she never listened. She pulled harder and was finally able to pull through. Her ear was going to hurt from that silly move.

"Let's not try that again," Sen said. "We're going to have to wait."

Dree rubbed her sore ear. "I'm not used to you giving up. It makes me nervous."

"I'm not giving up," Sen said, as she joined him on the floor. "I just think nothing we do right now will help. We need to wait for an opportunity. If we act too soon we could make things worse."

"If you don't stay when I'm queen, what will you do?" Dree asked. That was causing her more stress than being locked in a pirate ship.

"I don't know. I might go back to Boztoll. I spent most of my life there."

"If you don't know what you want to do, why not stay? There are lots of things you could do in my kingdom. Lots of opportunities. I'm sure there would be something to interest you. If you don't want to be on my council, there are plenty of other options."

Sen looked at her and frowned. It made a lump form in Dree's throat. Sen rarely frowned, and he was doing it at her.

"Once you get everything settled, you won't need me anymore. Mace will be there for you. I'll stay until everything's official."

Dree nodded. She couldn't force him to stay—well, she could, but she wouldn't. He'd already given up two years of his life to make sure she was alright. Still, she'd never thought about what life would be like if he weren't there. He was her best friend. Sure, she would have Mace, but they didn't seem to connect the way she did with Sen. Why hadn't Sen just agreed to marry her?

Tears pricked her eyes as she realized Sen meant more to her than she realized. She raised her knees and wrapped her arms around them. How had she hidden her feelings so deeply that she hadn't even recognized them? She rested her head on her knees, facing away from him. It didn't matter how she felt. Sen had already refused her.

"Don't worry," Sen said. "We'll get out of this."

"I'm just tired," she said, keeping emotion from her voice. She let a few tears run down her cheek and onto her dress. She didn't move to wipe them because she didn't want Sen to know.

Sen sighed and put a hand to his head. Great. Now Dree was crying. They had been through a lot together, and he'd never seen her cry. She was trying to hide it, but he could tell. He wasn't sure if she was crying because they were locked up or because he wasn't going to stay in the Northern Kingdom. It was probably being locked up.

He didn't know what to do in these situations. Should he pretend he didn't notice? She seemed to be going through a lot of effort to breathe normally and not let him know. The sniffs and the slight tremble to her shoulders gave it away.

"These pirates aren't like the ones they talk about on Earth," he said, deciding to change the subject.

"Oh?"

"Did you look closely at their hats? They almost seemed like they were crocheted. The flag outside seemed home-made as well."

"What does that mean, though?" she asked, not looking at him.

"I'm not sure. I wonder if they're some type of copycats that don't have a great objective yet. That's my hope. They might just let us go."

She raised her head but didn't turn toward him. She pulled a handkerchief from her pocket and wiped at her nose. "That would be nice. We need to search for the crown."

"Right." How had he forgotten about the crown? "I don't think we should just ask if they have it. That might make them keep us longer." He pulled at the metal cuff on his arm. "I wonder how these bracelets come off? If we escape and still have them on, we might not get them off."

Dree fiddled with hers. "There isn't a keyhole."

"I've never heard of an object that can stop magic like this."

"The pirates have to have magic, right? Everyone has magic now, so why are they using a lantern?"

"Making an orb of light can be convenient, but you have to keep your focus on it. You can't just leave it to light the room. A lantern takes care of that."

She nodded. Even with the dim flickering light, he could see her red eyes. He swallowed hard and wanted to kick himself. If he was a good friend, he would wrap her in a hug, which would be completely out of character for him. Why hadn't he agreed to marry her? Even if she never fell in love with him, it would be better than turning her over to someone else she didn't love. She trusted him, and he let her down.

Sen prided himself on going into situations with a clear head, and he had failed today. He should have known better than to go on a ship like this. They should've watched from a distance. Now, he was here with no plan and no magic.

"How many crew members do you suppose they have?" she asked.

"I don't know what it takes to sail a ship. It has to be more than the two of them."

"So, if they open the cell and we knock them out, it probably won't do us any good?"

"No. There are sure to be others."

Dree ran a hand over her blue dress. "When we don't come back, do you suppose Mace will come looking for us?"

"I'm sure he will."

"I wonder if Captain Lenzo will come."

Sen looked thoughtful. "Possibly. I'm not sure whether that would be a good or bad thing. He might prefer it if we disappeared."

"He can't take over without me. He isn't connected to the throne in any way, so he should hope I make it through this. People like him are hard to read." She sighed. "I'm not sure what's more dangerous. Captain Lenzo or these pirates."

Chapter 6

Captain Lenzo was up to a lot more than anyone knew. Mace was still unsure what it all could be, but he was spending his time doing more than being the captain of the guards. The soldiers were out investigating the missing crown, and Mace was inside the captain's room to try to prove his own suspicions. Sen and Dree had been gone for two days and hadn't sent word, but this was the first time he'd been able to get into the room.

The whispers that said Lenzo was studying to be a sorcerer seemed valid in his opinion. There were strange things hidden all over the room. He discovered a box of what appeared to be marbles and had been burned by one when he tried to pick it up. When he examined the walls, he found one that had a secret latch that opened. Behind it was a shelf full of different vials. Mace didn't know what was in them because Lenzo had labeled them in an unfamiliar language.

On the other side of the room, the wall also opened and was full of spell books. No one used spells except sorcerers and witches. A person had to reach an entirely different level of magic than the normal person to be considered a sorcerer or witch. Mace could only remember three times that anyone had held the titles in the last hundred years.

Mace circled the room one last time to make sure there were no signs that he'd been in there. He'd found a lot, but no crown. That didn't make Lenzo innocent. It just meant he wasn't stupid enough to leave the crown in his own room. He locked the room and hoped he was leaving it the way he found it.

"There you are," a soldier said, rushing toward him.

Mace's heart pounded in his chest. Had someone seen him go into Lenzo's room?

"I shouldn't be telling you this," the soldier said. "I was guarding the drawbridge today, and a young woman came to us and asked us if she could talk to you. She wouldn't say why, so she was turned away."

"She was searching for me?" Mace asked, gesturing to himself. Who could be looking for him?

"Yes. She seemed distressed. I thought you might want to know."

"What did she look like?"

The guard looked at the ceiling as he thought. "Um—Brown skin, black hair, and dark eyes. Really pretty. She said she knows you, and it's an emergency. She was young. Probably no older than eighteen."

Mace shifted from one leg to the other. "Do you know where she is?"

"When they wouldn't let her in, she just appeared rejected and went toward the village."

"Alright, thank you."

He couldn't imagine anyone like that looking for him unless it was Halla. The girl had never spoken to him before, but Dree said she was coming eventually. He rushed from the castle and hurried down the road to the village. It wasn't far from the castle, so he got there in good time.

Mace shook his head. She could be anywhere. Halla was a quiet soul, and she didn't like to stand out. If it was her, she would not be standing in an obvious spot. People crowded the village square, buying and selling from temporary stands. The smell of warm bread entered his nose, reminding him he missed breakfast.

"Mace!" He turned when he heard his name. Halla was bolting toward him, her black hair flying behind her. She plowed into him, giving him the most unexpected hug of his life. "I didn't think I would find you!" she said, pulling away from him and turning her attention to the ground.

"Let's go back to the castle, and you can talk on the way," he said, leading her away from the crowd. She kept up with his fast pace and kept her eyes averted. When they got to the road, he turned to her. "What's wrong?"

She rubbed her arm nervously and kept her gaze down. "I overheard something at Vetta's," she said, her voice shaking.

He didn't know if she was worried about what she had to say or if she was scared of him. Possibly both. He had a reputation for scaring the maids. He didn't mean to, but he didn't have time to be pleasant. "What was it?" he asked.

She pushed a stray lock behind her ear. "There was a man talking to Vetta. He was wearing armor and had a sword. They were making a deal about her crops and talking about Dree. He said he was supposed to marry her."

Mace nodded. "It must have been Captain Lenzo."

"I can't remember everything they said, but what I took away from it is that you are in danger. I suspect the man means to kill you and marry Dree."

"Yeah, I already know that. I wonder why he would go to Vetta, though."

She glanced up, then back to her boots. "He wanted information about Dree's time there and about you and Sen."

"Hm. I'm sure Vetta was thrilled to tell him everything."

"I expect so. I didn't hear what she told him because they went in to have tea. I packed my bag and left. I'm sorry I didn't learn more."

"It would have been foolish to follow them and eavesdrop. I appreciate you coming to warn me. Where's your bag?" he asked, glancing at her. She wasn't carrying anything.

Halla looked into her empty hands and raised her brows. "I had it a minute ago. I was so relieved when I saw you, I must have dropped it."

"Someone probably snatched it already."

"I didn't have much anyway," she said, staring at her feet. She was walking slower, so Mace matched her speed.

"I'm sure we can find you what you need." Mace wasn't sure who to talk to at the castle, but they had to have some extra clothing somewhere. If not, he could buy her something. He should have asked Dree who to talk to in situations like this.

"Um—I don't know how to ask this," Halla said quietly. "I can't return to Vetta's. I left without her permission, and she won't forgive that, especially from me."

"Dree told us you were coming eventually. It won't hurt anything to have you here early."

The girl glanced up with hopeful eyes. "Really? Thank you. I don't have enough money for an inn, and I'm not acquainted with anyone here."

"Let's get you to the castle and figure things out, alright?"

She smiled shyly and nodded.

"Dree and Sen aren't here right now, but I'm sure we can get you a room." They walked in silence toward the castle. Mace rarely had trouble knowing what to say, but Halla was quiet, and he didn't know her well. She'd always caught his eye, but he ignored things like that. He'd had bad experiences with pretty girls before.

He grimaced. This situation he'd gotten himself in with Dree was eating at him. He wasn't sure what had come over him when he agreed to the marriage contract. The more he thought about it, the more he realized he didn't want to be a prince. Commanding the army would be a great honor, but he would much rather be on the Queen's Council. He liked the political side more than the military. He hoped they could defeat Lenzo, find the crown, and convince the council to let Dree marry who she wanted.

He let out a heavy sigh. Dree didn't seem to realize who she wanted to marry. Mace had been watching Dree and

Sen for two years. As far as he knew, nothing romantic had ever happened between them, but they spent all of their free time together. The problem was, they didn't seem to realize what they meant to each other. He might have to tell them because they weren't figuring it out.

Mace shook his head. Most people didn't try to figure out ways to get their betrothed to fall in love with someone else. He liked Dree. She might have a lot to learn before she became queen, but she was determined and hardworking. Dree was the worst maid he'd ever seen, but she never stopped trying. She was pretty too—still, there just wasn't any emotion involved when he thought about her.

Why was his life always such a mess? He'd decided years ago he wouldn't ever get married, and then he'd agreed to, much too quickly. And now, he was thinking about Halla's pretty face and quiet personality. He'd made his decision, and he had no right to be thinking about Halla. It was possible he could get out of the contract if he could get Sen to open his eyes.

Halla stumbled, and he reached out and steadied her. "Careful."

"Thank you," she said, looking up at him with her big, beautiful eyes.

His heart thudded in his chest. It was betraying him. He nodded at her and cleared his throat. He had issues.

Halla hoped Mace wouldn't see how embarrassed she was. She couldn't believe she had hugged him! She'd never hugged a person besides her mother in her life, and she started with one she was both attracted to and scared of. Not only that, but someone with a marriage contract! Her mother would roll over in her grave.

She'd gotten here as fast as she could, and it sounded like Mace already knew about the plot against him. She didn't even need to come. She wouldn't dwell on that. Working here had to be better than working for Vetta. If it wasn't, it couldn't be worse.

"Are you hungry?" Mace asked as they entered the castle.

"I'm fine," she lied. She hadn't eaten anything since yesterday.

"*Fine* can have so many meanings," he said, looking sideways at her. "Let's get you something to eat. Is there anything else you need?"

"No. Well, I lost my alicorn," she said. "Do you think there is a way to find it? I flew her here and didn't tie her up when I talked to the guards."

"I can ask around."

She was sure he didn't have connections here after only being around a few days, but he wasn't shy. It would be easier for him to figure things out than her. "Thanks."

"I didn't know you had an alicorn."

"That's another reason I can't go back to Vetta."

He grinned. "You stole an alicorn from Vetta?"

Halla felt heat creep up her neck. "I don't consider it stealing. I brought her with me when I came to Vetta, and Vetta confiscated her."

"Vetta stole your alicorn?" Mace asked, scratching his chin. "I know she doesn't let maids house their own animals on her property, but that seems pretty low."

Halla kept her eyes on her boots. She usually avoided talking to people, but when she did, she got to know her boots really well. Why was it so hard to look a person in the face?

She shrugged. "She said it should have been hers."

Mace raised his brow. "That doesn't make sense."

Halla let out a long sigh. "The alicorn first belonged to my father. Vetta and I have the same father."

Mace came to an abrupt stop. "What? Vetta's your sister?"

"Yes."

He whistled. "I never would have guessed."

"Because she's white?"

"No, because you're quiet and she's loud. I've never respected Vetta, but I didn't think she would be low enough to make her own sister her maid."

"It has been hard, but I'm putting that in the past." She really hoped it was true. When she was young, she had longed to meet her sister. She imagined the fun adventures they would have together. Meeting Vetta had shattered that dream. Getting over that heartache wasn't easy.

"Which alicorn is it?"

"Windy."

"I can probably find her. Windy loves me. I bet if I call for her, she'll come."

Halla didn't doubt it. "Thank you."

Mace cleared his throat. If Halla didn't know better, she would suspect he was nervous about something. "If you need anything, let me know," he said. "I know all the maids were scared of me, but I'm harmless."

Halla smiled. The maids were scared of him? Most of them were half in love with him. He intimidated Halla, but she was that way with most people. This place was a new start. Perhaps, Halla could try to be more social. Sometimes, she went for days without talking to anyone.

"I'll talk to someone about getting you some clothes," Mace said. "All the maids seem to wear the same thing, so they probably have a pile of dresses somewhere."

"Thank you." There was something thrilling about the thought of getting a new dress, even if it was a maid's dress. She was fairly certain maids in a castle would have nice clothing. Royalty wouldn't want their servants to be sloppy. It had been a long time since she'd had something nice. Vetta didn't let her maids look dirty, but she didn't seem to mind their clothing being worn.

Halla knew there were probably lots of shady things going on at the castle, but she couldn't help feeling like this was the new start she needed.

Lenzo sat in his room in his comfy chair, studying his spell book. Things couldn't be better. Well, that wasn't completely true. It would be nice to not have to deal with Lesandri's *friends*. Still, Lenzo couldn't believe his luck. Mace had brought in a pretty young maid, and from his informants in the castle, he couldn't keep his eyes off her. He was told Mace helped the girl for several hours and ate two meals with her. What a fool Mace was. Lenzo would use this to his advantage. He wasn't sure how, but he could see an opportunity when it was presented to him.

Lenzo would be king. There was no doubt about it. He had waited long enough. He would be a more competent ruler than King Miadd or his bratty son. Prince Raz had been a spoiled, self-absorbed waste. His sense of entitlement should have been a disgrace to the king and queen, but they had been blind to his faults.

Lenzo didn't blame Princess Lesandri for running away. Her family had treated her like an embarrassment. It was rare to see her at public events, and rumors circulated she was sickly. As an important part of the king's inner circle, Lenzo had been one of the few that knew the princess hadn't had magic.

If Lenzo had been smart, he would have befriended the princess before she disappeared. He should have tried to be sympathetic to her plight. That would have been a lot easier than what he was up against now. She would never like him, but he wouldn't let that change his plans.

It had been too easy to get rid of King Miadd and Prince Raz. Neither one of them was loved in the kingdom, so it was no chore to find a group of no good criminals willing to kill them for a few pieces of silver. The criminals would never tell. They were taken out by the king's guards, just as Lenzo had planned. It was nice to have everything wrapped up so neatly.

Lenzo drummed his fingers on his book. He had a tough decision. Should he marry Lesandri and rule through her or have her killed? If she could be tamed, he would prefer letting her live. If he killed her, he wouldn't be crowned king without a lot of fighting. He wasn't in line for the throne, so people would expect one of Lesandri's cousins to take over.

Perhaps, he could put a spell on her to make her subservient. She had changed since she left two years ago, and he could tell she wouldn't obey him without a fight. It was too bad she disliked him. He could admire her spirit and beauty, but not when she was against him.

It had irritated him when he found out about her marriage contract. That had made things more complicated. She must have grabbed the first man she could find to avoid obeying the council. It was obvious she wasn't in love with Mace, and from the way he stared at the new maid, he wasn't in love with her, either.

It was convenient that she chose a hired hand as her fiancé. He would be easier to get rid of, and fewer people would wonder when he disappeared. If she had ended up married to the governor's son like the original plan, that would have caused more complications, but Lenzo had been plotting even then.

"Aha," he said, when he came to a spell to make a protective bubble. No one had possessed the ability to make a protective shield in over five hundred years. If he could manage it, he would have a significant advantage.

Lenzo had a feeling he would need some tricks in the coming days. The princess's friend Sendo was more of a threat than Mace. Two years ago, it had been impossible to go through an entire day without hearing that boy's name. He and his friends had made quite the impression on the world.

It was hard to tell the rumors from the truth when it came to Sendo and his friends, but from the gossip that reached the Northern Kingdom, they possessed magic that no one else had. What magic, Lenzo didn't know, but he needed to be careful. It was also obvious Sendo was protective of Lesandri.

It had been almost too simple to steal the crown since Lenzo was in charge of the security protecting it. He didn't have the satisfaction he might have if it had been a challenge. It worked well to get Sendo and Lesandri out of the way. If Lenzo was lucky, Garin wouldn't let Sendo return from the search for the crown, but Lenzo had never been lucky, so he better have a solid plan.

Chapter 7

Dree was ready to stick her head through the bars again. They had been on this ship for two days! The space was too small, and she was sure she was going to smell soon if she didn't already. The pirates only let them out a few times a day to take care of personal needs. There were around twenty pirates as far as she could tell, and all but three had the magic restricting bands they wore.

They hadn't seen the original two pirates since the first time they came down. The only pirate they spoke to was a man named Garin. He was the third person without a magic restrictor. He was somewhere around thirty with dirty blond hair and wild eyes. There were other pirates that brought their food, but they didn't say anything.

"Time to go up top," Garin said, unlocking their cell. Dree hoped that would be a good thing. They hadn't been up top since they came here. She hoped they weren't going to have them walk the plank. They stood, and the man motioned for them to go in front of him. They walked up the stairs and onto the deck of the ship.

Something about Garin made Dree uneasy. Most of the pirates seemed almost awkward around them, but Garin sent out a superior vibe she couldn't explain. He didn't dress like the others. They were all slightly tattered and dirty, and he looked more like a royal. He was clean and held himself upright to the point of appearing rigid.

"Well, if it isn't our prisoners," Ernesto said, taking a step toward them. Garin turned and walked quickly away.

Dree squinted at him. The sun was bright after being below.

"I am Captain Ernesto, and this is first mate Oscar. We assume we are far enough from shore that you won't be jumping."

"What magic is this?" Oscar said, walking up to Sen.

Ernesto rolled his eyes. "What are you talking about, Oscar?"

"Look at him," he said, pointing at Sen. "It's Rosendo, and he hasn't aged a day!"

Sen took a step back, and Dree raised her brows.

"That's not Rosendo," Ernesto told the other man. "That would be impossible. He looks an awful lot like him, though."

"Rosendo is my father," Sen said. "You must be his friends. The ones he came from Mexico with."

"Well, what do you know?" Ernesto laughed. "We always wondered what happened to Rosendo. He wanted to farm, of all things. Oscar and I wanted adventure, so we left him to the farm, and the farmer's daughter."

Oscar grinned. "He married the farmer's daughter, right?"

"Yes," Sen said. "They returned to Mexico a couple of years ago."

"How did they manage that?" Ernesto asked.

Dree was starting to feel hope. These men might let them go.

"I can teleport to Earth. I could take you two back if you want."

"Nah," Oscar said. "We like it here now that we have magic."

Ernesto nodded in agreement. "There was a time we would have given anything to go back. Now that we have magic and goals, everything is different. Come, let's have lunch." He motioned them toward a door, and they entered to see a large table that ran almost the length of the room. Ten chairs surrounded it.

Sen sat down without an invitation, and Dree sat beside him. The pirates didn't seem to mind. They plopped down on their own chairs, and Ernesto yelled for someone to bring food.

"So, what are your names?" Ernesto asked.

"I'm Sen, and this is Dree."

"Sen, Sen... The same Sen that helped with the silver eclipse?"

"Yes."

Ernesto laughed. "So, Rosendo's son is a celebrity. We owe you one. You're the reason we have magic!"

Dree felt even more hope. Sen just looked serious. A man entered with a tray carrying four plates, placed it in front of them, and left.

Ernesto grabbed a roll and took a bite. "Is it a coincidence you were on our ship, or were you hunting us down?"

"I don't hunt people down," Sen said, staring intently at the captain.

"No? That's not the rumor we heard."

"When I was working on the silver eclipse, that was different. We had to stop the people who were trying to prevent it."

"And what about your friend here?" Oscar asked, spearing a piece of chicken with his fork. "Did she help?"

"I wasn't one of the members of The Silver Eclipse, if that's what you mean. I helped a little."

Sen nudged her boot with his toe. "I considered you a part of it."

She blushed and focused on her food.

"I thought it was kinda funny. The group was called The Silver Eclipse, and that was also the name of the magic that saved everything," Oscar said through a mouthful of chicken.

Sen didn't give an explanation. He just kept eating.

Ernesto pointed his fork at Sen. "What do you do now that you aren't saving the world? Getting into trouble? Is that why you were on our ship? Boredom can lead to mischief."

Dree snorted. "Says a pirate."

Oscar laughed. "She's got us there."

"Do you really want to be pirates?" Sen asked. "I know people aren't feeling very threatened by you, but eventually, people will come after you."

"It takes a while to make a name for yourself," Ernesto said, taking a bite of chicken. "People will fear us soon enough."

"Because you spread butter on things and egg political buildings?" Dree asked, tearing a piece off a roll.

"You have to admit the butter was funny," Oscar said with a chuckle. "Every time I picture someone entering the room and touching anything, I laugh."

Dree sat up tall. "It seems juvenile to me. You're grown men."

"We've done more than silly pranks," Ernesto said, giving Oscar a warning stare. "Our latest endeavor is going to have us set for life."

Dree tilted her head. "Not if you get caught and end up in jail. Or dead."

"What did you do?" Sen asked.

"We can't talk about it now," Ernesto said. "Maybe some other time."

Sen narrowed his eyes. "Where are we going? We've been sailing for two days, and the further we get from land, the fewer islands there are. What's the point of sailing away from anywhere you can dock?"

Oscar laughed. "We aren't trying to dock. Have you heard of Mermaid's Demise?"

Sen shook his head, and Dree nodded. The two continents in Basura were both on the same side of the world.

On the other side was only the ocean. Very few people sailed over there because there wasn't anything to see.

"Mermaid's Demise was rumored to be a misty part of the ocean where ships frequently disappeared throughout history," she told Sen. "Some suspect there is a huge whirlpool. There isn't a reason to go near it, as there is nothing else around it."

Ernesto grinned. "Maybe not around it, but what about under it?"

"Don't tell me you're trying to find Riviand?"

"Not on this trip, but who wouldn't want to find a lost continent full of gold?"

"Full of gold?" Dree asked. "I've studied mythology surrounding Riviand and nothing says it has any gold."

"I'm still confused," Sen said.

Dree turned to him. "Riviand was supposed to be a continent that was on the other side of the world. In theory, the people there wanted to get away from the rest of the world, so they used some powerful magic to pull the entire continent under the ocean. It supposedly happened a few thousand years ago."

"I remember something about that, now that you mention it." Sen threw a grape into the air and caught it in his mouth.

Dree tried to not look impressed. "It wasn't supposed to have gold, though."

"Every city hidden in the ocean has gold," Ernesto said. "Why else would they hide?"

"It's all just a myth."

"Well, we're going to hunt for it," Oscar said. "After we take care of something."

Sen took a bite of his roll. "Something at Mermaid's Demise?"

"Yes."

Dree frowned. "People don't go there because they don't want to drown. Why would you try to go there?"

"It's a good place to dispose of something you never want found," Ernesto said.

Dree shivered and hoped he didn't mean them.

"Once we finish, we can take you home," Ernesto said. "Or you can help us search for Riviand. We have a theory that it's under Mermaid's Demise."

"And you get there how?" Sen asked.

Oscar frowned. "We haven't figured that out yet."

"You could take these cuffs off us and let us teleport home," Dree said hopefully. "Then we wouldn't be in your way."

"I don't think so," Ernesto said. "Just because he's Rosendo's son doesn't mean we trust him yet."

"Did your eye patch change sides?" Sen asked Oscar.

Oscar coughed and rubbed his eyepatch. "Nah, it's the same one."

Dree held back a smile. The patch covered his right eye, and his left eye had marks around it from where the patch had been. These pirates were frauds in so many ways. It was surprising none of them were walking around with a fake peg leg.

Ernesto shoved an entire roll into his mouth. "Since you can't do magic, and there is no possible way for you to swim to shore, we will allow you to move freely around the ship. You can sleep down below or up on deck. We don't have any beds. Most people sleep above deck to avoid everyone else's smell."

Sen leaned his elbows against the railing and gazed into the ocean. Dree stood beside him, scanning the water for fish. Every now and then one would jump out of the water.

"This would be fun if we weren't captives," she said. "I've never been out to sea before."

"What do you suppose the pirates want to dispose of?" he asked.

Dree shivered. "So long as it isn't us, I don't care."

"If ships all disappear there, shouldn't we be worried?"

Dree regarded him. "There are lots of stories about ships disappearing at Mermaid's Demise, but none of it has ever been confirmed. I'm not sure if it's any more real than the lost continent of Riviand."

"I can't believe those guys are my dad's friends. He always wondered what happened to them. I wonder what they've been doing for all the years before they got magic. I'm glad they gave me my sword back at least."

"Don't you find them funny?" she asked.

Sen nodded. "They're trying so hard to be pirates, and there isn't anything scary about them... Well, maybe

Ernesto's teeth. Oscar's eye patch is definitely for show. They don't even talk like pirates."

"How do you think they got an entire crew of men to work for them and wear magic blockers?"

"They must pay a lot."

"Garin is creepy. He has mean eyes. None of the others do."

Sen glanced at her. "Yeah, we should probably stay away from him."

Dree smiled and gazed out at the sunset. "I'm glad they let us out. It's nice. I wouldn't want to live on a ship or anything, but it might be fun to go out occasionally."

Sen nodded and scanned the ocean. Ever since he'd realized he cared about Dree, it was harder to talk to her. Maybe not harder, but more painful. He wanted to kick himself every time he thought about it. What were the chances Dree and Mace would decide to break their contract? It was possible. If they could somehow make sure Lenzo wasn't a threat anymore, Dree wouldn't have to be in a hurry to make that kind of decision.

"What is it?" Dree asked, raising her eyebrow.

Sen blinked. He hadn't realized his gaze had left the sunset and was now on her.

She frowned. "Is everything alright?"

"It's fine," Sen said, shifting back to the ocean. "I was just thinking."

"About Garin?"

"No. Nothing important."

"Do you think Mace is searching for us yet?"

"Probably not. Since we didn't know what we were up against, he probably assumes it will take time. I hope he finds something out about Lenzo. I don't want to leave you with that man still holding so much power."

Dree nodded. "I keep pondering on that. I don't want him to be captain of the guard, but I'm scared to do anything about it. He's obviously after power or he wouldn't want to marry me. It's annoying to know that anyone who wants to marry me only wants power."

Sen shifted. "That's not true. I don't believe Mace is after power."

"He wants his voice to be heard. He doesn't really want to marry me. If we can get the council on my side instead of Lenzo's, I think Mace would be happy to break the marriage contract and become part of my council."

Sen's heart sped up. "Is that what you hope happens?"

Dree frowned, staring out at the ocean. "I don't know. Kind of. Mace is turning out to be a better person than I thought at first. He's capable and, I believe, reliable. I don't think he wants to be the prince, though, and I'm not sure I want to spend my life with him. I wonder if I acted too hastily and so did he."

"I'm sorry I didn't agree to the marriage contract with you. Then, we could have figured out a way to get rid of Lenzo and I would have let you cancel it and marry who you want."

"It's fine. If I do have to marry Mace, it's still a lot better than Lenzo." She leaned against the railing and sighed. "I always knew I wouldn't get to choose who I married. I let myself have some hope after I ran away."

"Mace is a good guy."

"I know. I keep telling myself that. And he's handsome. All the maids were in love with the two of you."

Sen felt his face and neck heat up. There was no way the maids were in love with him. Mace maybe, but not him.

Dree laughed. "I can tell you don't believe me, but it's true. Maids are the worst gossips I've ever seen, and they talked about the two of you all the time."

"So, who did you gossip about?" Sen asked, trying to turn it away from him.

Dree looked at him and smiled. "I was only pretending to be a maid. I didn't gossip like one."

Sen turned to face her and leaned one elbow on the railing. "Come on. You're telling me in all that time at Vetta's there was never one guy that caught your attention? I know Vetta had plenty of gentleman callers that all the maids must have been peering at."

Dree's face lit up as she studied him. "I never thought I would see the day!"

"What are you talking about?"

"You're teasing me, and your eyes are twinkling."

Sen felt a small smile appear on his face. "My eyes never twinkle."

"I know! That's why it's so great. They're still twinkling!" She reached out a finger and poked him in the nose. Sen grabbed her hand, and time seemed to stop. Her smile slowly faded and was replaced by a questioning stare. All he could think about was kissing her. Sen's mind had never been in such a confused mess. He shook his head and dropped her hand.

"It must have been a trick of the light," he said, turning back to the water. They needed to get off this boat. What if he had actually kissed her? He would have lost his best friend. Everything would have become awkward between them. He was going to lose her anyway. He was more sure than ever that he was going to have to leave as soon as they settled everything. Now that he knew his own heart, he wasn't going to stay around and watch her fall in love with Mace.

"I guess not all maids gossip," Dree said. "Halla doesn't. She doesn't really talk to anyone. I hope she comes sometime. It sounds like Vetta has it out for her. It's strange, since she never flirts or gossips. She seems like a model maid. She should probably get a bonus."

Sen nodded but didn't look at her. She was talking fast, which meant she was trying to cover the uncomfortable feeling that had settled into the conversation. People were always commenting on Sen's lack of emotion, and he hoped whatever emotion he had been showing hadn't been obvious.

"Maybe we should get Oscar a parrot," he said. "If they are trying to be stereotypical pirates, he should have one."

"I wonder where they got all of their pirate information."

"Well, they came here as teenagers. I'm guessing they saw a lot of movies before they came here. My dad sure thinks television is one of the greatest things ever. I bet most of their ideas were from movies."

"I didn't pay a lot of attention to the pirate movie we watched."

"I could tell it scared you," Sen said, watching the sun disappear. "I thought it was funny the way you would suddenly get tired and fall asleep every time a movie scared you."

Dree frowned. "I'm actually glad Basura doesn't have television. It was interesting, but a lot of it scared me. I had bad dreams every time we watched it. Do you ever want to go back to Earth?"

"Only to visit. How about you?"

"There isn't anything there for me. I have too many responsibilities here."

"I wonder if my brothers will ever want to come back. They spent most of their lives here." Sen thought of his five brothers and frowned. It had been a long time since he had been with them.

"They seemed happy when we were there."

"I bet it's harder on Mateo. He's my only brother that has magic. Now, he has to hide it so he doesn't freak anyone out on Earth."

"Your mom seemed to like Mexico."

"Yeah. She didn't use magic that often, even when she was here. I don't think they'll ever be back. At least not permanently."

"How did your father get from Earth to Basura without magic?"

"There was a witch living near his village," Sen said, trying to remember the story. "He and his friends found out she had magic and threatened to tell people. She told them they could get their own magic if they jumped off a waterfall and said a certain word. Instead of getting magic, they fell through a portal and ended up in this world."

"Aye," Oscar said from behind them. "And a miserable time we had here too. We were back and forth from one horrid job to another. Sometimes, I think we would have been better off following Rosendo's example. He jumped right into this world and made himself a life. Me and Ernesto jumped from place to place and tried to return home."

"What did you do?" Sen asked.

Oscar scratched his head. "Well, we usually found odd jobs. We carried things or ran errands for people. We didn't want anything permanent because we figured we would be going home. Looking back, that wasn't the best idea because we never learned any good skills. It's good Ernesto had this pirate idea or we would have no occupation."

Sen just shook his head. He didn't know if what they did was exactly an *occupation*.

"Ye might be wantin' to find a place to sleep for the night. It's going to be dark soon." He handed both of them a blanket and disappeared into the ship.

"That almost sounded like pirate talk," Sen said.

He looked around. Pirates were bedding down on the deck. Sen wasn't sure what would be worse. Sleeping up top or below deck. He could sleep anywhere, but Dree had a harder time feeling safe.

"They said more people sleep out here," she said. "So, I'd rather sleep below."

"Alright," Sen said, following her downstairs. It was dark except for one lantern. A few pirates were placing down bedrolls. Sen found a deserted area and threw his blanket down. Dree placed hers beside his and sat on it.

She pulled off her boots and placed them next to her. "I wish I had a change of clothes. I'm going to smell terrible soon, if I don't already."

"You don't smell," Sen said, lying down on his blanket. "Or if you do, everyone else smells worse and blocks your smell out."

Dree laughed and wrapped her blanket around herself as she laid down. "Thanks, I think."

Chapter 8

Halla swiped her dusting rag over the stair railing and tried not to hum. There was something fulfilling about cleaning the beautiful intricate patterns that were carved all around the castle. It was also easier to breathe knowing Vetta would not pop out and punish her for something.

Mace had talked to the head of housekeeping and gotten her a job right away. She hadn't been this content in a long time. They even gave her a room with only one roommate. The maids had all been crammed together at Vetta's, even though she had plenty of empty rooms.

When the rail was clean, she walked down a long hallway, taking in all the tapestries. She wasn't familiar with the stories they told, but she liked to make up her own when she saw them. One of Halla's favorite things to do when she cleaned was to make up stories in her head. It made work fun.

The hall made a sharp turn, and Halla paused when she heard angry voices around the corner. One sounded like Mace. Her stomach fluttered, and she peeked around. Mace was talking to the soldier that had been at Vetta's house. She pulled back and flattened herself against the wall, bringing back memories of the time the man had talked to Vetta. Eavesdropping wasn't something she had done a lot of, but she wanted to hear what the man was up to.

"I know you took the crown," Mace was saying. "It won't help you, though. Whatever your plan is, Princess Lesandri will not marry you."

Halla covered her mouth with one hand. Everyone was talking about the missing crown. If the man he was accusing was guilty, then he was possibly dangerous and Mace shouldn't be accusing him like this.

The man laughed. "The only thing standing between me and the princess is you."

"You might be the captain of the guard, but that doesn't make you above the law."

"It actually makes me the law in most situations. Once I'm rid of you, no one will try to stop me."

"Yes, well—" Mace stopped talking as Halla heard a crash. Her forehead furrowed, and she kept still.

"Taken out by ailam powder," the captain said. "Tsk, tsk. I thought it would be more challenging than that."

Halla's eyes widened, and she peeked around the corner. Mace was unconscious on the floor, and the captain was leaning over him, his back to Halla. If he had been hit with ailam powder, he would be unconscious for a while. Ailam powder was illegal and had been for the last two years. Only the giants who made the powder were allowed to use it now.

The captain stood tall and raised his arms, levitating Mace. He made his way in the opposite direction of Halla, floating Mace in front of him. They disappeared around a corner. Panic filled her from head to toe, but she couldn't let this man do anything else to Mace. Halla tiptoed after them as quickly as she dared. If she was caught, she wouldn't be of any help.

Being brave wasn't Halla's strong point, but she had to save Mace somehow. She could go for help, but if the captain of the guard was corrupt, some of the other soldiers might be as well. If she couldn't trust anyone, it was all up to her.

After they turned a corner, she heard a scraping sound. Slowly turning a corner, Halla frowned. It was a dead end, and Mace and the man were gone. There must be a secret passage. The maids told her there were several in the castle but only the royal family could use them. Halla rubbed her hands around the stone wall, but nothing happened. She tapped her lip with one finger and studied the stone.

"Open, please," Halla muttered, pushing on the wall with both hands. It creaked, and the wall moved. She couldn't believe that worked. Her heart raced as she entered the dark passage. The wall closed and left her enveloped in darkness. How was the man navigating in the dark? She held out her hand and caused a small orb of light to appear. It was too faint to see where the path went, but she didn't dare make it any brighter.

Halla took one slow step after another. A mouse scurried near her foot, and she held in a shriek that wanted to slip out. Turning a corner, she saw a light bouncing up ahead. She covered her light and watched the man go up a small staircase. He opened a trapdoor above him. Light spilled in, and the man levitated Mace out of the hole. The man followed and slammed the trapdoor behind him.

Halla crept up to the trapdoor and waited, the hairs on her arms all standing on end. If she came out too early, he would see her. On the other hand, if she waited too long, she might miss them. She counted to one hundred in her head and walked up the steps to the trapdoor. She had to squat to get under it. Letting her light go out, she pushed up gently.

The smell of horses met her nose. She peeked out of the small crack. Straw littered the floor, and the sounds of a stable filled her ears. Her eyes darted around. She couldn't see anyone, but they could be behind her. If she was going to save Mace, she was going to have to take a chance. She pushed the trap door all the way open and still couldn't see anyone. Standing up straight, she pulled herself up and into the stables, closing the trap behind her.

"Nice of you to join us," the captain said.

Halla spun around and covered her mouth with one hand.

He smiled. "You are not who I expected, though I shouldn't be surprised."

Halla breathed hard and tried not to let her lip tremble. "Let Mace go," she managed.

"How sweet. The quiet little maid wants to save her benefactor."

"Where is he?" she asked, trying to sound confident and failing miserably.

"In the wagon," the man said, gesturing to a beat up wooden wagon. It wasn't the type of transportation Halla had expected to see in a castle stable.

He grinned and ran a hand over his graying beard. "I suppose this is fortunate. Vetta sent me a message about her dear, little runaway sister. She wants you back almost as much as she wants Mace."

Halla's eyebrows knitted together. "You're sending him to Vetta?" She couldn't see any sense in that. He would just leave.

"Perhaps, I will eventually. Right now, I'll keep him locked away until the princess marries me. Later, if he begs, I'll send him to Vetta. I'm sure Vetta will make a deal with me to get the two of you back. This is actually quite fortunate. I thought we would have to put on a fake search for Mace. Now, we can tell everyone he ran off with the maid. That will speed things along nicely."

Halla took a step back and swallowed hard. The captain put his hand into a pouch and pulled out a handful of gray powder.

"Don't worry," he said, sauntering toward her. "It won't hurt."

"Ailam powder is illegal," she said, her eyes jumping nervously around. She would have to run around him to get to the door.

He laughed. "That's why I'm glad I had a nice supply before that law came out." He tossed the dust into her face, and she held her breath. It didn't matter. She felt herself falling.

Mace opened his eyes and yawned. Where was he, and why couldn't he move? It took him a few moments to clear his head. He appeared to be in a wagon, and it was night. The moon shone through the trees, casting eerie shadows across the area. He doubted they were on a trail because of the way the wagon bounced. His legs and hands were tied, and slowly, he remembered his conversation with Lenzo.

A small groan caused him to roll over. Halla slept near him. She was tied up as well. She didn't appear to be hurt, but it was hard to determine with only the moonlight to see by. Why would Lenzo take Halla? A heavy-set man was driving the wagon. Mace couldn't make out who he was, but he could tell it wasn't Lenzo.

Something wasn't right. This was too messy to have been planned by Lenzo. His hands were tied in front of him. Lenzo was known all over the Northern Kingdom for his strategies. He wouldn't tie a person's hands in front of them and throw them in a wagon to get rid of them. He would make sure they couldn't move at all. There was nothing to stop them from jumping out the back.

Mace lifted his hands and blew into the palm of one of his tied hands and tried to summon a knife from his room in the castle. Nothing happened. The ropes shouldn't stop the magic. He rolled close to Halla, so he was touching her and tried to teleport, but once again, nothing. He cursed softly under his breath and then rolled his eyes. Cursing, fixed nothing.

The man driving the wagon began whistling. He was oblivious to what was going on behind him.

"Mace?" Halla whispered.

His eyes darted to her. "Shhh. I'm going after the driver," he whispered. "If it doesn't go well, jump out the back." He wasn't sure because of the lack of light, but he thought she was frowning. He got onto his hands and knees and pulled himself quietly toward the driver. The ropes bit into his wrists, but he ignored it. When he was close enough, he got clumsily to his feet. He fisted his hands together and swung them as hard as he could at the driver's head. Instead of connecting with the driver, he hit an invisible barrier. It shocked him and threw him backwards. He heard Halla scream as he hit the wagon bed.

The driver laughed, not turning around. "I'm sure it was a noble try," he said in a voice much too cheerful for the situation.

"Are you alright?" Halla asked, pushing herself into a sitting position.

"Fine," he lied, ignoring the pain tingling through his body. He pushed himself up and leaned his back against the side of the wagon and concentrated on his breathing.

His chest felt tight, and his lungs burned like they were on fire.

"I don't imagine that was pleasant," the man said. "Lenzo knows some crazy magic. I'm Jolly, by the way. It's my name, not a character attribute. The force field goes around the entire wagon box, so I wouldn't try anything if I were you. That's not a threat, by the way, I'm just letting you know. Also, those metal cuffs on your arms restrict your magic."

Mace held up his arms and studied the metal bracelet on his arm right above the ropes. Halla was examining hers.

"Might as well hang tight and enjoy the ride. Lenzo doesn't leave any holes in his plans."

"Where are you taking us?" Mace asked.

"Up into the mountains. There's a hole in the rocks up there. I suppose you could call it a cave, but you can only get in from the top."

"You're going to throw us in?"

"Don't take it personally," Jolly said. "Disobeying Lenzo has never been an option. I learned that well and good when we were boys."

"You knew him when you were young?"

"Sure. He's my second cousin once removed. Or possibly my first cousin twice removed. I can't ever remember. All I know is you don't want to mess with Lenzo. That's why I'm doing this now. I hope you'll forgive me."

Mace pulled at the knot binding his ankles. Halla handed him a small knife. Her ropes had been cut. He raised his eyebrow, and she shrugged. Mace cut through the rope on his ankles and then tried to free his hands. He couldn't get the knife at the right angle with his hands tied the way they were.

"Let me help," Halla said, taking the knife. She sawed at the ropes. How had she freed her hands? She was struggling now, even though she had both hands free.

Jolly turned and watched them. "Sorry. I would have untied you earlier, but I was in a hurry." He went back to whistling.

The rope finally snapped, and Mace rubbed his wrists. "Thanks."

"Cutting a rope that thick is hard," Halla said, pushing a curl out of her eyes.

"How did you cut yours when your hands were tied?"

She looked down at the knife. "My ropes were loose. I just pulled my hands out."

"I didn't expect you to have a knife."

"It was my mom's. I always keep it with me."

Mace nodded. "Why did Lenzo take you? You aren't a threat to him."

Halla kept her head down. "I saw him take you, so I followed to try to help. I guess I wasn't as quiet as I thought."

"You followed?"

"Yes."

Mace wasn't sure what his rolling stomach was trying to tell him, and his heart was beating in time with the horse's hooves. Halla had come to save him. He wondered what she'd been planning to do before Lenzo caught her.

He shook his head. He couldn't think of Halla the way he was. Mace had sworn off love a long time ago, and now, he had to marry Dree. Not that there was anything wrong with Dree. She didn't make his heart pound like this, though.

If only he could get Sen to stop being an idiot. Dree and Sen were meant to be. Hopefully, he would figure that out before it was too late. Not that it would matter. Halla was too sweet and quiet to want to be with someone like him.

"I couldn't let you go missing," Halla said quietly. "The princess was so kind, letting me come to the castle. I owe her for getting me away from Vetta."

"So, you tried to save me for Dree?" he asked. It wasn't exactly what he wanted to hear.

She shrugged. "I should have known I wouldn't succeed. I've never been brave."

"Following Lenzo seems pretty brave to me."

"I was scared the whole time," she admitted.

Mace resisted the urge to rub his hand over her face. "Being brave doesn't mean you aren't scared. It means you do something even if you are scared."

"I agree," Jolly said. "And good for you, lady. I wish I was brave, but I'm not."

"You could be," Mace said. "You could let us go now. I can tell you aren't a bad guy." He wouldn't have guessed Jolly and Lenzo were related. The only similarity was their hair. The moonlight made it hard to know for sure, but it looked like he had gray hair. Lenzo was a large man, but it was all muscle. Jolly looked like he was the type to indulge in a dessert or two after dinner.

"I don't want to be bad, but agreeing to help Lenzo makes me bad. Sorry. I'm scared of him, and I can't go against his wishes. You don't know what he can do. Lenzo has been studying to be a sorcerer for almost as long as I remember. If I make him mad, he'll turn me into a sheep."

"He can do that?" Halla asked.

"I've never seen him do it, but he threatened me with it."

Mace was skeptical. "I've never heard of anyone that could turn people into animals."

"Have you ever heard of anyone making a force field?"

Mace thought about it. "Not in our lifetime."

"Lenzo can do things that others never dreamed of."

"He can't teleport."

"No, but it's on his list of things to learn."

Mace couldn't figure out why Lenzo would send Jolly for this job. The man was friendly, and Mace wasn't as worried as he could be. They might get Jolly to let them go.

"Why would he turn you into a sheep?" he asked. "There are lots of animals that would be worse."

Jolly snorted. "Worse than a sheep? Have you ever been around sheep? Their eyes are scary enough. Next time you see a sheep, look into its eyes and try not to soil yourself. Rectangle eyes. They see almost everything. Why do they need to see to the sides? It's unnatural."

"It's probably so they can see predators."

"All I know is they make me shiver. Plus, they stink."

Mace held back a grin. "As do most animals."

"But their stink is unholy."

The sun was peaking over the mountain as the wagon began slowly climbing. It was generous to call it a mountain. It was more like a large hill. The Northern Kingdom didn't have any gigantic mountains.

"I am sorry I have to do this," Jolly said.

"So, don't."

He looked down in shame. "I have to. I've thought of moving away somewhere Lenzo couldn't find me and make me do things. It would never work. Lenzo can find anyone."

Mace felt bad for the man, but he needed to stand up for something in his life. "How are you going to get us out of this force field? And once you do that, how are you going to get us into the cave?"

"No need for you to worry about that. It will all work out. It is Lenzo's plan, after all."

Chapter 9

"Land ho!" a voice yelled, startling Sen from his thoughts. He glanced around until he saw an island in the distance. A cheer rose from the pirates.

"I thought there weren't any islands out this far," Sen said, joining Oscar at the railing.

Oscar grinned. "This be the last island. It isn't very big, but we like to stop there every now and again."

It was still far in the distance. Sen squinted at it. "Is it inhabited?"

"Nah, only the islands near the continents are inhabited. We stay away from them because they tend to have older, less forgiving people living on them."

"Are we going to stop?"

"We are indeed."

"What do you do there?"

Oscar's eyes lit up. "We have us a relaxing day of competition."

Sen just nodded. He wasn't sure relaxing and competition were words that were usually used in the same sentence, but he was up for it.

"If yer anything like your father, yer going to love it. Yer father sure loved a good competition."

Sen nodded again. He was exactly like his father in that way. Sen and his brothers had spent hours every day trying to outdo each other at one thing or another. It drove his poor mother crazy. He wondered what kind of competition pirates would have. Hopefully, nothing too violent.

"Hey, you want some peanuts?" Oscar asked, holding out a handful of nuts.

"No, thanks," Sen said, holding back a smile. It was funny to hear Oscar's bad pirate accent come and go.

"Where's your lady friend?"

"She's still asleep."

"She's a pretty one, she is. Yer a lucky man in the love department."

Sen's neck felt hot. "No, it's not like that. We're just friends."

"Aye? And how's that working fer you?"

"Just fine," he lied. There was no way he was opening up to anyone about those feelings.

Oscar cocked his head and stared at him. "If ye say so. I saw you watching her yesterday. I think you're interested."

Sen raised one eyebrow as he looked at the man. "I'm watching you right now, and I'm not interested. Everyone watches people."

"Mayhap," Oscar said, "But you watched her differently."

"Mayhap?" Sen asked, trying to steer to a safer subject. "Can you just speak normally? It's hard to follow you with your fake accent."

"I've been in this world for a long time. For a good part of it, I couldn't understand the language. I could only speak Spanish. The language people speak here is like a strange form of English. We learned it, but it was still hard. When we all got magic, it was a miracle. I could understand everyone perfectly, and I no longer had an accent."

"What does that have to do with your pirate accent?"

Oscar shrugged. "I'm just saying it's not easy to force an accent in a language that isn't your first."

"So, why try?"

"Because we're pirates!"

Dree hopped out of the small white dinghy and sighed with relief. The small boat had swayed back and forth, making her nervous and a bit nauseous. She took a few steps onto the sandy beach and inspected the island. Palm trees shaded a good portion of the sand. There wasn't a lot to see.

The air was dry and hot. Her feet were going to be sweating in her boots. She looked around and noticed that she and Sen were the only ones wearing anything on their feet. The pirates were barefoot. Another dinghy came to shore, and more barefoot pirates came out.

Sen sat on the ground and pulled off his boot. Dree didn't want her dress getting any dirtier than it already was, so she lifted one foot and tried to get her boot off. She wobbled and fell backwards. So much for that.

She glanced at Sen. A smile spread across his entire face. Butterflies attacked her stomach as she stared at his perfect teeth. She had always believed Sen was good looking, but he was even more so when he smiled. She would have to get him to smile more. No, she didn't need to find him attractive. That would only add to the problem.

"What are you grinning at?" she asked, trying out her best glare.

He kept smiling. "Now that you know how to cook, I should teach you to take off your boots."

She pulled off her boot and threw it in Sen's direction. "Ha, ha."

"Or I could teach you to throw," he said, glancing at the non-threatening boot lying a foot away from him.

"I missed you on purpose."

"Sure."

Dree smiled at the sparkle in Sen's eyes. She took off her other boot and chucked it at him. He caught it before it could hit him in the face.

"Alright, everyone," Captain Ernesto barked. "If you want to be part of the games, come over here."

Sen popped up and grabbed Dree's hand, pulling her to her feet. "Come on."

"I'm not going to participate," she protested.

"Why not? It might be fun."

"They are pirates. Who knows what they might think is fun?" She followed him over to the gathering of pirates and made sure she didn't stand anywhere near Garin. He was standing near Ernesto with his arms folded and a glare on his face.

"The first competition will be crab fighting!" Ernesto said, smiling.

"Crab fighting?" Dree asked.

"Aye. Everyone has fifteen minutes to find a crab, and then the crabs fight to the death!"

"That's barbaric!" Dree protested.

"You only have to participate in the events you choose," Ernesto said with a roll of his eyes. "Alright, fifteen minutes. Go!" Most of the pirates went running.

"You aren't going to do this one, are you?" Dree asked Sen.

"No."

"For those of you who are still here, we will have a staring competition," Ernesto said.

"A what?" Dree asked.

"Haven't you ever had a staring competition?" Sen asked.

"No."

Ernesto grinned. "Two people stare at each other and try not to blink. The person who blinks first loses."

"I guess I can handle that." Dree wasn't sure what she'd thought about pirates before this, but she'd assumed they would do more dangerous things.

"Dree and Sen will start," Ernesto said. "Okay, face each other."

Dree turned and gazed up at Sen. His expression was serious, and she was sure she was going to lose. If there was anyone that could focus, it was Sen.

Garin ran a hand through his hair. "This is such a waste of time."

Oscar fiddled with his eye patch. "It all depends on your point of view now, don't it? If ya work all the time and don't take time for fun, you're in danger of becoming boring."

"Ridiculous," Garin muttered.

"Let's get started then," Oscar grinned.

"Okay, now for the rules. No looking away," Ernesto explained. "You have to stare at each other until someone blinks. Ready? Go!"

Dree tried to appear as serious as Sen. He stared intently into her eyes. A few pirates stood by, watching. It made her self-conscious. How did Sen keep that expression? It made her want to giggle, but giggling probably wasn't part of a pirate contest.

Her eyes felt dry, and she blinked. "Blast!"

"Best out of three," Ernesto said.

"Are we allowed to do anything besides stare?" Dree asked.

Ernesto scratched his head. "Such as?"

"Can we talk or try to scare each other?"

"It's not usual, but I say yes. No jumping in the other person's face, though. Alright, ready? Go."

"I doubt you can scare me," Sen said with a straight face.

"I bet I can," she said, matching his expression.

"Oh yeah? Let's see it."

"You're really hot when you smile." Dree grinned as Sen flinched and blinked. She hoped she used the expression correctly. One of Sen's friends from Earth had always been saying it. Perhaps, it wasn't an Earth expression, but it was definitely not something princesses grew up saying.

"Aha! Dree wins," Ernesto proclaimed. "Okay, last time. Go."

Sen narrowed his eyes as he stared at her. She could tell he was hyper-focused this time. It would be pointless to try the same tactic again. He would be ready. One pirate started chanting her name, and she smiled.

"You're pretty proud of yourself, aren't you?" Sen said.

"I am," Dree admitted. "I'm proud of myself every time I get you to react. It's not an easy thing to do."

Sen smiled for the second time that day, and Dree felt her insides turn to goop.

"Sen wins!" Ernesto called out.

"Wait, what?" Dree asked, looking at the captain. "I didn't blink."

"You did," Sen said.

"How did I blink and not notice?" Dree complained. She knew why. Somehow, she'd let that smile distract her. She had to get better control of herself. Dree sat quietly as Sen beat three pirates at the contest. She fiddled with the metal cuff on her arm, hoping it would come off. More pirates joined the group, all holding crabs.

Dree didn't believe in having animals fight each other, but a few minutes into the crab fight, she realized she had worried for no reason. None of the crabs seemed to be in the mood to fight. The pirates tried to poke and prod the crabs, but the crabs seemed more interested in trying to leave. After a few more minutes, the pirates gave up.

"Now, fishing," Ernesto said. "Everyone has an hour to bring a fish to me. You must be crafty because you must use your hands or something you find on the island. Ready, go!"

All the pirates ran to the trees, but Sen ran straight to the ocean. Dree followed Sen at a regular pace. She was sure she couldn't catch a fish, but she didn't want to stay with Ernesto and Garin. Sen dashed into the waves and disappeared. Panic filled Dree as she rushed toward him. He popped up from the waist deep water and pushed his hair from his eyes.

Dree stepped into the ocean and waded toward him. "Don't do that! I thought you were going to drown."

Sen slogged toward her. "Nah, I'm a great swimmer."

She put her hands on her hips. "Of course you are."

He grinned again. "Were you coming to save me?"

Dree ignored the grin. "Yes, but we both would have drowned. I can't swim."

"I remember offering to teach you last year. You seemed to think that was a waste of time."

"It is. When will I ever need to swim?" Dree went deeper into the water. "I do want to wash the smell off me and clean my dress."

Sen chuckled. "Have you ever worn clothing covered in salt water? It doesn't dry comfortably."

"Anything has to be better than the mess I am now."

"I could teach you to swim now, but I'm afraid your huge sleeves would pull you under."

Dree lifted her arm and studied her long wet sleeves. "It's fashionable, you know."

"I'm sure."

Dree pointed toward the island. "Here come some pirates. It looks like they have sharp sticks. Maybe you should have gotten one."

Sen glanced at her and tilted his head. "What would I do with a sharp stick?"

"Spear a fish?"

Sen shook his head. "They aren't going to spear a fish. All they are going to do is make fools of themselves." Sen didn't even care about winning the competition. He just wanted to stay near Dree. For him, that was saying something. He should forget about Dree and join the competition, but he couldn't make himself care.

Small waves splashed up against her, and she bent enough to get her entire dress wet. "It would be nice to smell good again. I want to get my hair wet, but I'm afraid I'll fall in."

"I can help," Sen said, pushing his palms across the water and slinging it at Dree.

"What are you doing?" she squealed, wiping water from her face. "I can't believe you did that!"

Sen remained stoic. "I was helping you wash your hair."

Dree's mouth formed a thin line, and Sen knew he was about to get it. Dree cupped her hands and threw it into his face.

"Real mature, Dree."

She grinned and splashed more water in his direction. Sen stood still and refused to react. He knew it drove her crazy. He wanted to smile, but he held it in. She splashed harder, and all he did was close his eyes.

"Are you finished?" he asked when the splashing stopped. "I have a fish to catch." He turned and scanned the water.

Dree jumped on his back, catching him off guard. They both plunged into the waist high water. Sen quickly found his footing and stood. He coughed a few times and pulled Dree up and helped her stand. She must have realized they were going down and held her breath because she wasn't coughing.

"That backfired," she muttered, pushing her hair out of her face.

"Lucky for you, you still look cute when you're soaked."

Dree's eyes widened, and Sen winced inside. He should have kept that to himself.

He turned away from her and looked back at the water. "Now, help me find a fish."

Chapter 10

The fishing competition was a bust. Not a single person had caught a fish. Dree and Sen hadn't even spotted one.

"What next?" Oscar asked, rubbing his eyepatch. Dree grinned. Oscar had switched the eye the patch was on at least four times today.

"I thought pirates would have better competitions," Dree said. "You should probably ask Sen for some pointers because these have been rather lame."

Ernesto nodded. "We had to ban some competitions due to safety problems."

"What were they?" Sen asked.

"Well, we had a drinking game," Oscar said. "We banned that on account of some people not being able to hold their ale." The pirates all laughed, and some of them were looking at a short, blushing pirate. "Now, we've banned drinking altogether. All it does is turn us into bigger idiots than we already are."

"That's for sure!" one pirate called out and some others laughed.

"We did an archery tournament," Ernesto said, scratching his head. "Most of us aren't the best aim. After the third person got hit by an arrow, we stopped that one."

"I still have a mark!" a dark haired pirate exclaimed, rubbing his thigh. "Poe shouldn't be allowed any weapons."

"You shouldn't have run in front of my arrow," said a tall pirate, who must be Poe.

"I was at least fifty feet away from the target."

The pirates all laughed, and Dree shook her head. When the time came, it wouldn't be too hard to round up these pirates. They would be lucky to make the history books. She wondered how Ernesto had picked his crew. Had he stood on the street and asked for the least experienced men to apply? This was the first time any of them seemed to have any personality. Most days, they all did their jobs quietly with little interaction.

The only pirate that didn't seem to be enjoying himself was Garin. He'd spent most of the day standing with his arms crossed, glaring at the lot of them. Dree wondered why he was even here. He didn't fit in with the rest of the pirates.

"Then, there was the dragon egg contest," Oscar said. "That was one we came up with on the spot because there just happened to be two nests of dragon eggs one time we came."

"Do we even want to know what that one was like?" Sen asked.

"Well, we got into two teams, and we decided the team that stole the most dragon eggs would win," Oscar said. "No one came out a winner that time."

"I nearly lost my hand," one pirate said, cradling his arm at the memory. "Once those dragons bite, they don't like to let go."

"I'm pretty sure I got seventh degree burns," another man said.

A different pirate shook his head. "There isn't such a thing as a seventh degree burn."

"Is so."

"Is not."

The pirate lifted his shirt and showed the other pirate his scars. "Then, what do you call this?"

"Alright, maybe there is such a thing."

"How about we have the pepper contest?" Ernesto said, holding up a bag. "No one can call that a lame contest. Everyone sit in a circle."

All the pirates, along with Sen and Dree, sat on the sandy beach. So much for washing out her dress. Being wet and touching the sand was disgusting. She could feel it sticking to her legs and feet. It was gritty and uncomfortable. Ernesto dumped out an array of peppers. Dree didn't know this many types existed.

"Who's first?" he asked.

Sen tilted his head. "What's the competition?"

Ernesto's grin spread across his entire face. "The winner is the person who can eat the hottest pepper."

"I'm in," Sen said.

Ernesto studied his crew. "Who wants to go up against the landlubber?" All the pirates refused to make eye contact. "What, nobody?"

"I still haven't recovered from last time," one man said.

Oscar shook his head. "I can't ever get past the third round."

Another man held out his hands. "I probably have a hole in my stomach from the last time I played."

"I'll do it," Dree said. This was a competition she might be able to win.

Laughter answered her.

"Some of these peppers are incredibly spicy," Ernesto told her.

"I can handle it."

"I don't think it's a good idea," Sen said.

"I grew up eating spicy food," Dree assured him. "Besides, you're doing it."

"You won't be able to beat me," Sen informed her. "I can take it. I'm half Mexican. My dad used to grow ridiculously hot peppers."

Oscar laughed. "Being half Mexican isn't going to save you, boy. I'm a full-blooded Mexican and I can't take it."

Sen ignored Oscar and looked at Dree. "I've eaten really hot stuff competing against my brothers. I don't want you to make yourself sick. If you do this, you'll regret it."

"We'll see," Dree said, smiling. Dree's father had liked to eat spicy food. He said it was what separated the men from the boys. It would be hard to find something too hot for her to eat.

"Alright, the two of you sit in the middle of the circle and face each other," Ernesto said. They both moved in, and Dree gave Sen a sassy smile.

Sen shook his head. "You're going to regret this. It's going to give you all sorts of digestive problems if you aren't used to it." Dree just shrugged. She was a little worried, because the food they had been eating at Vetta's hadn't been very spicy. It was possible she wasn't used to it anymore.

"Last call," Ernesto said, looking over the pirates.

"I'll join," Poe said. He moved into the middle and sat next to them. He rubbed his hands together and pushed back his greasy brown hair.

Ernesto pulled out a small knife and cut a yellow pepper into pieces. He handed a piece to all of them. "You have exactly one minute to have your piece swallowed." They all put their piece in their mouths and chewed. It wasn't hot at all.

"Weak," Sen said.

Dree nodded. "I agree."

"Even my mum could handle that," said Poe.

"Let's skip the next two then," Ernesto said, taking out a thin, shriveled pepper.

"Gross, but not too hot," Dree said, chewing.

Sen nodded. "Yep."

Poe made a face. "Tasted like my mum grew it."

Ernesto handed them a piece of purple pepper.

"I've never had a purple pepper," Dree said, putting it in her mouth. It was sweet with a small hint of spice. She would have to find out what it was called and get the castle chef to add it to their menu.

"I like that one," Sen said.

Poe swallowed it and stuck out his tongue. "Tastes like old boots."

Oscar laughed. "How often do you eat old boots?"

"Only did it once, and it was in desperate circumstances."

"I wanna try it," said a pirate Dree didn't know. Ernesto cut a piece and handed it to him. The man stuffed it into his mouth and chewed. "Don't taste like boots. It tastes like happiness covered in frosting."

Dree raised her eyebrow. She liked it, but it didn't taste a thing like frosting. These pirates were a strange lot.

They went through the next three peppers without a problem. They were getting hotter, but nothing Dree couldn't handle.

Poe spat out the next one. "My mum can't even make anything that tastes that bad. I can handle the heat, but not the taste."

"Alright, Poe is done," Ernesto said. Poe stood and joined the other pirates as a spectator.

Dree bit the pepper. Poe was right. It was nasty. She forced herself to swallow it and hoped it wouldn't give her a stomachache.

Ernesto cut an orange piece from a thick pepper and gave it to them.

"You should give up before you hurt yourself," Sen said, popping a piece in his mouth. Dree ate her own. "You're just trying to get me to stop so you can. I'm fine."

The pirates would lean in every time they took a bite. Dree smiled to let Sen know she was feeling fine. Her stomach was protesting, but that was to be expected after eating so many peppers. Sen wiped his brow but kept chewing.

"Who is ready for the last one?" Ernesto asked, holding out a green, shriveled pepper. The crew cheered. "Let me warn you," he cautioned. "This one is much hotter than anything you've ever tried. It's a hundred times worse than the last one. Would either of you like to back out?"

Sen shook his head.

"No, I'm ready," Dree lied.

"For the last one, you will take turns. I'll cut it into several small pieces. Very small pieces. We don't want anyone dropping dead. Oscar and I cultivated this pepper ourselves. It's called the J. Lo pepper because it's hotter than Hades."

Oscar laughed, and Sen and Dree shared a confused look.

Ernesto grinned. "For your first turn, I only want you to lick it. When you do, I won't be surprised if you both give up. Oscar, give them a water flask." Oscar handed them both some water, and Ernesto gave them both a small piece of pepper.

"I'll go first," Dree said, licking the pepper. Fire filled her tongue and ran through her body. Eating lava couldn't be any worse. She gagged and coughed. This was the worst feeling her mouth had ever experienced. It was like the heat of a thousand suns, burning through her innocent tongue. Pressing the water to her lips, she gulped it down as quickly as she could. Her entire body was covered in sweat.

"Looks like I'm going to win," Sen said.

"Don't eat it!" Dree croaked. Her tongue felt swollen. It was going to blister.

Sen held his hand out to Ernesto. "Give me the rest of the pieces."

"Don't eat them all at once," Ernesto warned, as Sen popped it all into his mouth. The pirates cheered. Dree shook her head as he swallowed. He turned and smiled at her. After a couple of seconds, his eyes widened, and his face turned red. He grabbed his water and drained it.

"Why did you do that?" Dree demanded, her mouth feeling numb.

Sen wiped the sweat from his face and groaned. He jumped up and ran into the trees. The pirates laughed. Dree frowned as she watched Sen disappear. She'd give him a minute before she went after him.

Oscar grinned. "No one can handle that pepper. Remember when you tried it, Ernesto?"

Ernesto cringed. "Aye. Worst experience of my life. It's painful going in and painful coming out, and I only had a small piece. I don't envy your friend."

Dree side eyed the pirate. "Why do you do contests like this? I can't believe I let myself do it. What if something bad happens to Sen?"

"Oh, it's going to be bad. Don't worry, though. He'll be over it by tomorrow."

Dree rubbed her watering eye. "Tomorrow? That's a long time to be miserable."

"Don't be rubbing yer eyes," Oscar cautioned. The warning came too late. Dree's eye was on fire.

"Quick, give her some water," someone said. They pushed a flask into her hand.

"Wash it out," Ernesto commanded.

"This is all so stupid," Garin said. "This is only going to delay us more than it already has."

"I don't see why you are in such a hurry," Oscar said.

Dree poured the water directly onto her face, hoping to wash away the pain from the evil pepper. She could hear Garin and Oscar arguing, but she couldn't focus on what they were saying. Hoping to her feet, she walked away from the pirates. She must be a horrifying sight. Her eye was swollen, and her nose wouldn't stop running. The pirates were calling to her from behind, but she ignored them. When she had gone a considerable distance, she stopped and poured more water into her assaulted eye.

When all the water was gone, Dree reached into her dress pocket and pulled out her handkerchief and wiped at her nose. Why had she gotten pulled into the competition? Sen loved to compete. He'd given up trying to get her to play games or compete early in their relationship. It wasn't her thing. Why had she changed her mind this time?

It had been a long time since Dree had cried from pain. She wasn't sure if she was crying, or if her eyes were watering. Perhaps both. How could a person feel numb and on fire at the same time? She would never tease the pirates about having lame competitions again. This one should go on the list of the competitions that should be outlawed.

Sen groaned as he rolled around on the hard ship deck. He'd tried going below, but the air down there made him feel worse. He ignored the curious stares from the pirates and kept his face away from their curious glances. Stomach acid had taken up permanent space in his throat, and everything that could run out of a person's face was leaking.

He wasn't completely sure how he had gotten here. He remembered puking on the island, and then Oscar had come and led him somewhere. Probably to the dinghy. The pepper coming up had been more painful to his throat than when it went down. His mom always told Sen and his brothers that they would regret their competitive natures someday. This was that day. Why hadn't they left him on the island and just let him die?

"Sen?" Dree asked, kneeling next to him. "Are you alright?"

"Just leave me alone," he grumbled.

She ignored him. "Ernesto gave me this medicine. He said it might help you."

He wiped his face on his sleeve and glanced up. Dree's right eye was swollen shut. "What happened to your eye?"

She handed him a vial. "I touched my eye before I washed the pepper off."

He watched her as he swallowed whatever was in the vial. "It looks bad."

She tilted her head and studied him. "Have you seen yourself?"

"No, but I can imagine. Are you okay?"

"Better than you. Are you going to be alright?"

"Probably," Sen said, sitting up. "I feel better than I did before I drank this." The acid wasn't as strong, and he could swallow without wanting to cry.

"What were you thinking?" Dree asked. "You could have taken one bite and won. You didn't have to show off."

"I know," Sen admitted. "I'm too stubborn. I couldn't let you win."

"Well, you won," she said with a slight smile. "Do you feel fulfilled?"

"I feel stupid."

"Why would you feel you need to beat me at something? You're better at everything than I am."

"Not everything. I know it's ridiculous. You saw the way me and my brothers were in Mexico. Everything we did was a competition. I miss it sometimes."

"Well, next time, let's play chess or something. That has to be a lot less painful."

"Deal."

Garin stopped in front of them and looked down. He held one of the offensive peppers in his hand. "Nice day to be out on the open ocean." He popped the pepper into his mouth and chewed it.

Dree's eyes widened, and Sen frowned. He waited for Garin to bend over in pain. Didn't he learn anything from watching them?

"Horrible flavor," he said, brushing his hands together. "I'm disappointed."

Sen watched him closely. The heat should have hit him by now. He wasn't reacting in any way.

Garin smiled and ran his hand through his blond hair. "I hope you enjoy the rest of your day." He nodded at them and walked away, his cape flapping behind him.

"That was not normal," Dree said, glancing at Sen.

"No. There's something off about that guy. More than just his eyes."

Oscar walked up and squatted next to them. "There's a lot wrong with him, in my opinion. Just some advice. Stay away from Garin. He makes my skin crawl. How are you feeling?"

"Better than I was."

"Good, good. You look horrible, but not as bad as the drooling idiot you were when we got you off the island."

Sen sighed. "Thanks a lot, Oscar."

"Sure thing. It's always good to have someone to tell you the truth about things. Especially if it's something you can change—I guess you can't change the way you look. I'm sure you'll be back to your natural state in no time. Before that happens, you might want to stay away from Dree."

Dree's eyes narrowed. "Why would he need to stay away from me?"

"He doesn't need to be scaring you off. What woman wants to kiss someone that looks like that?" he asked, gesturing at Sen.

Dree opened her mouth to say something, then shut it.

Sen didn't have it in him to argue.

Oscar laughed. "See what I mean? You should hide below until you look a bit less—like that."

"Don't you have anything better to do?" Sen mumbled.

"Unfortunately not."

"Well, why don't you find something?"

Oscar grinned. "I can take a hint. I'll see you around." He bounced up and wandered away.

Why couldn't everyone just leave him alone?

Dree stood. "Well, I guess I'll leave you to roll around on the deck. Let me know if you need anything."

"Thanks."

Sen watched her walk away. His stomach was still cramping, but he wasn't in agony anymore. He sighed as he laid back on the deck and stared at the blue sky. It was good he wasn't trying to impress Dree. If so, he would be failing immensely.

Chapter 11

Dree pulled her fingers through her long, wet hair. Captain Ernesto had allowed her to use his cabin to take a bath. He had even had the men bring her fresh water from the island and had it heated. It must have taken them a long time to haul. She should have taken a bath on the island like the others, but she hadn't felt good enough to protest when Ernesto offered. She was feeling so much better after the bath and a good night's sleep. Her eye was only slightly puffy today.

One pirate had given her a tunic and a pair of britches. They were too big, but it was nice to have something clean. When the salt water dried on her dress it had become stiff and itchy. After her bath, she'd washed her dress in the tub, but it would take a while to dry.

Dree scanned the captain's cabin. There was a large bed, a wardrobe, a desk, and an old, weathered chest. It smelled musty, but not as bad as the stink below deck. She wondered what was in the chest. Her eyes kept landing on it and eventually her curiosity got the best of her. It wouldn't hurt anything to take a little peek. She grabbed hold of the lid and pulled up, expecting to see some type of treasure. This was a pirate ship, after all.

The lid opened without trouble, and Dree frowned as she spotted a mess of old clothes. What did she expect? It wasn't even locked. She put her hands to her waist as she stared inside. She glanced at the door and then kneeled by the chest, sticking her arm through the clothes, and searched through the bottom of the trunk. Her hand touched something hard, and she grasped it.

Why was she being so snoopy? She should leave whatever it was and mind her business. She knew she couldn't do it, though. Pulling the item up, she gasped. In her hand, she clutched the amethyst crown. The gold and gems sparkled up at her. The pirates weren't as incompetent as they seemed.

The crown pulsed in her hand. Legends said that the crown held magic, but only for the queen. Dree had never held it before. She'd never even been allowed to get within twenty feet of it. The purple gems glittered as she held it up to the light. A pounding at the door had her scurrying to replace the crown.

She stumbled to the door and pulled it open. Sen stood there with a half smile. Even his half smile made Dree's heart speed up. He was handsome, even with slightly swollen eyes. How had it taken her so long to realize how she felt about him?

"Hey," he said. "It sounds like we are going full speed toward Mermaid's Demise. I tried to talk Ernesto out of it, but he's determined."

"We need to talk," she said, glancing around the deck. No one was paying them any attention. "In private."

"We can go toward the back," he said, linking his arm with hers. He led her leisurely toward the back railing. Sen released her arm and leaned back with his elbow on the rail. "What do we need to talk about?"

Dree glanced around to make sure no one was close enough to hear. There was a pirate scrubbing the floor only fifteen feet away, but he didn't seem to be paying attention. She stepped nearer, so she was right beneath Sen's ear. If this didn't look suspicious, she didn't know what would. If she went on her toes, it would only take a couple of inches to kiss him.

Sen's eyes narrowed in confusion as he gazed down at her. "What is it, Dree? You're making me nervous." She took a half step back and shook her head. She needed to get better control of her thoughts.

"My crown is in the captain's cabin," she whispered.

His eyes widened. "You saw it?"

"Yes, it's in an old chest."

"Just kiss her, mate," Oscar said, coming up beside them. "She gave you plenty of opportunities."

Dree glared at the pirate and his fraudulent eye patch. "We're just friends."

"So you both say."

"Because it's true," Sen said.

He grinned. "I think yer both just scared."

"Dree has a marriage contract."

Oscar scratched his chin. "They can be broken."

Sen rolled his eyes. "Yes, but it's not going to be."

Dree swallowed hard and scanned the ocean. She wished Sen would beg her to break it. It was a silly hope, since he'd already told her he didn't want to marry her.

"Look at her," Oscar said. "She wants ya ta kiss her."

Dree folded her arms and frowned. "I do not!"

"She's just never kissed anyone, perhaps?" Oscar smirked, moving his eye patch to his other eye. "She's nervous."

"I have kissed someone," Dree said, wondering why she was having this argument with a pirate.

Sen's head whipped around, and he studied her. "You kissed Mace?"

"No!"

"Then, who?"

"Does it really matter?" Dree asked, ignoring Oscar's wide grin.

Sen frowned. "Sort of."

Sen ground his teeth together and tried to rein in his annoyance. It wasn't any of his business who Dree had kissed.

"It was Tal," Dree said. "Happy?"

"Tal kissed you?" Sen asked, clenching his fists. "After the awful way he treated you?"

Dree sighed. "He didn't kiss me. I kissed him."

"Why?" Sen asked, completely dumbfounded. Tal had wanted nothing to do with Dree and had been pretty vocal about it.

"It was the most awkward experience of my life, and I'd rather not talk about it."

"I'd like to hear about it," Oscar said.

"I can't believe you kissed him," Sen said, shaking his head.

"It isn't as bad as you kissing Ming Li. I was supposed to marry Tal. You kissed her to prove something to everyone."

Sen crossed his arms and glared at her. "I wasn't proving anything." He knew it was a lie as soon as he said it. Ming Li was one of his friends and part of The Silver Eclipse. She'd been worried about dying without being kissed and insisted on someone kissing her. Sen had done it when her other friends wouldn't. "How do you know about that anyway?"

"Ming Li told me."

Sen didn't try to hide his emotions. It just happened naturally. Ever since he realized he'd messed up with Dree, he couldn't seem to hold them in.

"Why are you so angry?" Dree asked. "I've never seen you like this."

"It's because he's jealous," Oscar said, leaning against the rail and watching with amusement.

"I'm not jealous," Sen muttered. "And what kind of pirate butts into people's love life?"

Oscar chuckled. "We're what you might call unconventional pirates, and it doesn't seem like you have a love life."

Sen took a deep breath through his nose and turned to storm off. He'd never stormed off in his life. What was happening to him? He took a few steps and stopped when Dree tugged on his arm.

"Sen!" she said, causing him to look down at her. "You're scaring me. Are you alright?" She placed a hand on his cheek, and he swallowed. He wasn't sure if he wanted to scream or cry. Both options went against his nature.

"I'm fine," he managed.

Oscar shifted. "Stop being a chicken and kiss her."

Sen stared up at the sky in one last attempt to control himself. Dree's hand felt like it was burning into his cheek. He peered back into her concerned eyes. Sen gently took Dree's wrist and removed her hand from his face. He meant to let go and walk away, but instead, he leaned down and kissed her.

Sen was sulking. Dree had never seen him like this, and it made her nervous. Ever since he kissed her yesterday, he'd been avoiding people and grunting at anyone who tried to talk to him. Now, he was sitting on the deck with his back against the wall, staring into space.

"You need ta talk to that boy," Oscar said, coming up behind her.

Dree's eyes narrowed. "It's completely your fault! If you hadn't been bothering us, he never would have kissed me. Now, he's regretting it."

"I did you both a favor. You needed a little shove."

Dree crossed her arms. "No, we didn't. We are friends, and now, you made it weird."

Oscar raised one brow. "If he only wanted to be your friend, he wouldn't have done it."

"Sen is calm most of the time, but you challenged him. For some reason, he can't back down from a challenge."

"That is a personality flaw. He should work on it."

Dree rolled her eyes and tried to walk away. Oscar followed her to the railing. There was nowhere to go on a ship to have privacy.

Oscar fidgeted with his eye patch. "Don't tell me you didn't want him to kiss you. I see you watching him. He means more to you than a friend."

"He's my best and only friend. He means a lot to me. I'll never forgive you if he avoids me from now on."

"He's just confused. Give him some time. It wasn't a bad kiss, was it? It looked fine and natural from my view."

Heat enveloped Dree's cheeks. "You are insufferable." Dree had little experience with kissing. When she'd kissed Tal, it had been terrible. Part of that might have been because he wasn't kissing her back. When Sen kissed her, her knees had barely held her up. Why hadn't he agreed to marry her? How would she ever be happy with someone else?

"The look on your face tells me everything," Oscar said with a grin.

Dree shook her head and walked away.

Sen wondered what Oscar was saying to Dree. He seemed amused, and she appeared furious. Sen sighed. He couldn't seem to gain control of his emotions. He didn't know how to deal with it because it was a strange sensation for him.

Why couldn't he walk away from a challenge? He should have ignored Oscar. Now, things with Dree were going to be awkward. He knew it wasn't fair to blame the ridiculous pirate. Sen had been ready to ignore the taunting until he gazed into Dree's eyes. He'd wanted to kiss her. Now that he'd done it, he wanted to spend the rest of his life doing it.

Sen pulled at the metal cuff around his wrist. He needed to convince Oscar to take it off. They needed to get off this boat. The memory of Dree whispering that she'd found the amethyst crown popped into his head. He had forgotten about it until now. They needed to get the cuffs off, grab the crown, and then get off the ship.

"Acting a bit immature, aren't we?" Oscar said, plopping down next to him.

Sen took a deep breath through his nose. "I'm acting immature? You're a grown man pretending to be a pirate."

"It's not pretend."

"You wear an eye patch, and you don't even need one. You're like a little kid in a costume."

"I suppose that's true," Oscar admitted, taking off his hat. His black hair was plastered to his head with sweat. "This whole pirate thing was Ernesto's idea. I'm not complaining. It's been fun. I worry we might get in too far and not be able to claw our way out. Most things we've done have been harmless."

"Whatever you two are up to now might get you into trouble," Sen warned. "People stay away from Mermaid's Demise for a reason. It sounds dangerous."

"Very dangerous. From what we've heard, it's a huge whirlpool. That's why we need to go there."

Sen tried to remember what they'd said. "To throw something in?"

"Yep. Something thrown in there will never show up again."

"What are you trying to get rid of?"

"I can't talk about that. We met a man when we were in the Northern Kingdom. He offered us a lot of money to dispose of something. He won't pay until we return."

"Sounds shady. How will he know you actually did it?"

Oscar scratched his greasy head. "Garin."

"What does he have to do with anything?" Sen had only seen the man a few times. He was one of the few people with his own room, and he must spend most of his time there.

"Yes. Garin isn't a part of our crew. The man who gave us the task insisted on Garin going with us to prove we did it."

"I see." Sen's mind whirled. The item they were supposed to dispose of must be the crown. Why would someone want to get rid of it? Selling it would make a person rich. It must be someone who didn't want Dree to become queen yet. Mace was probably right. It must be Lenzo. Who else would benefit from delaying the coronation?

"I don't care for Garin. He makes me skin crawl," Oscar admitted. "There's something about him I don't like. I didn't like his master either. If it was up to me, we wouldn't have agreed to this plan."

"What are the chances of you taking this cuff off me?" Sen asked, holding up his arm.

"I can't do that. The man we made a deal with gave them to us. He demanded the crew wear them. He said he would take them off when we came back."

Sen ran a hand over his face. "So, you don't even know how to take them off?"

Oscar shrugged apologetically. "No."

"Great," Sen muttered. "You realize that if we get sucked into the whirlpool, the man won't have to pay you? Maybe that was his plan. Get rid of the crown and the crew."

"Maybe," Oscar said with a heavy sigh. "We'll just have to be careful. When we get close to the whirlpool, we can levitate the crown from a safe distance."

Sen nodded. "I think I'll go talk to Dree."

"Good idea," Oscar said. "Kiss her again, and things will be better."

"What makes you credible when it comes to kissing?" Sen asked, standing. "You're as old as my dad, and I don't see you in a relationship."

"I read a lot. I prefer the romance type, so I'm pretty much qualified to give advice."

Sen laughed and went searching for Dree. The pirate was crazy, but he had improved Sen's mood. It wasn't easy to get Sen to laugh.

"If yer looking for yer woman, she be up there," Ernesto said, as he stomped past him. "I won't be held responsible if she falls."

Sen glanced up to see Dree twenty feet up in the rigging. She was leaning against the ropes, staring out at the ocean. He grabbed hold of the ropes and climbed up. Dree peered down and smiled cautiously. He couldn't blame her. He'd been acting ornery since yesterday.

"This isn't where I expected to find you," he said when he got to her level.

"It's not where I expected to be," she said. "I've never seen Oscar up here, so I figured it was safe. It's liberating and terrifying. I probably can't hold on for much longer, though."

"You do seem to have a death grip," he observed, pointing at her white knuckles. "The pirates are planning on throwing your crown into Mermaid's Demise."

"I wondered if that was the plan. Did Oscar tell you?"

"He said they were throwing something in. He wouldn't say what. I said something about throwing the crown in there, and Oscar agreed without realizing it."

"I never thought I would wish I could teleport."

"We're stuck," Sen told her. "They don't even know how to take our cuffs off. The person they made a deal with about the crown is the one who can take them off. Garin works for that man. He might know how to do it."

Dree sighed. "That doesn't sound promising."

"Not at all. Somehow, we need to get the crown and get out of here."

Dree nodded. "It won't be hard to get. It's not even locked up."

Sen kept his eyes on the ocean. "Getting out will be a problem."

"So, what do we do?"

"I have no idea." They both stared out at the water for a moment. He hated that he had no plan. He glanced at her. "Sorry, I've been a jerk today. It really irritates me that I gave in to Oscar."

Her cheeks turned pink, and she kept her gaze averted. "It's alright."

"It isn't."

She gave him a half smile. "You haven't been a jerk. In all the time I've known you, this is the only time you seemed so irritated. I can't even count the times you've had to calm me down."

"I get irritated often enough," he admitted. "I'm just good at ignoring it."

"I'm not. I need to climb down. I'm getting a cramp in my foot."

"You want to race?" he asked.

She laughed. "Why? Just for your ego? I never climb, and I've seen you climb impossible things." She started slowly down the rigging. He started at her speed and then gave up and scurried down. She was going too slow.

"Do you think Mace misses us yet?" she asked, as she joined him on the deck.

"I'm not sure. He knows it might take a while. We thought it would be faster, though."

"Don't you think he has tried to contact us telepathically? I've never learned to do it, but he probably knows you could. When he can't reach you, he might suspect something is wrong."

"You can't send anyone a message unless you know where they are. He might just assume we found a lead somewhere else and moved on."

Dree sighed. "There are so many flaws to magic."

"I would still rather have it than not."

They both stopped talking as Garin walked past them. He didn't say anything, he just glanced at them and walked away.

Dree shivered and said something under her breath about Garin's eyes. "I wonder if I can use the crown's magic," she said. "When I touched it, it felt like it was pulsing."

"What kind of magic does it have?" Sen wondered if they could use the crown's magic to escape somehow.

"I'm not sure. No one has used it in so long. There are stories about one queen that people claimed could go invisible. I don't know if it was related to the crown, though."

"I'm surprised your father didn't have you study something that's so important to the kingdom," Sen said.

It was hard to believe how blind King Miadd had been when it came to raising children. Had it never crossed his mind that something might happen to Prince Raz that would leave Dree queen? Things happened all the time, and he had done nothing to prepare her. It was the opposite, really. He'd kept her more clueless than was natural.

"The crown is only important if a queen rules. Since I wasn't supposed to rule, he probably didn't care. The crown was only a trinket for him, as he couldn't use it. He only cared about things that benefited him. I should know."

Dree frowned out at the ocean, and Sen wished the king was alive so he could tell the man what he thought of him. The man couldn't even take time for his daughter, just because she had no magic.

"Your father was a fool. If he had taken time and opened his eyes, he could have realized how amazing you are. You learn fast. If he had allowed you to do things, you would have blown him away."

"Thanks," she said, her cheeks turning a rosy pink. "Sometimes I wonder if I was too passive. Perhaps things would have gone differently if I insisted on my parents' attention. I could have tried to learn more, but I held in my anger and obeyed their rigid rules."

Sen tilted his head as he watched her. "Until you ran away. That was a pretty big act of defiance." He wanted to take her in his arms and comfort her and tell her to break her marriage contract, but that wouldn't make anything less awkward. Sen had always prided himself on being brave and up for anything. Now he realized he was a coward.

"I probably shouldn't have run away," she said with a tired smile. "It really didn't help anything."

"Mermaid's Demise ahead!" someone yelled.

Dree's eyes widened as she gazed at Sen. "It appears we're out of time."

Chapter 12

"We need to keep a safe distance," Captain Ernesto said, as the crew all squinted into the fog, trying to see the whirlpool. He held the amethyst crown in his hands.

Garin shook his head. "We need to get closer. From this distance, we won't know if the crown gets into the whirlpool."

"If we get too close, we could get sucked into it," Oscar said.

Dree swallowed. She didn't want to get sucked into the whirlpool. They needed to get the crown, but what were their options? They couldn't take on an entire pirate crew, especially when they didn't have the advantage of using magic.

Garin leaned over the rail, his blond hair blowing in the wind. "We need to get closer to the fog."

"I don't like it," Ernesto said. "The closer we get, the stronger the wind. If we levitate it now, we can get it far enough in."

"If we can't see the whirlpool, we won't be sure it gets in," Garin protested.

Ernesto shook his head. "I won't risk the crew."

The nervous pirates all looked relieved. They weren't any more excited about sailing into the unknown than Dree was.

Garin's eyes narrowed and appeared to be on fire. He turned and took a step toward Ernesto, and stopped. "You don't need to worry. You know the magic I am capable of."

"Causing intruders to fall through the deck might be helpful, but I doubt anyone has the power to keep an entire ship from being destroyed in a whirlpool."

Garin's eyebrows came together as he frowned. "I can do things you can only imagine. Would you like a demonstration?"

"There might not even be a whirlpool," Dree said, hoping to buy some time to think. "No one has ever seen it after all."

"No one who lived to tell about it," Oscar agreed.

"Oh, it's there," Garin said. "I have no doubt about it."

"Well, we aren't going closer," Ernesto said.

Garin's nostrils flared. "Fine, but I'll levitate the crown over. I won't take the punishment for your failure."

"If you do it, we might not get our money," Oscar protested.

"You'll get your money," Garin snapped, grabbing the crown from Ernesto. Dree wasn't surprised to see Ernesto take a step back. Garin's eyes were unsettling.

"Do it fast, and get it over with," Oscar commanded.

Dree sighed. She wasn't going to be able to save the crown. It wasn't worth letting anyone get hurt.

Garin placed the crown around his arm and smiled. He flung out his arms, and Oscar and Ernesto fell to the deck.

Dree squeaked in surprised protest and stepped forward, but Sen took her elbow.

"Let me up!" Ernesto protested from the ground. Garin must be using some type of magic to keep them down. The crew was all slowly inching away. They were all useless without magic.

The man laughed. "I don't think so. You are all fools. You realize this crown is worth one hundred times more than you were offered to get rid of it?"

"What of it?" Ernesto growled.

"You could've easily taken it and sold it."

"We made a deal," Ernesto said. "We keep our word."

Garin barked out a laugh. "Strange, coming from a pirate."

"Pirates can keep their word," Oscar said, struggling against his invisible bonds.

Garin laughed again. "Well, that was your mistake. I'm not as daft as you are. I'm taking the crown, and you'll never hear from me again. I can't let you go back and tell Captain Lenzo what happened. Better for him to believe we all drowned. I plan on being one of only a handful of survivors, of course."

Dree ground her teeth. So, it was Lenzo. It wasn't a surprise, but now they had confirmation. Sen kept a firm hold on her elbow. What did he think she was going to do? If only she could get the crown. She didn't know what magic it possessed, she only knew the rumors. It should protect her if she was wearing it. Of course, it might only work after she was crowned. Everything she knew was too vague.

"What are you planning?" Ernesto asked.

Garin kept his arms aimed at the two of them. He must have to do that to keep them down. If they could distract him, the two men would be free to use magic. She wasn't sure how good their magic was. They had only been doing it for two years.

"Luckily for some of you, I don't know how to teleport. I'll keep four men to help me sail to land. The rest of you will jump."

"It's called walking the plank," Oscar said from the deck. "At least get it right."

"How are you going to sell the crown?" Dree asked. "By now, the entire world knows it's missing."

Garin grinned. "You are quite innocent. There are plenty that would buy it. I haven't decided if I will sell it or try to figure out its magic. I've studied it extensively. If I can harness the magic, I'll be unstoppable."

"Only the queen can use the magic," Dree said.

"Perhaps. I'm willing to experiment. Now, who wants to jump first, and who wants to be one of the four to survive?"

"Walk the plank. Not jump," Oscar muttered.

Sen dropped his hand from Dree and lunged forward. Garin wasn't expecting it and crashed to the deck when Sen's shoulder made contact with the man's gut. The crown rolled to the floor. Dree sprang forward and grabbed it. She shoved it onto her head and watched Sen and Garin punch each other. Oscar and Ernesto jumped to their feet and watched the men fight.

"Hit him harder, Sen!" Oscar encouraged.

"Use your magic!" Dree scolded the two pirates.

Oscar scratched his head. "What for? Garin can't use magic when Sen's pounding him like that. Besides, we aren't what you might call good at magic."

Dree looked to where Sen was dominating the fight. His lip was bleeding, but Garin's nose appeared to be broken, and both eyes were going to be black.

Garin didn't look up to doing any magic. Sen stopped hitting the man and got to his feet, wiping the blood from his lip.

Garin sat up on the deck and glared up at Sen. "You're going to regret that," he said, raising an unsteady hand.

"Don't move a muscle, or you will be sorry," Dree commanded, pointing her finger at Garin. She didn't know what she would do if he defied her.

Garin laughed and spit blood onto the deck. "You think the crown will scare me? You said it yourself. Only one person in this world can use the magic of that crown."

Dree smiled. "And I was correct."

All the pirates stared at her, and Garin's eyes widened, then narrowed. "I will not believe you are the princess. Why would the crowned princess be on a pirate ship?"

"Perhaps she was searching for her crown," Sen said, standing next to her.

Oscar smacked his forehead. "You're the princess?"

Dree nodded, but kept her finger pointed at Garin. She hoped she didn't look as ridiculous as she felt.

Garin's eyes darted from the pirates to Dree. "It's a bluff. Give me the crown, and I'll let you all come with me."

Sen smirked. "You'll let us, will you? I don't think you're in a bargaining position right now."

"I'll share the crown," he said, licking his lips. "We can sell it and split it between everyone."

Dree's mouth turned down. "You'll share my crown with me? How generous."

Garin stood and pointed his palm at Dree. "You don't seem to understand the kind of magic I have. I've been learning from Lenzo, and there is nothing any of you can do that will compare to what I can do."

"Great, a standoff," Oscar muttered.

Dree kept her finger pointed and didn't let her stern expression falter. Could she do anything? She thought about being invisible. She concentrated on it as hard as she could.

"Where did she go?" Oscar asked.

It worked. She softly stepped away from where she had been standing in case Garin reacted and walked carefully toward him.

"She must really be the princess!" one pirate exclaimed.

Garin pointed his palm around and frantically scanned the ship. He finally settled on Sen. "Show yourself, or I will blast him!"

Dree kept creeping closer. Garin's blond hair was sticking out, and his swollen eyes flashed with fear. She moved behind him and paused. She didn't know what to do. What would Sen do? Probably have a knife at the man's throat. Dree didn't have a knife or any weapon. Reaching out her finger, she poked him in the back.

Garin yelled, and a ball of fire shot from his hand and busted through the deck.

"My ship!" Ernesto yelled, knocking Garin to the floor. "Go check below and see what the damage is." He sat on Garin and held his arms down. Oscar and Sen ran below.

"Get off!" Garin commanded, as he squirmed under Ernesto's weight.

Dree concentrated on becoming visible again. She looked down and watched herself reappear.

Sen came running back. "The fireball went through the bottom. The ship is filling with water."

Dree put her hand to her forehead. "Why did I do that?"

"It isn't your fault," Ernesto said, pulling Garin to his feet. He kept a firm grip on his hands.

"We can't fix this," Oscar said. "The ship is going to sink."

"Take my cuff off," Sen said to Garin.

Garin shook his head. "Why would I do that?"

"Because I'm the only one that knows how to teleport. I can get us out of here."

"Fine," Garin said. "Release me."

"Don't try anything," Dree said, pointing at him again. She was sure she didn't look threatening. Ernesto let him go.

Sen held his wrist out.

Garin smirked at the cuff. "Many people believe the lost continent of Riviand is under the whirlpool. I think I'm going to find out if it's true." Garin turned and leaped from the ship.

"No!" Dree cried, as she watched their only hope of survival disappear.

Sen ran to the railing and gazed down. "I don't see him."

"We're too far from any land to survive," Ernesto said, searching the water for Garin.

"Maybe the princess can help," Oscar said. "She has magic."

Dree swallowed hard. "I don't know how I can help. I don't know how to teleport. What about the smaller boats?" The ship felt lopsided.

"Right!" Ernesto said. "Everyone get in a dinghy!" The pirates all rushed to the small boats and began piling inside.

Sen studied the boats. "Those are full. Everyone isn't going to fit."

"I suppose I'll stay behind," Ernesto said, frowning. "The captain goes down with the ship, I suppose."

"I'll stay as well," Dree said. "Perhaps I can figure something out."

"Dragon!" someone yelled. The pirates quickly lowered their boats, leaving Ernesto, Oscar, Sen, and Dree.

Dree glanced up into the sky and saw a large orange dragon circling above them.

Sen smiled. "That's Tal's dragon."

"Tal?" Dree asked with wide eyes. "How would Tal find us?"

"He's the one I messaged for help."

Dree felt her stomach drop. "Of all the people you could call, why him?"

"I was sinking through the floor of a ship. I messaged the first person who came into my head. There wasn't a lot of time to plan."

"What a marvelous creature," Oscar said, as they watched the dragon slowly get lower.

This was the worst day ever. Being saved by Tal was only a little better than a sinking ship.

Ernesto kept his eyes up. "If you know that dragon, I'm assuming we're saved?"

"Probably," Sen agreed.

The enormous dragon landed on the sinking ship, causing it to rock.

Tal flashed his familiar lopsided smile and pushed his wavy brown hair from his eyes. "It looks like I came just in time. Everyone, hop on. There are only four saddles, so one of you will have to sit between them and hold on to me."

"Dree first," Sen said.

She scowled. She didn't want to be right by Tal, but she climbed on anyway. Sen probably wanted to be behind her in case she fell, but that meant she was the one without a saddle. Not that they were impressive. They were flat, but they had a place to hook in a person's feet. The dragon was hard and scaly and Dree felt her foot slip, but she caught herself. Sitting down between two saddles, she tried to figure out where to hold on.

"You're going to have to come closer," Tal said. "Sheba isn't as large as some dragons, so we're going to have to be cozy to get five on."

Dree wanted to protest, but the ship shifted suddenly. It was sinking faster. She got up right behind Tal and pushed his black cape out of the way.

"Hold on to me," he commanded.

She muttered something she didn't even understand as she put her arms around Tal's waist.

Tal chuckled under his breath. "It's good to see you again too, Dree. Nice crown."

Dree clenched her teeth together to stop herself from responding. Sen sat behind her in the saddle, and the two pirates were behind him.

"Everyone, hold on tight. I've taught Sheba to take off slower than some dragons, but it's still fast."

The dragon lurched forward and sprang into the air. Dree screamed and held on as tight as she could. She had never been on a dragon, and the speed was a shock. The dragon leveled out and slowed. She forced herself to take slow, deliberate breaths. She glanced down at the sinking ship and the smaller boats full of pirates.

"You think you can loosen your hold a little?" Tal asked.

"Sorry," she said, trying to release the tension in her arms.

"This is the most fun I've ever had!" Oscar said. "I can't believe I'm on a dragon."

"We're going to have to land on Marqurain Island," Tal said. "Sheba's been flying around for days with no good rest. She can't make it all the way to the mainland."

"Can we teleport?" Dree asked.

"I'd rather not," Tal said. "I did it once with Sheba, and she had a major meltdown. It took her three days to get over it. She's fast, though. It will only take us a couple of hours to get to the island."

Dree sighed and wondered how stiff she would be in a couple of hours. She loosened her hold when she realized she was still holding on fairly tight. This was going to be a rough ride.

"I've tied myself on," Sen said. "You can lean against me, and I'll hold on to you so your arms don't get sore."

Oscar snorted. "Nice line, mate."

"Be quiet, Oscar," Dree said loudly so the man would hear.

Sen put his arms around her and pulled her back. She let go of Tal and leaned against Sen.

"We won't look if you wanna kiss," Oscar said.

"We are only friends," Dree said. "You better knock it off or I'm going to have you locked up when we get back."

Oscar just chuckled.

They all walked around the small island, getting the kinks out of their legs. It had taken almost twenty minutes for

Dree to relax on the dragon. For a while, Sen had wondered if she might fall asleep. Her head had rested against his shoulder and his neck, and he'd resisted the urge to lean his head on hers. It wasn't hard since she had a poky crown on her head. He'd had to be careful, or he could've lost an eye.

Tal had been right about the dragon. She was exhausted. As soon as they dismounted, she curled up and fell asleep.

"I thought I'd made everything right with Dree," Tal said, walking up to him. "She sure didn't seem happy to see me."

"She's had a hard month."

"I heard about King Miadd and her brother. I guess that means she's going to be queen."

"Yeah," he said, watching Dree from a distance. She had taken her boots off and was walking in the shallow water.

"Are you going to stay with her?"

Sen shook his head. "As soon as she's crowned and we take care of a threat, I'm going to leave."

"Hm," Tal said, as they strolled across the beach. "I thought you two might end up together."

Sen sighed. "We've only ever been friends."

"That's what you said when you visited last year. I kinda thought you were trying to convince yourself."

"It's time for me to move on. Dree has a marriage contract, so she won't need me anymore. We had to get her one before she returned home because the King's Council wanted her to marry the captain of the guards."

Tal raised an eyebrow. "You helped her find someone to marry?"

"Yeah. I suggested him. He's a good guy. They'll be fine."

Tal stopped and stared at him with narrowed eyes.

Sen stopped. "What?"

"If it's all good, why is your eye twitching?"

Sen put a hand to his eye. "I ate a hot pepper the other day. My eyes have been having problems ever since."

"Why are you wearing a magic restrictor?" Tal asked, pointing at the cuff.

Sen glanced at his wrist. "The pirates put them on us."

Tal sighed. "I guess I know who stole them, then."

"Stole them?"

"It's partially my fault. Ming Li warned me not to make them."

Sen shifted. "You made them?"

"Yeah, sorry. I had help. They seemed like something that would be a nice precaution to use on the prisoners in Akkron. I figured if they escaped, they still wouldn't be able to do magic, and they would be easier to catch. We had a prison break a while back. Here, let me see." He took Sen's wrist and started twisting the cuff back and forth. There was a click, and it opened. Tal put the cuff in his pocket.

Sen rubbed his wrist. "How does it work?"

"It's mixed with rednax venom. We heated the metal and the venom together."

Sen nodded. Rednax were smelly animals that had venom that could block magic. "I guess we're even."

Tal grinned. "Not even close. You still owe me. You rubbed the venom on my arms, and you knocked me out with ailam powder."

"Yeah, well, you shouldn't have been sneaking around like you were up to no good."

"That's true, but I hope you've stopped reacting before you know what's going on."

"I've gotten better. Thanks for coming for us. I wasn't sure if you got my message."

He laughed. "I got it loud and clear."

"Too loud?"

"It was the loudest message I've ever gotten. I believe you said 'HELP! CAPTURED BY PIRATES!' It bounced around in my head and caused my girlfriend, who I may have been kissing at the time, to be concerned."

Sen grinned at the image that popped into his head. "Sorry. I was sinking into a wooden floor. I didn't have time to be quiet."

"It took a while to find you. Since we didn't know where you were, we couldn't teleport. A few people have been flying over the ocean looking for you. I sent them all a message and told them I found you."

Sen rubbed his sore wrist. The cuff hadn't been super tight, but he'd messed with it enough to make it chafe.

"So, there was a prison break? Which prison? Akkron?" he asked.

"Yeah, Akkron. It happened a while back. It wasn't pretty. The prison should have been completely secure, but you know how that goes."

Sen tried not to be bothered by the fact that no one had asked for his help. "How many people escaped?"

"Just a handful, but they were all high security prisoners."

He nodded. "Did you catch them all?"

Tal frowned and looked out at the ocean. "Almost all."

"You should have gotten me. I could have helped. I still can if you need me after I help Dree."

"We thought about asking you a few times. It happened right after you visited and we knew you were busy helping Dree."

Sen nodded. "I still could have helped. Did I know any of the people that escaped?"

Tal sighed. "It would take me hours to tell you about all the crazy things that have happened. You probably don't have that kind of time."

"Maybe I'll come find you when everything is settled with Dree." Sen hadn't wanted to stay around Akkron after the silver eclipse, but there was something annoying about not being included in the group.

Oscar and Ernesto approached them and Oscar rubbed his eye. "How long will we be here?"

"It will take a few hours before Sheba can make it back," Tal told him.

Sen tilted his head. "But now I can do magic, I can teleport us back."

"So, you're going to leave me here?" Tal asked, grinning. "I've spent days by myself searching for you. I'm tired of my own company."

"We shouldn't stay long," Sen said. "The captain of the guard is evil. We think he's trying to take over."

"So, that's why he wanted to marry Dree?"

Sen nodded. "Probably. And we should send out a search party to pick up the other pirates. They aren't going to make it back in those tiny boats."

"So, who are these two? Pirates or more prisoners?"

Ernesto puffed out his chest. "I'm the pirate captain."

"Didn't they capture you?" he asked Sen. "Are you taking them to prison?"

"It's complicated. They aren't actually bad. Remember the story my dad told about how he got here from Mexico?"

"Something about him and his friends bothering a witch and she tricked them into coming here?"

"Yeah. These are my dad's friends."

Tal laughed. "That's hilarious. We could send them back to Mexico."

Ernesto shook his head. "We don't want to go back now that we have magic. We like being pirates."

"You can't keep being pirates," Sen said. "Eventually, people will hunt you down. And now you don't have a ship."

"We'll think on it."

"I've heard about you," Tal said with a grin. "Everyone's talking about you, in fact. It's not every day you hear about pirates that wipe butter all over a building."

"We should go," Sen said. "There are so many things we need to fix."

"Alright," Tal said. "Let me talk to Dree first. I want to make sure we're okay."

Chapter 13

"Hey," Tal said, as he sat next to Dree on the sand.

"Hello," she said, pushing down her nerves. She was holding her crown, turning it slowly in circles.

"I thought we were good last time we talked, but you didn't seem too thrilled to see me."

Dree pursed her lips. Tal had apologized, and they had been good. After two years of reliving the awkward moments in her mind, it made her not want to see him again. She had nothing against him, she just didn't want to remember.

If she was honest, he hadn't done anything to begin with. Neither one of them had wanted to go through with their arranged marriage. It just hurt her ego knowing he had been so excited to not have to marry her.

"Sorry. It's embarrassing to think back on some memories from before," she admitted. "I cringe when I dwell on them."

"Don't be embarrassed. It's a waste of time. If I dwelled on every weird thing I've said or done, I would be a wreck."

"I kissed you," Dree said, feeling her cheeks heat.

Tal grinned. "That was awkward, but you were just trying to fix things between us."

"It's still horrifying to reflect on."

"It's been two years. That's time enough. We can laugh at it now."

Dree smiled. "I guess. You did look terrified. I can still picture your face."

He winked. "I was terrified."

"I have that effect on guys."

"That's not true. Sen told me you're getting married."

Dree covered her face with her hands. "Ugh, yes."

"You aren't happy about it?"

"It's fine," she said, dropping her hands. "He'll be good for the kingdom. Mace wants to make a difference. He's good looking and strong. He's great."

Tal tilted his head. "But you aren't in love with him?"

"Not at all."

Tal nodded. "I'm surprised you didn't just ask Sen. You two have been good friends."

Dree frowned as she fiddled with the crown. "I did. He said no."

"Interesting," Tal said, rubbing his chin. "Did he say why?"

"He wants to have a marriage like his parents, not be forced into something. It would be weird anyway since we're just friends."

"No weirder than someone Sen picked out for you."

She sighed. "There must be something wrong with me. I'm a princess, and I still can't get a guy to actually want to marry me. Even the guy who's marrying me doesn't want to."

"There's nothing wrong with you. I was just a jerk that didn't want to be bossed around by my father. Who knows what Sen's problem is. I think he's regretting his decision to let you marry someone else, though."

She wished that was true. "I seriously doubt it. He said no pretty fast."

"Maybe too fast? If he didn't take time to think it through, it might have been too late when he let it sink in."

Dree laughed. "I can't believe I'm having this conversation with you."

"It is kind of funny, but I'm right. Are you in love with him?"

She frowned. "We're just friends."

"That's not what I asked."

Her lip quivered, and she swallowed a lump in her throat. She would not cry in front of Tal. If she tried to talk, she would cry. She settled on shaking her head and decided he could interpret that however he wanted.

Tal gave her a sympathetic look. "You are in love with him. Have you told him?"

She shook her head again. Two tears slid down her cheeks, and she angrily wiped them away. "Sorry, I'm ridiculous. I didn't even realize how I felt until it was too late."

"It's not too late," Tal said, putting his arm around her. "Marriage contracts can be broken."

"But Sen doesn't want to marry me," she said, as more tears fell. Dree hadn't been hugged much in her life, and Tal's arm around her made her feel like a little girl.

"Maybe Sen didn't understand how he felt, either," he said. "All I know is, Sen's been following you around for two years. A guy isn't going to do that for no reason. He could've gotten a job anywhere, but he worked on a farm to stay with you. Did you know Governor Zara offered him a job? A really good job."

Dree wiped her eyes. "She did?"

"Yes, and he turned her down to follow you. He could have made a lot of money."

"Did she offer the rest of you jobs?"

"Not me," Tal grinned. "When I asked her why, she said she wouldn't even hire me to clean her floors. She might have been joking, but with Zara, it's hard to know."

"I'm sure she was joking," Dree said. Tal had been as important as anyone in The Silver Eclipse.

Tal shrugged. "I don't want to work in the government. I don't have the temperament and Zara knows it. It's the same reason the two of us would have been terrible together. I would make a better jester than a prince. Now, back to the subject at hand. We all had important people from all over the world trying to get us to come work for them. We really have more options than we know what to do with, and Sen chose you."

Dree frowned. She was holding Sen back. "He only stayed because he loves a challenge. Stopping me from being helpless was probably the biggest challenge of his life."

"That's not true. Tell him how you feel."

"I can't," she said. "He doesn't feel that way about me."

Tal raised his eyebrow. "How do you know?"

"You remember how Sen is with competition? Well, Oscar baited him into kissing me. Afterwards, he was so mad. Sen's usually so stoic, but he was angry that he had done it. It scared me. I thought he would never talk to me again."

Tal leaned forward. "Are you sure he wasn't angry that he kissed you when he knew he couldn't be with you?"

Dree stood up, and he followed. "Still into matchmaking, I see."

He smiled. "I have a pretty outstanding record. Seriously, though. Tell him how you feel. Then, at least you'll know."

Sen watched Dree and Tal talk from a distance. It would be great to be able to hear from this far away. He forced himself to stop grinding his teeth when Tal put his arm around Dree's shoulder.

"You gonna let that boy waltz in and steal your girl?" Oscar asked, causing Sen to jump.

Sen glared at the pirate. "She's not my girl, and Tal has a girlfriend. We're all just friends."

Oscar's eyes sparkled. "If that's true, why are you working on busting your teeth?"

Sen relaxed his jaw and crossed his arms. "Because you won't let it drop. It's irritating."

Dree and Tal stood and continued talking. Tal took her wrist and removed her cuff.

Oscar raised an eyebrow. "Is he holding her hand?"

"He's taking off her cuff."

"He knows how? That's good. I've been feeling guilty about putting them on you."

Sen looked pointedly at the pirate. "You should. If you hadn't, we all could have teleported home."

"Well, now yours is off, so you can take us back."

"I will after Tal and Dree finish talking."

"Talking," Oscar scoffed. "I can't believe yer allowing it."

"For the last time, I don't care who Dree is with. It's her life, and she's just my friend."

"Oh, lookie there," Oscar said, pointing. "Now he's hugging her, and she's hugging him back."

Sen's head jerked back to Tal and Dree. He didn't realize he'd moved until he was halfway to them. He could hear Oscar chuckling behind him. Tal and Dree turned and watched him. There was no use stopping now, so he continued stomping toward them. Dree's eyes were red. Had Tal made her cry?

Sen shoved Tal, causing him to take a few steps back. "What do you think you're doing? She has a marriage contract!"

"It was just a friendly hug," Tal said, flashing his famous half smile. "You want one?" he asked, opening his arms.

Sen clenched his fists. "I will knock that stupid smile off your face."

"Stop, Sen," Dree said. "Nothing happened."

He pointed at Tal. "Did you make her cry?"

Tal kept smiling and winked at Dree. Sen took an angry step forward, and Dree grabbed his arm. She pulled on it until he looked down at her.

"It was a hug, Sen," she said. "Don't get angry."

"I'm already angry," he growled. "Why would you hug him? Why are you crying?"

Dree wrapped her arms around his neck and gazed up at him. "Don't let me marry Mace. Please." She blinked, and a tear rolled down her cheek.

Sen frowned as he wiped it away with his thumb. She didn't want to marry Mace? "You don't have to marry him."

She gazed intently into his eyes. "But I have to marry someone."

Sen's heart was trying to break free from his chest. "We can find someone else."

Tal snorted. "Sen, stop being an idiot." He grinned and wandered off.

Dree kept her arms locked around Sen's neck. He wondered if she could hear his heart. Was she trying to tell him something? Could she like him, or was he just a better option in her mind?

"I hate it when guys make me kiss them," Dree said.

Sen's eyes widened as she went onto her toes and pressed her lips to his. Butterflies swarmed his stomach as he wrapped his arms around her.

Dree pulled away and gazed into his eyes. "Give me a chance, Sen. I know you said—"

He leaned down and kissed her. He didn't want to hear her repeat anything he'd said. Hope filled his heart as she clung to him.

"I called it, didn't I?" Oscar said from behind. Dree jumped back, and her face turned a fiery shade of red. Oscar and Ernesto stood there grinning. They really were a lame excuse for pirates.

Sen narrowed his eyes. "Have you ever heard of bad timing? You definitely have it." Sen put his arm around Dree, ignoring Oscar's laugh. "Come on. Let's say goodbye to Tal. We need to teleport and send a rescue group for the other pirates."

They walked in silence with the two pirates following behind them. Sen's heart was still pounding. Why did they have to get interrupted? They needed to talk, and the longer they waited, the longer he had to fret about what he should say. Tal was sitting by the sleeping dragon, smiling at them.

Sen titled his head. "Don't say anything."

Tal lifted both hands in surrender and grinned. Sen still had a slight urge to punch his friend, but all things considered, it probably wouldn't be the best idea.

"We're going to go. We can't waste any more time."

"Alright," Tal said. "Do you need any help? I can tell Sheba to wait here for me."

"Is that safe?" Dree asked.

"Sure. Dragon's love beaches. She's probably safer here than most places."

"I remember when riding dragons made you sick," Sen said, remembering the first time they had ridden a dragon. Tal had gone and puked when they landed.

"Yeah, it still makes me sick occasionally, but I've taught Sheba to be a little smoother than other dragons."

Ernesto ran his hand over her orange scales. "Aren't you worried she might fly away if you leave her here?"

"No, I'll explain it to her."

Oscar laughed. "Explain something to a dragon?"

"Tal can talk to animals," Dree said. "It's some kind of mind connection."

Tal bobbed his head. "I've gotten really good at it too." He rubbed Sheba's head, and she lazily opened her eyes. He stared into her eyes and rubbed her head.

Oscar leaned closer to Sen and whispered, "What's he doing? Looks like he's trying to hypnotize her."

Sen shrugged.

Tal turned to them. "Alright, she's going to wait here for me."

"Are you the same Tal that was a member of The Silver Eclipse?" Oscar asked.

Ernesto rolled his eyes. "Of course he is. He is Sen's friend, isn't he? How many friends named Tal would Sen have?"

"Can I maybe have your autograph when we get back? Yours and Sen's?"

Tal laughed and patted Oscar on the shoulder. "Sure."

"We're probably going to end up in prison and you want an autograph," Ernesto mumbled.

"Prison?" Oscar asked.

"We stole the princess's crown and captured her. Of course we're gonna end up in prison."

Dree shifted under Sen's arm. "We can make some sort of deal, I'm sure."

"Speaking of the crown," Sen said, "where is it?"

"Oh no!" Dree exclaimed. "I must have dropped it." She turned and darted back to where they had come. Sen could see the crown glittering in the sun. He smiled as he watched Dree try to run in the sand with her boots on.

"You're welcome," Tal said, slapping Sen on the back.

"Knock it off," Sen said, stepping away.

Tal grinned. "Nah, I think you owe me."

"For what?"

"That kiss."

Sen shook his head.

"You can't take all the credit," Oscar said. "I'm sure a lot of credit goes to me. I prodded where it was needed."

"You're both crazy," Sen said. "You might have just caused a bunch of problems."

Oscar scratched his head. "Problems how?"

"It doesn't matter." He didn't want to have this conversation. "Where did Ernesto go?"

They all glanced around the beach, but the pirate captain was nowhere to be seen.

"He's probably just using the bushes, if ya know what I mean." Oscar cupped his mouth and yelled, "Ernesto!"

Sen sighed. "Great. We don't have time to search for him."

"I'll stay and look for him," Tal volunteered. "Where should I meet you?"

"Come to the castle."

Dree rushed toward them. "The crown is gone!"

Sen's eyebrows came together. "Gone? How? I just saw it glittering over there."

"It disappeared. I was about to pick it up, and poof. It was gone."

Oscar scratched his chin. "I bet it was Ernesto. He enjoys being a pirate, and he's good at summoning things. It's one of the magical abilities he's become good at."

"What good would it do him?" Sen asked. "He doesn't know how to teleport, so he would be stuck here."

"Don't know, but I'd bet on it being him. I've been keeping us out of trouble for the most part. I try to talk him out of things that might send soldiers after us."

"Shouldn't there be a protection on the crown so people can't summon it?" Tal asked.

Dree shrugged. "There is a protection over the castle. Nothing can be summoned from it. I doubt there is anything on individual objects."

Sen took a deep breath through his nose and sighed. "We can't leave the pirates floating out there for long. They could be in danger."

"The island is small," Tal said. "You all go, and I'll stay here and hunt for Ernesto and the crown."

"It could be dangerous. He could be hiding anywhere." Sen might get irritated by Tal occasionally, but he didn't want anything bad to happen to him.

"I can probably find him fast enough. If you want to wait a few minutes, that's probably all I need. He couldn't be far."

"Five minutes," Sen agreed.

Tal nodded and jogged over to the nearest palm tree. He pressed his hand to it and bowed his head.

Oscar chuckled. "What's he doing? Talking to the tree like he talked to the dragon?"

Sen tilted his head as he watched Tal. "Something like that."

"I suppose if yer chosen to save the world, you should have powers no one else does. Do ya think your mate can find him?"

Sen shrugged as Tal walked up to another tree. "You know we can't let you continue being a pirate, right?"

"Aye."

"You should give up the pirate talk."

Dree nodded. "You're terrible at it. You should ditch the eye patch as well."

Oscar let out a defeated breath and took off the patch. "I suppose it feels better to be without it."

Tal took a step away from the tree and smiled. He raised his hands into the air and twirled them around above his head.

"Come on!" Tal called to them. "I've got him."

Oscar shook his head. "Your friend might be a bit off."

Sen just smiled and made his way toward Tal. Dree and Oscar followed.

"He wasn't far," Tal said, leading them into the trees.

"So, where is he?" Oscar asked.

Tal pointed up into a tree. "Right there."

Ernesto was upside down, halfway to the top of the tree. Vines were holding him up and wrapped around most of his body. The amethyst crown laid on the ground under him. Dree scooped it up and stepped back.

"Wow," Oscar muttered. "I don't want to be on your bad side."

Tal laughed and raised his arms. He moved them slowly, and the vines holding Ernesto lowered him to the ground.

"What's the big idea?" Ernesto growled from the dirt.

"That's what we want to know," Sen said. "You took the crown. Again."

"Let me go," he protested, struggling against the vines.

"We will once we get to the castle."

Dree placed her hands on her hips. "And by letting you go, we mean from the vines. I can forgive you for stealing the crown once, but twice is ridiculous."

"The first time we didn't technically steal it," Oscar said. "Someone else stole it and gave it to us."

"We can figure it out later," Sen said. "Everyone, hold on to me, and I'll take us to the castle." Oscar touched Sen's shoulder. Tal bent over and grabbed Sen's leg with one hand and Ernesto with the other. Dree grabbed Sen's hand, and he tried not to smile. He was doing a lot more smiling and frowning this week. Concentrating on the castle, he whisked them away.

Chapter 14

Halla didn't know how long she and Mace had been in the cave. It had been three days at least. When they had gotten close to the cave, Jolly had given them instructions to open a crate. Mace pried it open, and blue smoke billowed out. That was the last thing they remembered before waking up in the pit. Cave felt like too friendly of a word for this place. There was a hole at the top that let in light, and it had about thirty feet to move around in. Three narrow tunnels led to smaller caverns, but they were small with low ceilings.

The pit was filled with food, blankets, lanterns, and even clothing. It was all men's clothing and much too large for her, but it was clean at least. She was wearing an overly large men's tunic as a dress. It went past her knees, and she cinched it with the belt she'd been wearing when they were brought here.

This had been the most awkward few days of Halla's life. She had never spent much time around men, and she didn't know what to say. Mace spent most of the time trying to figure a way out, so it spared her from having to converse much. He had tried to make handholds on the rock walls, but none of the supplies were strong enough to break into the walls.

There was a book about goblins mixed in with the supplies, and she had read it three times. She knew more about goblins than she would ever need to know. Still, reading the book was better than watching Mace. He was so much better looking than anyone she had ever seen, and when she watched him, it led her to having ridiculous daydreams about the man.

"Have you memorized it yet?" Mace asked, breaking her out of her stupor.

Her head jerked up. "Excuse me?"

"The book. You've read it quite a few times."

"I'm sorry. I should try to help you."

"There isn't a lot to help with. I don't think we're getting out of here unless someone lets us out. We could rip the blankets up and tie them into a rope, but there isn't any way we could anchor it to anything up there."

Halla glanced at the scattered supplies. "What if we stacked the crates?"

"I thought about that. There aren't enough. If I could just get this cuff off," he muttered, pulling at the metal contraption. Halla looked at her own bracelet. She's tried several times to get hers off.

He ran his hands through his hair and sighed. "I wonder what Lenzo's plan is. I'm a little surprised he didn't just get rid of me permanently." He sat next to Halla with his back against the rock wall.

"It's going to be bad if we get out, and I'm afraid part of it is my fault," she admitted.

Mace arched his eyebrow. "Oh?"

Halla took a deep breath. She might as well get it all out. "From what Lenzo said, it sounded like he wanted to get you out of the way long enough for people to give up on finding you. Eventually, after he marries the princess, he will turn you over to Vetta."

"That sounds terrifying. I don't see how that's your fault, and I'm not scared of Vetta. She can't keep me anywhere against my will."

"He changed part of the plan when I interfered," she said, not brave enough to look at him. "He's going to tell people that, um, that—"

"That we ran off together?" Mace finished for her.

"Yes," Halla nodded, heat creeping into her cheeks. "Even if we escape, I'll never be able to go back."

"You will. People will believe us, and Dree won't ever marry Lenzo. She'll figure something out, and Sen will help her."

"How long have you loved her?" Halla asked, and then immediately slapped her hand to her mouth. "Sorry, I didn't mean to ask something so personal."

He shrugged. "You can ask me anything. We might as well get to know each other better. We could be here for a long time."

Halla couldn't believe she asked that. There were so many other things she could have said. She wasn't a nosy person, but he probably thought she was.

He scratched at the stubble on his chin. "Dree and I aren't in love."

"Oh." She didn't know what to say to that. It wasn't what she expected but she wasn't too surprised. The only times she had heard Dree mention Mace, it hadn't been in a favorable manner, and she had been muttering under her breath. She hadn't ever seen them together back at Vetta's.

"We entered into the marriage contract so Lenzo couldn't marry her." He said it so matter-of-factly that it made Halla frown. Marriage shouldn't be like that.

"Hm. I always thought she liked Sen."

Mace nodded. "I'm sure she does, and he likes her."

Halla was confused, but she had already pried enough.

"I don't think we will end up married. I'm hoping Sen will stop being an idiot and admit he's in love with her. If he does, we can cancel the contract."

"I see," Halla muttered, ignoring the flutter in her heart. A prickle of hope sprung up inside of her, and she tried to squash it. Even if Mace was free, there was no reason he would turn his attention to her. She could barely hold up her side of a conversation.

Mace picked up a dark rock and examined it. "I never wanted to get married, but I couldn't let Lenzo take over."

"You never want to get married?" Halla blurted out.

"Probably not. I was in love with a girl once when I was younger. It didn't end well and kind of soured me on love."

"Oh." She tried to think of something to say, but she couldn't think of anything. There weren't a lot of situations that required her to talk and so she was out of practice. She couldn't be less boring in a conversation if she tried. Mace probably wished he was stuck with anyone besides her.

He tilted his head and watched her. "So, I told you about my love life. How about you? Any special person in your life?"

"No," she admitted, ducking her head. "Vetta didn't allow things like that." Even if she did, it wouldn't have changed anything. Being shy was such an obstacle.

"That sounds like Vetta. Did you have your eye on anyone? Most of the maids were half in love with Eral. They were always sneaking up to the stables to get a glimpse of him."

Halla smiled. None of the maids were sneaking up to see Eral. They were all trying to see Mace, and Eral just happened to be with him most of the time. Not that there was anything wrong with Eral. He was a talented farmhand, but he couldn't be over sixteen.

He leaned forward and grinned. "Did I guess it? You're secretly enamored with Eral."

"No."

"Then, why are you grinning like that? I've never seen you smile that big."

Her cheeks felt warm. "I think it's sweet that you don't know that all the maids were sneaking to the stables to see you."

Mace snickered and tossed his rock into the air. "That's a good one. The maids were all scared of me."

"They weren't. Well, maybe a little, but they all liked you anyway."

Mace shook his head.

"I shared a room with them. Your name came up at least every other night, usually more."

Mace grinned. "Are you trying to get on my good side?"

Halla's insides melted. It was unfair for a person to be so good looking. She gripped her book and tried not to look nervous. "Was I on your bad side?"

"No," he chuckled. "Far from it. So, what were the maids saying about me?"

"I probably shouldn't tell you. It would make you far too conceited." Was she flirting? She'd never done it before, so she wasn't sure.

His white teeth flashed. "I'm already too conceited, so it won't hurt anything."

"They liked to talk about how handsome you are." Heat crept up her neck.

"Hm, and which of my attributes did they like?"

Halla let out a small laugh. "This conversation is getting strange."

He rolled the rock in his hand and winked at her. "Strange circumstances call for strange conversations."

She tilted her head and studied him. "You're a lot different than I always thought."

"Oh?"

"You seemed so serious."

"I can be. Working for Vetta was hard work. Stop trying to change the subject, though. I want to know what the maids said. It was my hair, right? You have to admit, I have nice hair."

Halla smiled. He did have nice hair.

"Did Dree ever talk about me?"

Halla paused. Dree rarely took part in the night time gossip. The two times Halla had heard Dree talk about Mace, it hadn't been something a person should pass on. "Not the same way the others did."

"I'm not surprised. We didn't talk much, but when we did, we butted heads. So, what about you?"

Halla swallowed hard. "Me?"

"Did you ever talk about me?" His eyes sparkled and Halla willed her heart to keep beating.

"Why would I talk about you?"

"My nice hair?" He grinned mischievously.

She put her book on the floor. "I didn't talk to many people about anything."

"But if you talked about me, what would you say?"

"Are you really this starved for compliments?" she joked, fiddling with the metal cuff.

"Perhaps." His brows knit together. "In reality, I'm trying to take my mind off our situation. I wish I could figure out a way out of here. Dree and Sen might need me. Sen might be in danger if Lenzo sees him as a threat. Dree's probably safe since he needs her for his plan."

"What if they leave us here?" she said, voicing her concern. She'd tried ignoring that fear, but it wouldn't be pushed away.

"They probably won't. Why fill the place with supplies if they just want us to die here?"

"It would be easier for them, though. Then, we couldn't ever tell anyone what happened."

"We'll get out."

Halla nodded and twisted the cuff back and forth. She wondered if he was saying what he felt, or if he was trying to make her feel better. She glanced at his lips, then away. What was wrong with her? He wasn't ever going to kiss her regardless of what her daydreams seemed to want, and he shouldn't. He was linked to Dree.

Hoping to her feet, she made sure her tunic was straight, then she heard a clink. Her metal cuff had fallen to the floor.

"It's off!" Mace exclaimed, grabbing the cuff and getting to his feet. "What did you do?"

"I was just twisting it back and forth."

Mace clasped the cuff back together and studied it. "Twisting it how?"

"I don't know. I wasn't paying much attention."

He pulled on the round cuff and it remained closed. "Can you levitate us out?"

She took a deep breath through her nose. "I'm not very good at levitating. My mother didn't like us to use magic too often, so I'm not good at most of it."

"I could try to teach you to teleport, but that takes a lot of concentration. It's harder to take another person. If you could get yourself out, you could get help to come back for me. Are you up for it?"

Halla wasn't sure, but she nodded. They weren't getting out any other way.

Mace watched Halla wipe the sweat from her brow. They weren't going to get out by teleporting. Halla gave it a good effort, but she wasn't getting it. He'd tried moving his cuff all around, but it wouldn't come off.

"Perhaps you could try sending someone a message," he said doubtfully. Communicating telepathically was a fickle bit of magic. If you thought deeply about the person you wanted to talk to, and you knew where they were, it was possible to whisper and send a message directly to them. It had to be someone you had a connection with. From what Halla said, she didn't know many people. It also gave you a massive headache if you talked for more than a minute.

"I know how to do that," Halla said, her shoulders slumping. "I used to do it with my mom. I've never tried with anyone else, and I don't know if there is anyone that would be able to hear me."

Mace put a hand to her shoulder. "It's worth a try, though, right?"

Halla took a step back. She couldn't think if he was touching her. "I don't know anyone except some of Vetta's maids and a few from the castle. Even then, I only observe. I don't have any connections."

"Dree and Sen might be back at the castle. Could you try one of them?"

"I've only talked to Dree a few times, and never Sen, but I can try." Halla closed her eyes and whispered something Mace couldn't make out. She paused and waited, then tried again. Mace tried not to be captivated by her lips. He paced back and forth across the pit. He needed to knock some sense into Sen. Halla was getting deeper under his skin.

"Stop," he muttered when she rubbed her temples. "You'll give yourself a headache."

"Sorry," Halla said, staring down at her hands.

He put a finger under her chin and lifted her face softly. She hesitantly peeked up at him. "Don't be. We'll figure this out."

She took a step away and looked up at the opening. "I used to levitate myself up to the top cupboard in my house. It was as far as I could get before I started shaking. What if we stack the crates as far as they will go and then I try to levitate the rest of the way?"

Mace looked skeptically at the crates. They wouldn't be able to put them one on top of another or she wouldn't be able to climb up. It would also be unstable. "I'm not sure how high we could make them. You would still have a ways to go."

"Can we try?"

"Sure," he said, pushing the first crate into position. "You realize how high you levitate has nothing to do with ability, right? If you can levitate a foot, you can levitate to the sky. The only thing that stops people is their own insecurities."

Halla's mouth turned down into a perfectly cute pout. "My mom used to tell me that. I can't seem to get past it, though, and I haven't tried in a long time. Vetta forbid me from doing magic."

"Are you scared of heights?"

"No, but I'm scared of falling."

"That's what's blocking you, then." Mace pushed four crates into a square and then placed two more on top. "If you can get over the fear, you could go all the way to the top."

Halla nodded and bit her bottom lip.

Mace studied the crates. "This isn't going to work like this."

"Could we put them more like steps? Four in a row and then three and so on?"

"That makes a lot more sense. Let's try that." They unstacked the crates and began rearranging them. "If you haven't levitated very high before, we should probably have you practice for a while first."

"That is probably a good idea."

"We can put all the soft stuff under you, but it won't do much if you fall from that high. I wish I could get my cuff off." Whoever had invented these cuffs better hope Mace never ran into them. This was the most helpless he had ever felt in his life.

Chapter 15

Dree placed the amethyst crown in a box under her bed. They had decided not to tell anyone that they had the crown. If Lenzo believed it was still missing, he wouldn't try to steal it again. She glanced around the room. Under the bed was the most obvious place to hide something, but she didn't know where else to put it.

As soon as they arrived, Sen and Tal had teleported Ernesto back to Earth. There was a chance he would come back if he still remembered where the waterfall with the portal was, but they hoped he would stay there and stay out of trouble. She sent Oscar to an inn and told him to stay there until things were calmer. She would not have him arrested, but they couldn't have him accidentally running into Lenzo.

Dree jumped when there was a pounding on the door. "Who is it?"

"It's Sen. We have a problem."

She hurried to the door and unlatched it. "What is it?"

He entered the room and shut the door. "Mace is gone."

"Gone? Gone where?"

"No one knows. Rumors say that a maid he knew came to the castle, and they ran off together."

Dree frowned and sank down onto her bed. "Am I really that bad? What do I do that scares every man away? It has to be my personality because I have a mirror and I'm sure it's not my looks."

Sen's mouth turned up slightly at the corner, and he sat beside her. "You haven't scared me away."

Dree rolled her eyes. "But you wouldn't marry me. And Mace—"

"Didn't you just beg me not to let you marry Mace?"

"Yes, well, that doesn't mean it feels good to know he's run off on me."

He looked pointedly at her. "I don't think he ran off."

She threw her arms into the air. "Well, where is he, then?"

Sen ran a hand over his curls. "The maid that came was Halla."

Dree blinked twice. "Oh. I never would have expected that. She's so quiet."

"I bet Lenzo is behind it. You and Mace might not have been in love, but Mace wouldn't just run off. If he decided he didn't want to stay, he would have told you."

"What do we do? This is something the guards would take care of, but we don't know who is loyal to Lenzo."

"I don't know. We can talk to Tal. He might have some ideas."

"Where is he?"

"He teleported to Grenta to tell them about the stranded pirates. Once he gets a search party together, he's coming back."

She shook her head. "I shouldn't be letting Lenzo get away with this. We need to replace him, but I worry we won't know which guards are corrupt."

"Was Garin a guard?"

"I'm not sure. He didn't look familiar, but I was gone for a long time."

Sen arched his brow. "Can we trust your mother? She might know."

Dree shrugged. "Probably. It wouldn't hurt to talk to her."

"Let's start with her." Sen stood, and Dree followed. "And, Dree? I was stupid when I said I wouldn't marry you. We can talk about it later because there is too much going on right now. Alright?"

Dree bit her lip and nodded. She wished he would kiss her, but he was right. They needed to stop Lenzo and find Mace and Halla.

Sen clenched his jaw and tried not to insult the queen. She had made them wait over two hours to speak to her. She sat on a bench in the courtyard with her long golden dress neatly arranged around her.

"I hope you have learned not to be so impulsive, Lesandri," Queen Navina said. "If you had left the guards to do their job, perhaps you wouldn't have lost another man. He probably felt neglected. A princess should not be galavanting around the world searching for criminals. What kind of image do you want to portray to your subjects?"

"We didn't ask to speak to you so you could insult us," Dree said, standing tall in front of her mother. "There are some questions we need answered, if you can manage to do that without being rude."

The queen raised her perfectly shaped eyebrows.

"Was there a guard named Garin?"

Navina crossed her arms and tapped her fingers against her arm. "I don't believe so. Why do you ask?"

Sen looked at Dree. "If she doesn't know him, the 'why' isn't important."

Dree nodded. "Mother, we need to have Captain Lenzo put into prison. Do you know where we can find him?"

Navina laughed. "Put Lenzo in prison? He's the best captain this kingdom has known."

"You mean the most corrupt," Tal said, walking toward them with Oscar in tow. Oscar cleaned up well. Sen almost didn't recognize the man.

"He shouldn't be here," he said, pointing at Oscar.

Tal shrugged. "If we're going to capture the captain, I don't see any reason he should have to hide."

"Who are these people?" Navina demanded.

"I'm Tal, and this is Oscar."

"Tal?" she sniffed. "As in Talon?"

"The same."

She narrowed her eyes. "How dare you show your face in this kingdom!"

Dree crossed her arms and glared at her mother. "Tal is helping us."

"Why would you work with someone who so unceremoniously dumped you? He should have honored the agreement made by his parents."

"Mother, we have bigger problems right now."

"You are really going to forgive him?"

Dree rolled her eyes. "Tal and I would have been terrible together. We're friends now."

"Marriage has nothing to do with being good together. Talon's father was a great political figure. Your marriage would have been advantageous to both of you. Now you've shackled yourself with a farmhand. Not just a farmhand, but one who ran off the minute your back was turned."

"Mace wouldn't do that," Sen said. "Lenzo has to be behind it."

Navina smacked her hand against the bench. "Who gave you permission to speak?"

"He doesn't need permission to speak," Dree said.

"You could have at least chosen that one," she said, gesturing at Sen. "At least he has the distinction of helping save the world."

"Do you or do you not know where Lenzo is?" Dree muttered in what Sen assumed was an un-princessly way to speak. Fire flashed in Navina's eyes. "If you don't, then you are wasting our time."

"I haven't seen Captain Lenzo today, but he usually exercises his unicorn at this time. Probably in the southern pasture."

Tal snorted. "The famous captain of the guard rides a unicorn? That's hilarious."

"You ride alicorns," Sen said, remembering Tal's stable full of alicorns and pegasi.

"Yeah, and I have nothing against unicorns. It's just funny that he rides one of the most delicate and graceful of all magical creatures. I mean, I've never met the man, but from the way you describe him, it's giving me a funny picture in my head."

"How does this man fit into all of this?" Navina asked, pointing at Oscar.

"He's a friend, I believe," Dree said, smiling at Oscar.

Oscar stared at the queen without speaking. The man didn't appear well. Sen couldn't tell if he looked sick or scared.

"Hey, Oscar?" he said. "You alright?"

"What?" he asked, blinking at Sen. "What are we talking about?"

"You seem a little distant."

"Oh, um, I was just thinking," he said, glancing quickly to Navina and away.

"We should go," Dree said. "The sooner we take care of this, the better."

"I hope to see you all again," Navina sneered. "I can't imagine I will if you are planning on messing with Lenzo."

"Come on," Dree said, leading them away from her mother and out of the courtyard. They hurried through the castle and out the back. "The southern pasture isn't far."

"Your mother is everything the rumors say about her," Oscar said.

"What do people say about her?" Dree wondered.

"That she is the most beautiful woman to walk the planet."

Sen just shook his head, and Tal laughed.

"Do they also say she's scary and mean?" Dree asked.

Oscar grinned. "I bet she's just misunderstood."

"Don't let her beauty cloud your mind," Dree warned him. "She's not misunderstood, she's just rude."

He narrowed his eyes. "I've read so many books over the years. I think I recognize someone who is misunderstood."

Tal chuckled. "So, what would happen if this was a book?"

Oscar scratched his chin. "Well, a man would come along. They would meet and probably hate each other in the beginning. After a lot of effort, he would break down her hard exterior, and they would fall in love."

"And you want to be that man?" Tal asked.

"Oh. Not me," Oscar said. "I don't know what to say to a woman. Especially a queen."

"She's not the queen anymore," Sen said.

"I have a perfect match making record," Tal said. "If you need my help, I'm here."

"Do not try to match Oscar with my mother," Dree said with a shiver. "He may be a pirate, but he still deserves someone who would be nice to him."

"Is that him?" Sen asked, as he spotted a rider in the distance.

Dree squinted. "I think so."

"A white unicorn, of all things," Tal said with the hint of a laugh. "I don't understand why you guys don't find that funny. A white unicorn is a ten-year-old's dream."

Sen studied the captain for a moment. He did look funny. Captain Lenzo was a strong man, and he was tall. He was also wearing armor. He appeared too large for the creature.

"Shall we speed things up?" Tal asked. He stared at the unicorn and got a serious expression on his face. He focused on the animal and mumbled something under his breath. The unicorn turned and began trotting toward them. Lenzo pulled on the reins, but the unicorn kept coming.

Sen was impressed. "You've gotten better at controlling animals."

"I'm not controlling them, but I've gotten better at communicating with them. They usually get excited when they realize we can understand each other."

"That man doesn't look happy," Oscar said, putting a hand to his sword.

Lenzo's unicorn stopped in front of them, and he dismounted. His eyes flashed with anger as he turned to face them. "What did you do to Keekee?"

Tal turned a laugh into a cough. "Keekee. Nice name."

Lenzo narrowed his eyes. "I recognize you. You are one of the obnoxious kids that we had in our prison a few years back."

Tal smiled. "Glad you remember."

"Everyone remembers," he said with a smile that was nowhere near friendly. "You made an idiot of yourself."

"So I hear," Tal said, shrugging. "The king had my memory erased, so I'll have to take your word for it."

"You're the one that was supposed to marry the princess. You're lucky the king isn't still alive. He was angry you chose to go against the agreement."

"Why would he care?" Dree asked. "It's not like I was here anyway."

"Yes, well, it works to my advantage, I suppose. As does the fact that your latest fiancé has run off with someone else."

"I'll never marry you."

He glared down at her. "We shall see what the council says."

She smiled sweetly. "Yes, we shall. Let's call them together."

Dree sat at the head of the council's table. Sen sat to one side of her, and Tal on the other. Oscar was keeping out of sight. Lenzo hadn't recognized him earlier, but they didn't want to chance it again. Twelve council members sat around the table. The council was composed of six men and six women.

The head of the council was an older man named Hevnin. Dree didn't know him very well, but he had been on the council for a long time. Lenzo sat at the other end of the table. He seemed a lot more confident than Dree thought he should. She was glad to have Sendo there and even Tal.

"You've got this," Sen said under his breath. "You're in charge, not them."

Hevnin glared at a Dree. "Princess Lesandri, the council has decided that you will marry Captain Lenzo. We understand you had a marriage contract with Mace, but as he seems to have run off, the council has voted unanimously."

Dree narrowed her eyes and let her gaze fall on all the members of the council. "I hope you all know that as soon as I'm queen, I will have the power to dismiss any of you I choose. It would be good for you to all rethink this decision. I would also like to make an accusation against Captain Lenzo. Mace wouldn't have run off, and I believe Captain Lenzo had something to do with his disappearance and the disappearance of Halla."

"That's quite the accusation," Hevnin said. "Do you have any proof of this?"

"No, but I know it's true the same way you do. I'm just not scared of him the way you are."

"It's all very entertaining," Lenzo said. "But let's get to the matters at hand. The man has disappeared, and that makes his contract no longer valid. The kingdom needs to know that everything is secure, so the sooner we crown the princess, the better."

"I agree," said Hevnin.

Dree tried not to grind her teeth. "If you choose to make me marry him, I will have every single one of you replaced as soon as I'm crowned." The members all shared looks. None of them wanted to be replaced. They also all looked at Lenzo.

"I don't know how Lenzo's threatening or bribing you, but you all know that you are wrong, and something needs to be done about it. I'm fairly certain he's the reason that Halla and Mace disappeared. Do you want to have a new vote?"

No one on the council made eye contact with Dree or each other.

"I'm also sure Lenzo is the reason the amethyst crown was stolen. I'm almost one hundred percent certain."

Lenzo leaned forward in his seat. "How can you be sure of that?

"Because we found the pirates that you bribed to take the crown and throw it into Mermaid's Demise. We also talked to your friend Garin, and he confirmed he was there to make sure the crown was destroyed."

One of the counselors gasped.

"And who is Garin?" Lenzo asked.

"We aren't playing that game. You stole the crown and gave it to the pirates. We met the pirates and Garin. I have no doubts in my mind. You are guilty."

Lenzo smiled, but Dree could see the tension in his face. "That is a delightful story you've invented, but you have no proof."

"And yet everyone believes me," Dree said, looking at the guilty expressions on the councilmembers' faces. "Do you all want to lose your positions?"

"They won't lose their positions," Lenzo said. "I'll be sure of it."

Dree swallowed and tried to appear calm. If he was already making statements like that, he wasn't even masking the fact that he was going to take more power than the husband of a queen should have.

"Do you want to spend the rest of your time answering to him?" Dree's head was beginning to ache. She wished Sen or Tal would chime in, but they were being quiet so the council would know she was in control.

A councilwoman with a tight black bun stood and observed her fellow members. Dree couldn't remember her name, but the woman had always scared her when she was a child. "I am with the princess," she said. "We should not force her to marry the captain."

Lenzo's eyes narrowed, and his lips formed a thin line. "You will regret that, Marvna."

Dree stood and placed her fists on the table. "Do not threaten my council."

Hevnin peered quickly at Lenzo, then to Marvna. "Marvna, don't."

"No, Hevnin. We were wrong to agree to Captain Lenzo's plan in the first place. We are here to help the kingdom be strong, not fall to a power hungry man who will end up a tyrant."

"I agree with Marvna," a tall, dark-haired man said. Dree tried not to smile. One by one, each member stood to support her. All except Hevnin. He remained frowning in his seat.

Dree stared into Lenzo's eyes. Her stomach was a mess of nerves, but she kept a calm outward appearance. At least, she hoped she did. "Where are Mace and Halla?"

Lenzo sneered. "How should I know?"

"Where are they? Don't make me angry."

Lenzo laughed and stood. "Are you threatening me, little girl?"

Sen and Tal stood by her.

"Do you think your little bodyguards are going to stop me?"

"Captain Lenzo, I strip you of your command. I will go easy on you if you tell me where Mace and Halla are."

He flashed his teeth. "Easy on me? I wish I could say the same." Lenzo thrust out his arms, and a bright blue flash shot from his hands. Dree ducked, not knowing what he was doing. Sen, Tal, and all the councilors fell to the floor. Dree popped up in time to see Lenzo run from the room.

Grabbing her long, billowing dress, Dree ran after him. She wasn't the best runner, but Lenzo was going slow with his heavy armor weighing him down. When she got close enough, she jumped onto his back and tried to hold on to his smooth armor. He jerked to the side, causing Dree to fall. On the way down, she grabbed Lenzo's beard. He yelled and fell down with her.

Dree landed on her back and took a few deep breaths. Lenzo got up on his hands and knees and glared at her. She leaned back on her elbow and kicked him in the side with all the force she could muster. He fell over, then rolled and lunged at her.

"Help!" she yelled, rolling out of his way. With any luck, some guards would hear her. Scrambling to her feet, she rammed into him with her shoulder, causing him to fall again. Pain from hitting into his armor shot from her shoulder to her hand. Sen and Tal came running into the hallway.

Lenzo stood up and held one arm in the air. "You will regret this day for the rest of your life." He slashed his arm down, and red smoke filled the hallway. Dree coughed and waved the smoke away with her hand. She could hear Sen and Tal coughing as well. When the smoke cleared, Lenzo was gone.

The members of the council trickled into the hallway.

"He got away," Dree said. "If anyone sees Lenzo and doesn't inform the guards, we will arrest them for treason. Does everyone understand?" The council all nodded. "Marvna, will you please tell the guards what happened? Tell them Lenzo must be captured at all costs."

"Yes, Your Majesty," the woman said, bowing before disappearing down the hall.

"You," she said, pointing at the tall man. "Find my mother and tell her what happened. The rest of you plan the coronation. It will happen tonight."

"Tonight?" Hevnin protested. "That's much too soon."

Dree glared at him. "Putting it off will only cause problems. I don't care if no one comes. It still happens tonight."

Hevnin sputtered. "But you can't be made queen without the amethyst crown."

"I have the crown."

Chapter 16

Sen couldn't imagine what the castle would have looked like if they had more than one day to prepare. It was packed. Everyone in the surrounding village must have come to see Dree become queen. She had commanded half of the guards to stay around the castle and half of them to go out in search of Mace and Halla.

It had been hard for Sen to pay attention to the ceremony because he couldn't keep his eyes off her. Her long burgundy dress cascaded to the floor, and her brown ringlets fell loosely around her shoulders. When the amethyst crown was placed on her head, a ripple of energy went through the castle. Sen wasn't sure if he was the only one that felt it, but from the look on everyone's faces, he didn't think he was.

Now that the ceremony was over, people were busy talking, dancing, and eating. It was amazing how much cake they had gathered in such a short amount of time. Dree made her way toward Sen, her lips pursed and her gaze fixed on him. He put his drink on a table and walked over to meet her.

"I'm going to leave," she said when she reached him.

"Are you allowed to leave your own celebration?"

"I'm the queen. Doesn't that mean I can do what I want?"

"You tell me."

She took a deep breath and blew it out slowly. "Then, dance with me."

He raised an eyebrow. "Is that a command?"

"No."

He held out his hand, and she gripped it. Sen placed his hand at her waist and frowned. Her eyes were full of tears. "What's wrong?"

"Nothing is wrong," she said, placing her hand on his shoulder.

"Liar."

"Stop," she said, as they started dancing. "Don't make me talk or I might cry."

"That means you aren't alright."

"Don't. Not here. Too many people are watching. I don't need the gossip." Dree let go of his hand and wrapped both of her arms around his neck and buried her face in his neck.

If she didn't want people to gossip, that probably wasn't her best move. Sen adjusted his head to not get poked by her crown. He wrapped her in both of his arms and ignored the moisture gathering on his neck.

"I can't have everyone see me like this," she sniffed.

Sen danced them toward the nearest exit and whisked her out the door. There was no way this would not cause a scandal. "Come on," he said, taking her hand and leading her outside to the courtyard. They made their way over to the large tree.

Dree wiped at the tears running down her face. "I hope no one saw that."

Sen didn't tell her about the glare her mother had shot at him as they left. "Don't worry about it. What's wrong?"

She sniffed. "What isn't? We shouldn't be celebrating when Mace and Halla are out there somewhere, probably in danger."

Sen nodded. He didn't want to mention that they might be dead. They would worry about that if it happened.

"I'm not fit to be queen."

"You are. You are going to be great."

"I almost had a panic attack today when I was talking to the council. And what type of queen chases a man down and jumps on him?"

Sen's mouth curved up in a small smile. "A great one."

"I haven't been able to concentrate since."

"Because you attacked Lenzo?"

She gave a short laugh. "No, because I got hurt from hitting him with my shoulder."

Sen grabbed hold of Dree's arms and peered into her eyes. "It's been a long day, but it's going to be alright. You are going to be the best queen ever, and I'll be here to help you."

She tilted her head, and her eyes fell to his lips. "Promise?"

He swallowed hard as he nodded. Why did she have to look at him like that? "And we are going to find Mace and Halla."

"Alright," she said, coming in a step closer.

"You've grown up a lot in the last few years."

She nodded. "We both have."

"I haven't changed much," he protested.

"You smile and frown a lot more than you used to."

She was right about that, but that had only happened in the last month. He still wasn't sure how he felt about it.

Her mouth turned up at one corner. "Your shoulders are a lot more impressive than when I first met you. It must have been all the work at the farm."

Sen groaned and shook his head. He let go of her arms and felt his cheeks burning.

She laughed softly. "Sorry, I couldn't help it."

"Does the crown feel different?" he asked, changing the subject. "Did you feel the room vibrate when the man put it on your head?"

"Yes, but I thought it was just me. I need to study the crown more. I don't know what it's capable of."

"Well, you can go invisible with it."

"I feel bad about the way I dealt with Garin," she said, chewing her lip. "I should have done something else. Then, the ship might not have sunk."

"It all ended alright. Tal said the pirates were all saved."

"What about Garin?"

"The pirates said he swam into the fog."

"Do you think he fell into the whirlpool?"

"I don't know. I doubt we will ever know. You don't need to feel guilty about him, though. He made his own choices."

She took another step forward. "I know."

Sen took a step back. Dree was getting awfully close, and he couldn't kiss her again. Not until he talked to Mace.

"I probably shouldn't have forced the council to crown me so quickly," she said. "I just felt like I needed to have more control, and I didn't want the council trying to manipulate me."

"You made the right decision. You can do what you want, but I think it would be wise to replace Hevnin as council head. He was the only one who didn't stand in your defense."

She tilted her head. "I've been considering that. Once we find Mace, I'm going to ask him to cancel our marriage contract. I hope he won't be angry. With luck, he will agree to be on the council."

Sen took another step back. "Mace and I spoke a while back. He offered to back out of the contract. He said he would like to be on the council."

Dree's mouth turned down. "What do you mean, he offered to back out?"

Heat crept up his neck. "He thinks I'm in love with you."

She looked down at her hands. "Oh."

Navina came bursting into the courtyard. "Lesandri! Get back in there this instant! It's one thing to go against tradition and choose the date of your own coronation, and a completely worse thing to dance away with a man that is not your fiancé and leave your guests.”

Dree put a hand to her forehead. “Mother, I hate to be rude, but you are not in charge of me.”

Navina’s jaw moved back and forth in barely masked anger. “You are not prepared to be the queen. You must let me guide you until you are.”

“Perhaps instead of hiding me away when I was younger, you should have taught me the things I needed to know. Then, you might not be so ashamed of me.”

“How was I to know you would end up as queen? Your brother should have ruled.”

Dree stood tall. “Yes, well, that didn’t work out, so now I’m going to have to figure things out myself.”

Oscar wandered toward them, his hands in his pockets. “Delightful party.”

Navina rolled her eyes. “Where did you pick this man up? He’s been inside stuffing his face with cake. It’s disgraceful.”

“I’m a pirate,” Oscar said. “Well, an ex-pirate. Pirates do a lot worse than overeat.”

Sen shook his head. Oscar was supposed to keep the pirate thing to himself.

Navina’s eyes widened. “Pirate? One of the pirates that stole the amethyst crown?”

“He didn’t steal it,” Dree said. “That was Lenzo.”

Oscar rubbed his neck and peered at Navina. “Perhaps, you would like to return to the party and dance with me?”

"Dance with a pirate?" Navina asked, pulling a fan from her sleeve. "I can only imagine the gossip," she said, fanning herself.

Oscar cleared his throat. "A little gossip never hurt anyone."

"Oh my."

Sen grinned as he watched the queen go from angry to flustered.

"I suppose one dance would be alright," she finally said. Oscar offered his arm, and she took it, letting him lead her back toward the castle.

"What just happened?" Dree asked. "I cannot believe my mother agreed to that."

Sen shrugged. "Why not? Oscar's not a bad looking guy."

"Yes, but my mother is not easily swayed by anyone. I would have been less shocked if she had smacked him with her fan." Dree sighed. "She was right, though. I should go back in. How do I look?"

Sen swallowed. "Beautiful."

Dree's cheeks flooded with color. "Do I look like I've been crying?"

"No."

"Then, we should return to the party."

Sen nodded and took her hand. They walked silently across the courtyard. So many thoughts were flying through his mind he couldn't even follow. He hadn't told Dree he was in love with her, but she must know. She might not be in love with him, but she had made it clear she would prefer marrying him to Mace. That had to count as something. And she'd kissed him.

When they entered the ballroom, the dancing was in full swing. Sen dropped her hand, even though it was too late to avoid gossip. Navina was being whisked across the floor by Oscar. His dancing was anything but conventional, but Navina actually appeared content.

"Can I have this dance?" a round man with brown slicked back hair asked Dree. Her lips formed a tight line, but she nodded. Sen watched as they disappeared into the crowd. He stood near the wall, watching the couples dance across the floor. After a few minutes, he made his way to the refreshment table. He didn't want to dance with anyone except Dree, so he might as well try the cake.

Dree tried to not to wrinkle her nose as she danced across the floor with the robust man. He smelled like garlic and sweat, causing her to count down the minutes until the song ended. Her eyes scanned the crowd for Sen, but she couldn't locate him. The man was talking about something, but she was having a hard time paying attention.

"Your Majesty?" the man said. She forced herself to look at him. "You aren't listening to me, and I'm trying to tell you something important."

"I'm sorry," Dree apologized. "Please, go on."

"I was saying that when I was a boy, I discovered an enormous crack in the rocks on the east mountain. Inside the crack was an enormous cavern. It isn't easy to get down because it is very deep."

Dree's eyebrows came together. She wasn't sure why the man was telling her this. "I see."

"Only a handful of people know about it. I showed it to my cousin, and we made it into our hideout. Of course, that was a long time ago. Since then, my cousin has used it for one thing or another. If someone were to capture a person, nobody would ever think to search there."

Dree's eyes shifted as she studied the man. What was he trying to say? Was he threatening her or just telling her a story?

"If someone were to disappear from your kingdom and get thrown into the cavern, it's likely they would never be found. You wouldn't need to panic or anything because my cousin keeps it full of supplies so they wouldn't be in immediate danger." The man released her hand and bowed, then slipped off into the crowd.

Dree stared after him until Sen came up to her, a plate of cake in his hands. "He disappeared fast."

"Yes," Dree agreed. "He might have told me where Mace and Halla are."

Sen arched his brow. "What do you mean?"

Dree told him what the man had said. Sen took a bite of cake, and Dree watched his face for any sign of what he was thinking. He chewed slowly, and Dree wondered if he was contemplating what she said or if he was just enjoying the food. He took another bite, and Dree fought the urge to poke him. She could be patient.

"Do you know where the east mountain is?" he finally asked.

"There isn't an exact mountain we call the east mountain. There are several east of us, so it could take forever to search."

Sen shoved the rest of the cake into his mouth and smiled when Dree rolled her eyes. He probably knew she was frustrated. He'd known her long enough to understand her impatience with him when he was thinking. Dree was too quick to answer, and Sen was too slow. They could probably learn from each other. She began tapping her shoe.

"Sorry," he said after he swallowed. "Were you expecting me to decide what to do?"

Dree crossed her arms and frowned. She *was* expecting him to tell her what to do. Life was easier if someone gave you the answers. She sighed. As queen, she needed to change that mindset.

"I would like your opinion," she said. "If Mace and Halla are in a crack on the mountain, it could take forever to find them. We could have all the guards searching, but that would alert Lenzo and he might move them."

"In a crack in the mountain?" Oscar said from behind them. "Let's move into the hall, shall we? No need to tell the entire party our woes, is there?"

Dree felt her cheeks warm. She should know better than that. "Yes," she said, heading out of the room. Sen and Oscar followed. Dree shook her head as she realized she liked

Oscar, and she trusted him. Trusting a pirate didn't seem like the most sound idea, but she had a gut feeling about it. After explaining the situation to Oscar, she watched him tap his chin and think.

"I might know of someone that can help," he said. "When I was young and living in Mexico, there were rumors of a witch."

"Right," Sen said. "She's the one who tricked you into coming here."

"Yes."

Dree chewed her lip. "But if she's from this world, why would she be any more helpful than anyone else?"

"The reason people thought Slosha was a witch was because she seemed to know about things before they happened."

"Like what?"

"Our village was far out from other cities and wasn't big. One year, we had a poor yield with our bean harvest. She turned up in town and had a truckload of beans she had been storing. The witch was always doing odd things that eventually helped people. She ran into town one day and yelled at all the people to get out of the inn. Everyone came out confused, but within a few minutes, there was an earthquake. The only building to be completely destroyed was the inn."

Dree wasn't convinced. "So, you think she could tell us where Mace and Halla are?"

"It's possible."

Sen shrugged. "It's worth a try. We don't have a better plan."

Tal came into the hall. Dree had forgotten about him. "What's going on?" he asked.

Sen caught him up as Dree paced across the hallway. She probably shouldn't be running off the moment she was crowned. It might seem irresponsible. Still, she couldn't leave Mace and Halla in danger.

"Dree shouldn't go," Sen said. "She's going to be needed here."

"Why don't you and Oscar go?" Tal said. "Dree can hold things down here, and I can fly over the mountains with Sheba to see if I can see anything,"

"Is that alright?" Sen asked Dree.

"That would be best," she agreed.

"I haven't been home in so long," Oscar said, almost reverently. "My parents have probably worried about me all these years."

"Would you rather stay?" Dree asked. "Sen's father could take him to see the woman."

"No, I'll come. I'm sure my parents know what happened. Sen's father probably told them when he returned. Still, I should go and see them. I want to return here, though. I've been here a long time, and it's grown on me."

"I'll go now," Tal said. "Sheba might even sense them." He waved and trotted off down the hallway.

"Don't forget to come back," Dree said to Sen, only half kidding.

"We won't," Sen said. "It shouldn't take more than a day."

"Don't worry, Princess," Oscar said. "I'll make sure he gets back."

She smiled. Oscar had already forgotten she was the queen now. "Thank you."

Chapter 17

S en knocked on his family's door and waited. He didn't want to walk in with Oscar and scare anyone. There was probably going to be a lecture from his mom. He hadn't visited in over two months. Sen smiled as he listened to his brothers tromp down the hall and crash into the door.

"Let me open it!" one of his brothers yelled from behind the door.

"No! You did it last time!" said another voice.

"Ouch!"

"I'm telling. Let go of the doorknob!"

"Mom! Javier hit me!"

"Did not, he's lying!"

"Am not—hey! Knock it off, no pinching!"

Oscar laughed. "Sounds like a house full of boys to me."

Sen pulled the door open, and his youngest brothers Pablo and Javier fell to the ground.

"Sen!" they both yelled, jumping to their feet. He wrapped both of them in a bear hug. He didn't want to live on Earth, but he missed his brothers.

"Sendo, is that you?" his mother Kraya asked, coming into view. She was drying her hands on a cloth and smiling. Sen released his brothers to give her a hug. "Who is this?" she asked, glancing at Oscar.

Oscar shifted uncomfortably. "We met a long time ago. I'm Rosendo's friend, Oscar."

Kraya smiled. "Oh, yes, I remember you. Rosendo will be thrilled to see you again. He's wondered about you over the years. Come in."

"We don't have a lot of time," Sen told her, as they followed her to the kitchen. Sen's brothers were close on their heels.

"Nonsense," Kraya said, handing Oscar a plate with a scone. "Please, sit." Oscar collapsed into a chair and started devouring it.

"We really need to leave soon."

Javier stuck out his lower lip. "You never stay long."

"It's about time you visited," Rosendo said, entering the room. He clapped Sen on the shoulder.

"Hola, Papá."

"Oscar? Is that you?"

Oscar looked up from his scone and smiled. "Good to see you again."

Rosendo laughed and sat next to his friend. "It's been years. I halfway believed you were dead."

Oscar grinned. "Not yet, but I've come close a time or two."

"Where's Ernesto?"

"You haven't seen him?" Sen asked. "I hope he didn't go back to Basura."

His father frowned. "Back? Was he in Mexico?"

"He was causing trouble and instead of locking him up, we sent him here."

"Who is we?" Kraya asked, handing Sen a scone.

Sen tossed the hot scone from one hand to the other. "A lot has happened since I've been here."

Kraya put her hands on her hips. "I hope you finally quit that farm."

"I did."

"Thank goodness. That woman you were working for sounded horrendous. I hope Dree left with you."

"She did. Dree's father and brother were killed, and she was just crowned queen of the Northern Kingdom."

Kraya put a hand to her mouth. "Oh my. How sad for her. It's too bad she wasn't able to reconcile with them before they died."

"Well, someone stole Dree's crown, and we had to go find it."

"Ernesto?" Rosendo asked.

"Yes. No. It's complicated."

"Not that complicated," Oscar said. "The captain of the king's guard stole it so he could get Dree to marry him. He gave it to me and Ernesto and wanted us to destroy it. We've been pirates lately, so we agreed. Sen and the princess snuck onto our boat. Dree got her crown back, but Ernesto tried to steal it again. Not me, I'm done being a pirate."

Kraya blinked twice, and Rosendo laughed. "So, why are you here?" he asked.

Sen sighed. "The man Dree has a marriage contract with is missing, along with one of the maids. We suspect the captain captured them and hid them in the mountains. We want to find them before they get hurt. Oscar thinks maybe the witch who tricked you into going to Basura would know how to help."

Rosendo scratched his head. "She might. There were a lot of things she knew that no one else did. Of course, she might not live around here anymore. We've been here for two years and never heard mention of her."

Kraya was frowning. "Dree has a marriage contract? You aren't talking about Tal, are you?"

Sen shook his head. "No. She needed a contract before she went back to the castle because otherwise the King's Council was going to choose a husband for her. He's a guy we worked with at Vetta's."

"I wonder why she didn't ask you. Does she like him?"

An inferno would be cooler than Sen's face. "Mom, come on."

Kraya smiled halfheartedly. "Sorry. I just thought the two of you might end up together someday."

Oscar nodded. "Their lips have ended up together a few times."

Sen chucked his scone at Oscar, and the man laughed. If Sen thought his face was hot before, he'd been wrong.

"Sendo!" Kraya scolded, her hands on her hips. "We do not throw things at guests. Let your father catch up with his friend. Go upstairs and talk to Mateo. That boy needs some positive influences in his life."

Sen would not miss the opportunity of getting away from this conversation. He dashed up the stairs and into his twelve-year-old brother Mateo's room.

Mateo sat on the floor playing a video game. "Get out!" he yelled.

"You don't really want me to leave, do you?" Sen asked.

Mateo jumped to his feet, dropping his controller on the floor. "Sen! Why haven't you been visiting? Mom was ready to go find you."

Sen rubbed his brother's head playfully. "Sorry. Dree's had some trouble, so everything's been crazy lately."

"Did Dree come?" he asked, sitting backward on a chair.

"Not this time."

Mateo stared at the floor. "I've been waiting for you to come. I need to talk to you."

Sen stepped over Mateo's clutter and sat on the unmade bed. "Oh yeah?"

"Sen, you have to get me out of here. I can't stand it anymore."

"Why? This house is a lot nicer than the one we had in Boztoll. You even have your own room."

"Do you know how annoying it is to be the only kid at school with magic? And I'm not allowed to use it. Mom doesn't even use her magic, and she told me to pretend I don't have any. None of the others understand what it's like."

Sen leaned forward with his elbows resting on his legs. "They don't understand? Having magic is amazing. I bet they all wish they had it. When we lived in Boztoll, they were all looked down on for not having any."

Mateo rested his chin on the back of the chair. "What's the point in having it if I'm not allowed to use it? I want to go back. Mom might let me since they let you stay there."

"I'm older."

"Yeah, but you've been there by yourself for two years."

"True, but I had responsibilities. And I was still a lot older than you when our family came to Mexico."

"I hate going to school here. It's so boring. And Mom and Papá are always on my case. They think I play too many video games, but what do they expect? No one likes me. I can't make friends here."

"Have you tried?" From what Sen remembered, Mateo hadn't had many friends in Boztoll, either.

"Come on, Sen. Be a good brother and take me with you. At least beg Mom."

"Right now isn't a good time. There's a man trying to force Dree to marry him, and we suspect he might be a sorcerer. Things are too dangerous right now."

Mateo's eyes lit up. "A sorcerer? That's so cool! I could help you defeat him."

"No, it's too dangerous. Maybe you can come for a visit when everything gets settled."

Mateo glared at him. "So, you get to save everything again and get all the credit? Didn't you get famous enough last time you saved the world?"

Sen rolled his eyes. "I don't enjoy being famous, and we aren't trying to save the world. Just Dree's kingdom."

"I bet Dree would let me come if she was here."

"Maybe in a few years. Right now, there are two missing people. We came here to get information and then we have to go right back. I don't have time to watch you."

"I'm twelve. I don't need anyone to watch me," he growled.

Sen felt bad for his brother, but now wasn't the time. "Maybe I can convince Mom and Papá to come for a visit soon. Dree is the queen now. I'm sure she would love to show you her castle."

Mateo's eyes widened. "I've always wanted to see a castle. Hey, if Dree is the queen, what would that make you when you marry her?"

Sen flinched. "What do you mean when I marry her?" Sen hoped in the end that was what happened, but why was everyone always assuming?

"Everyone wants you to marry her. She's always fun when she visits."

Sen grinned. "Most people don't describe Dree as fun."

"Well, she's funny. Remember when she caught her dress on fire when Mom was teaching her to make bread? Then she tried to make her bed and she couldn't even put the sheet on. It snapped back and scared her. I get that princesses don't make a lot of beds, but how hard could it be? She did a lot of funny things the first time you two came. Remember how scared she was when we turned on the TV?"

"That was two years ago. She's learned a lot since then."

"All us brothers want you to marry her. I bet Miguel would marry her if you don't. He talks about her all the time. He even told some of the neighbors that he was friends with a real princess."

Sen chose to ignore the last part. "Where is Miguel anyway?"

Mateo rolled his eyes. "He started college last month. He thinks he's so old and mature. Mom lets him live in a dorm there. He has a job in the cafeteria, so he thinks he's better than us because he has money. So, are you going to marry Dree?"

Sen let out a breath. "It's complicated. There isn't time to talk about it now. I've already stayed too long."

"Fine, but make sure you come back soon and talk to Mom about letting us visit. It isn't fair that we've only visited Basura once since we left. I bet Grandma and Grandpa miss us. Maybe Mom will let me go back and help them on their farm."

"I won't forget. Don't give Mom too much trouble, alright?"

Mateo shrugged. "I'll try."

Sen wasn't convinced. He could hear laughter as he got closer to the kitchen. When he entered, his father, Oscar, and his mom were sitting at the table. His mom was laughing so hard her eyes were watering.

"Oscar, you ready to go?" Sen asked. He wasn't sure he wanted to know why they were laughing.

Kraya pushed a blonde lock behind her ear and wiped at her eyes. "Oscar was just telling us about your pepper eating contest."

"I won, so why are you laughing?" Sen mumbled.

"That's my boy," Rosendo said with a smile.

Oscar grinned. "I don't know if you can call it winning. You looked awful."

"Did Oscar tell you he's been going around wearing an eye patch?" Sen asked. Two could play this game. "He moved it from one eye to the other and thought no one would notice."

Oscar grinned. "It was pathetic, but I was a pirate. Pirates need at least one crewmember with an eye patch."

Rosendo roared with laughter. "That is something I wish I had seen. One day, you need to come for a longer visit and tell me all about it."

Kraya stood and put her arm around Sen. "Oscar, give us five minutes and then you two can go." She eased Sen toward the door and led him outside, shutting the door behind them.

Sen turned to her. "Mateo wants to go back with me."

Kraya's smile slipped from her face. "He's too young."

"I told him that."

She rubbed her temples. "He's been so unhappy lately. He wants to practice magic, but I don't want anyone discovering he can do it and causing us trouble."

"Maybe you can come for a visit once we get things taken care of."

"We should. I miss my parents. Have you visited them lately?"

Sen felt guilty. He tried to visit his grandparents as often as he could, but he'd been slacking lately. "It's been a few months."

Kraya nodded. "Well, make sure you see them soon. I'll talk to Papá and make a plan to come. I worry about

Mateo. He's a smart kid, but all he wants to do is magic and video games. It's difficult to get him to do homework or help with chores."

"It sounds normal for that age."

"I suppose. Well, anyway, that's not what I wanted to talk about. I let it go earlier because I could tell you didn't want to talk about it—"

Sen shook his head. "Mom, I don't want to talk about Dree."

"Why not? Oscar told us everything."

"Oscar doesn't know everything. In fact, he hardly knows anything."

Her eyes danced as she studied him. "Well, he said you kissed her?"

"Mom—"

She held up a finger to stop him. "Did you?"

Sen kicked at a rock on the ground.

"I know you don't like to talk about things like this, or really anything, but I'm your mom. Part of my job is prying into your love life."

"Dree is supposed to marry Mace, and Mace is stuck in a pit somewhere. We probably shouldn't have taken time to come here."

"They can break a marriage contract from what I understand. If the two of you are in love—"

"Ugh, Mom, stop. I have enough problems right now. Dree likes me more than she likes Mace, but I'm not sure she's in love with me."

"She's only visited a few times, but I could tell she cares about you. And you care about her."

"Yes, but that doesn't mean we're in love. Mom, I really need to go."

Her eyes sparkled and she smiled. "Fine. Tell me you're in love with Dree, and I'll let you go."

"I don't have to tell you. You already know."

Sen couldn't believe Oscar had such a big mouth. They walked silently down a dirt road, and Sen secretly hoped Oscar would trip and fall on his face. He better remember where Slosha lived. They didn't have any more time to waste. This entire trip might be a bad idea. The longer they took, the more danger Mace and Halla could be in.

Up ahead sat a small cottage with a thatched roof. It was old but well kept. The entire yard was covered in beautiful flowers and flora. A woman with long black hair sat on a porch swing reading a book. If she was the witch, she didn't look it. She was wearing a pair of jeans and a red t-shirt. Her feet were bare, and she had them tucked up on the swing. She glanced up as they got closer.

"Is that her?" Sen asked.

Oscar nodded. "She is exactly the same as I remember."

She swung her legs down and watched them approach.

"Can I help you?" she asked, placing her book on her lap.

"Do you remember me?" Oscar asked.

Slosha studied him for a moment. "I don't believe so."

"I'm Oscar. We met a long time ago. It wasn't under great circumstances. Me and my two friends were behaving rather poorly at the time."

Her eyes narrowed. "You are one of the boys I sent to the other world."

Sen thought it was funny she referred to Oscar as a boy.

Oscar nodded. "Yes. I'm sorry for the way we treated you."

"What happened to the other two?" she asked. "Are they back?"

"Yes."

She blinked her eyes rapidly and sniffed. "Thank goodness."

Oscar raised an eyebrow. "You wanted us to come back?"

"You were only a youth," she said, gazing down at her book. "I was angry that the villagers were always spying on me. When the three of you came and called me a witch and tried to get me to do magic, I thought I was doing the right thing by tricking you. I figured if I sent you away from this world, I wouldn't have to worry about you telling anyone. I've felt guilty ever since."

"Well, it all worked out," Oscar said.

"It was awful," she said, looking up with unshed tears in her eyes. "The people in the village searched for you for so long. Every time a new search started, I wanted to die. I couldn't believe I was the reason so many people were grieving. I hope you can forgive me."

"If you can forgive me," Oscar said.

She smiled and nodded. "Is that why you came here?"

"No," Sen said. "We were hoping you might be able to help us."

"Who are you?" she asked. "You are too young to be one of the three I sent away."

"My dad is Oscar's friend. I was born in Basura."

Her brows came together. "Basura?"

"That's what we call the other world."

"That is a bizarre choice."

"It was an accident. My dad named it, and it stuck."

"Why do you need help?"

Sen quickly told her what was happening, and she listened attentively.

Slosha tilted her head. "I'm not sure I can help with your problem. I have no more magic than the other people in Basura."

Oscar scratched his head. "I was thinking about the earthquake and the inn. You knew it was going to happen before it did. I thought maybe you could tell us where Sen's friend is being kept."

"I admit I have a strange power. I can't even explain it. Often, I have dreams about things that are going to happen. I can't control it or see certain things. It's all very random and comes when I least expect it. I'm sorry."

Sen nodded. "Thanks for talking to us. Do you want to go back with us?"

She shuddered. "No, thank you. If I wanted to go back, I could jump through the portal at the waterfall. I live a quiet life here, and that's how I like it."

"How did the portal get there?" Sen asked. "Most people can't make portals, and the ones who can don't know how to make permanent ones."

"My father was brilliant at making portals. He made the one at the waterfall so I could return home if I ever chose to. He liked to explore different worlds, and this was where he met my mother. I had some trouble in the other world, and I'm content here."

"Isn't it lonely?" Oscar asked.

"I'm an extreme introvert. Everything I need and love is here. I have my gardens and my books. What more could a person ask for?"

Movement in the window caught Sen's eye. Someone was peeking out of the blue curtain. When they saw him watching, the curtain dropped back, and they disappeared.

"Does someone else live here?" Oscar asked.

Slosha frowned and glanced back at the window. "That's my daughter."

"You have a daughter?"

She shifted uncomfortably. "Yes. She was born here. She has nothing to do with the other world. She doesn't know about it, in fact."

Sen wanted to ask questions, but it really wasn't any of his business. "Well, thanks for talking to us," he said. "We should be on our way."

Slosha nodded and peeked back at the window. "I'm glad to know you are alright. Please tell your other friends I'm sorry."

"I will," Oscar said. They turned and went back down the path.

Sen turned to Oscar. "We need to hurry."

"I suppose I'm gonna have to come back later to see my family. I can't be socializing while your friends are in danger."

Sen nodded. He had been wondering how he was going to tell Oscar they didn't have time to stop. Oscar grabbed onto Sen's arm and they teleported back to Basura.

Chapter 18

D ree's eyes popped open when she smelled smoke, and she squealed as purple flames leaped around her bed. Her heart drummed against her chest as she jumped to her feet. The flames surrounded the entire bed. Taking a few fast steps, she jumped through the flames and rolled on the floor to make sure she wasn't on fire.

Quickly getting to her feet, she ran from the room. "Fire!" she yelled. "Everyone, out!" Her bare feet smacked against the cold stone floor, and she was relieved to see that the entire castle wasn't on fire. If it was only in her room, they might be able to put it out quickly and save the structure. "Fire!" she continued to yell.

No one answered, and there was no one in sight. Panic filled her as she wondered what was happening. There were always people around. Even in the middle of the night, it was rare to see empty areas. The night maids should be out.

Before Dree could run through the door to the courtyard, purple flames burst up in front of the doorway. She sucked in a breath and ran in the other direction. Purple flames! What could that mean? Dree sprinted toward the front of the castle and hoped she was the only one that hadn't gotten out yet. It was possible everyone else saw the flames before she did. It was strange no one had come to get her, though.

Dree jumped through the doorway as more purple flames shot at her. She ran across the drawbridge and stopped and turned. There wasn't any smoke coming from the castle, and there weren't any people out here. Where could everyone be, and what was going on?

A growling behind her caused her to freeze. So many thoughts raced through her mind. Was she supposed to run away from a ferocious animal or hold still? Perhaps play dead? She turned and shrieked when she saw a large blue dragon lumbering toward her. She wasn't normally scared of dragons, but this one didn't look tame. The way it came at her was like a lion stalking its prey.

Dree ran. The wind blew her curls, and her nightdress slapped at her ankles. She turned her head and watched the dragon charging toward her. She couldn't keep this up for long. Her bare feet were getting torn up. Lightning struck the tree in front of her, causing her to jump back and cover her ears. The tree was enveloped in purple flames.

The dragon stopped its pursuit, and Dree backed away from the unnatural fire and the dragon. The dragon turned its head and then broke into small pieces that resembled blue glass. Dree put her hand to her head and felt the amethyst crown. She hadn't been wearing it a moment ago. A flowing red dress had replaced her nightgown.

"It's a dream," Dree said. "It has to be a dream."

The ground she was standing on raised into the air, and she jumped, falling to her knees. Pain, unheard of in a dream, shot up her legs. Spots of earth began sinking all around her, and small tan creatures with pointed teeth crawled out of the holes. They almost resembled goblins, but they were smaller and had spikes covering their backs. The creatures surrounded her, but they weren't very big.

If this was a dream, it sure felt real. She tried to imagine the creatures away, but they all crept closer. She was wearing boots now. When one creature came too close, she kicked at it, causing it to fly high in the air. When it landed, it shattered. Scooping up an armful of her dress, she jumped over another creature and ran.

The ground sloped, and Dree was having a difficult time going forward. There shouldn't be a hill here. It slowly got steeper until she slipped, sliding ungracefully down to the bottom. She hopped to her feet and screamed as the tan creatures jumped on her. She began tearing them off her and throwing them as hard as she could. Every time one hit the ground, it shattered into a sparkling pile of glass.

"Why didn't I learn to teleport?" she asked out loud. If she lived through this, she was going to beg Sen to teach her everything he knew.

Purple flames surrounded her, but these were too high to jump.

"An excellent question," Lenzo answered. He stood in front of her in all black clothing with a dark cloak. Dree jumped to her feet and tried to concentrate on being invisible. Nothing happened.

"Let me go," Dree demanded. "Call off the flames."

Lenzo laughed. "Not until I get what I want."

"I won't marry you."

"You will. I have your worthless fiancé. If you don't cooperate, I might have to dispose of him."

Dree narrowed her eyes. "The kingdom won't support you. We have let them all know that you are corrupt."

"Yes, I know. It's an inconvenience, but nothing I can't handle. You've seen the power I wield. I'm going to leave you here while I find your friend. That will give you time to decide. You can choose me or I can kill your fiancé. I might kill off your friend as well. I think you might care more about him."

A dark circle opened behind him, and he walked through it. The hole swallowed him up and Dree's stomach was sick. Lenzo could open portals.

The top of Halla's body was out of the pit as she clawed at the rock solid ground. Her legs were still dangling in the hole.

"You can do it, Halla!" Mace called from below her. "You're almost there!"

If she had only levitated herself a little farther, she wouldn't be in this mess. There were only two choices. She could pull herself up or fall to her death. She stretched one arm out as far as she could and pulled with more strength than she thought she had. One leg made it out of the pit, and she pulled up the other. She rolled away from the hole and panted.

"You did it!" Mace yelled. "Are you alright?"

"Fine!" she called back. She got onto her hands and knees and glanced back down into the abyss.

Mace was smiling up at her. "Go for help. If things look too dangerous, skip the castle and go somewhere else."

"I'll hurry," she promised. She got onto her unsteady feet and rushed down the mountain. Her mind was a sea of worry as she tried to remember anything from the ride here that would give her any clues about how to get back to the castle. It had taken her two days and a bunch of bruises before she could levitate herself to the top of the pit. Mace had patiently given her tips, but after a few minutes of trying, she would get too tired.

Now, it was up to her. She might not make it to the castle. If she could find a farm or a house, perhaps she could borrow a rope and come back for Mace. A shadow passed overhead, and Halla glanced into the bright blue sky.

A dragon.

She darted into the trees and weaved her way into the dense foliage. She wasn't sure whether Captain Lenzo had a dragon, but she wouldn't risk it. Once she was sure no one could see her from above, she stopped. With luck, the dragon was just flying past and didn't have a rider.

Her eyes widened as the surrounding trees bent unnaturally away from her. Sun shone through, and she could see the sky once more. Halla pressed herself against a tree as an orange dragon crashed to the ground in front of her.

A boy about her age stumbled from the dragon's back and frowned at the creature. "Nice landing, Sheba. We're going to have to work on landing in tight areas." He pushed his brown bangs from his forehead and his eyes found her.

"Hi," he said, studying her. She must look awful. It had been days since her last bath. "Are you Halla?"

She stared at him, unsure of what to say. He wasn't familiar. He could work for Lenzo.

"My name is Tal. I'm friends with Sen and Dree."

"I-I'm Halla," she croaked.

"Are you alone?"

Her heart pounded, and she hoped he was telling the truth. "Mace is up the mountain. I need help getting him out of a pit."

"Show me," he said. Halla led him up the short distance she had come. Sheba walked lazily behind them. "It's lucky I saw you. I've been flying all over, searching for you two. How did you get out?"

"I levitated out. I'm not good at it, so I couldn't bring Mace out."

"Can't he do magic?"

"Someone put cuffs on our wrists so we couldn't do magic."

Tal frowned. "That keeps coming back to bite me," he muttered. "How did you get yours off?"

"I'm not sure," Halla admitted. "I was fiddling with it, and it fell off."

He cocked his head. "That shouldn't happen. They should be more secure."

"Mace is down there," Halla said, pointing to the crack in the rock.

"Hey, Mace?" Tal called down. "Are you alright?"

"Fine," Mace answered. "Who are you?"

"I'm friends with Dree and Sen. I'm going to teleport down."

Halla watched Tal disappear. A moment later, he reappeared with Mace.

"Here, let me take your cuff off," Tal offered. Mace held out his wrist, and Tal did something to the metal, then the cuff fell off. Tal placed it in his pocket.

"Why do you know how to do that?" Mace asked, eyeing Tal suspiciously.

"I helped invent them. We only meant them for use on criminals, but someone stole a box of fifty of them a few months ago. I'm guessing it was Lenzo."

"How do you know Dree and Sen?"

"We worked together a couple of years ago."

Halla's eyes widened. "Are you Talon? Part of The Silver Eclipse?"

Tal shrugged. "I was part of it."

Mace's eyes narrowed. "Your father was Governor Briggs."

"Yes."

"You were supposed to marry Dree."

Tal shifted uncomfortably. "Yeah, but that was a long time ago."

"We should go," Halla said. She hated tension. "Someone might come for us."

"I'll teleport us to the castle," Mace said, taking Halla's hand and glaring at Tal.

"Alright," Tal said. "I'll take my dragon. She doesn't like to teleport. Be careful. Everyone is on the lookout for Lenzo. Dree tried to have him arrested, and he escaped."

"How did you find us?" Mace asked, still irritated. Halla was confused. Shouldn't Mace be happy Dree didn't marry Talon?

"A man at Dree's coronation hinted at your location."

Mace frowned. "Coronation?"

"After Lenzo escaped, Dree demanded to be crowned at once. She didn't want the council to have any more control over her."

"Did they get the crown back?"

Tal nodded. "First, they got captured by pirates, but they got it back. Lenzo stole it and wanted the pirates to destroy it."

"Lenzo needs to be stopped. Did anyone clean out his room?"

"I doubt it."

"He has a bunch of stuff in there he probably shouldn't."

"We can check when we get back."

Mace crossed his arms. "Why are you here anyway?"

Tal grinned. "Saving you?"

"I mean in the Northern Kingdom."

"Sen messaged me when he got captured. I found them right before the pirate ship sank, but that's a story for another time."

Mace was still frowning. Halla couldn't understand it.

"Why don't you head back to Akkron?" he asked. "We can handle things here."

Tal raised his brows. "I'm getting some hostile vibes here. You aren't worried I'm here to get Dree back or something, are you?"

"Should I be?"

Tal chuckled. "Not at all. Dree and I don't mesh. She's great and all, but we were definitely not meant to be."

"Alright," Mace said, the tension going from his face. Halla sighed. She almost wished Talon had come back for Dree. Not that it would change things for her. Mace wouldn't like someone like her. He was kind to her, but he must be kind to everyone. She smiled when she had that thought. When they were at Vetta's, Mace had always been grumpy.

"I wouldn't relax that fast," Tal said with a mischievous smile. "I'm not sure you and Dree were meant to be, either."

Mace's eyes quickly went to Halla, then away, and he rubbed his chin. "I'm pretty sure you're right."

"Oh?"

"Anyone who's ever seen Dree and Sen should find it obvious that they belong together. In fact, I plan on knocking some sense into Sen when we get back."

"I'll help if you need backup," Tal said.

Mace laughed, and the two men shook hands. Halla's stomach was a mess of nerves. Mace didn't want to marry Dree? Why was she letting that affect her? She was only a maid. Even if he didn't marry Dree, he would not go back to being a farmhand.

After a quick bath, Mace met up with Tal in the courtyard. They hadn't seen Dree or Sen, but they must be around somewhere.

"I hope it doesn't take too long to get Sen to realize Dree is crazy about him," Mace said.

"They're getting there," Tal said. "I think they had some realizations when they were with the pirates."

"I hope so. I'm hoping it works out between them and that Dree will put me on her council."

Tal raised his brow. "That sounds so boring. You actually *want* to do that?"

Mace nodded. "I love politics, and I have some ideas I would love to put into practice. Dree is smart and learns fast, but she doesn't know a lot about what is going to be expected of her. I could be helpful. Your father was a governor. Don't you have ambitions toward that?"

Tal cringed. "Not at all. My father was corrupt and a great example of everything I don't want to be. It kinda soured me on politics."

Mace nodded. "There are too many corrupt people in power. That's another reason I want to be on the council. I can do good things."

Tal's eyes sparkled. "And that Halla is a pretty girl."

Mace's head jerked up, and he frowned. "I don't think she's your type."

Tal winked. "She's not. I saw how you were watching her. I have a girlfriend that's absolutely perfect for me. Halla seems to be shy and sweet."

"You don't like shy and sweet?"

Tal grinned. "I don't dislike it, but my girlfriend is definitely the opposite of those things. I need someone who can kick me in the backside if I need it."

Mace arched his brow. "Does she do that often?"

"Nah, but she threatens to occasionally."

Mace just shook his head. He supposed it was good that everyone liked a different type of person. Now that he had spent a few days confined with Halla, he was more sure than ever that he and Dree weren't a good idea. After his not so easy life, Halla was like a breath of fresh air. She was so kind and unassuming.

"Mace!" Sen exclaimed, rushing toward him. "I'm so glad Tal found you."

"Yeah, me too. Where were you? I thought you would be out looking," he joked.

"Oscar and I went and talked to a witch. We thought she might be able to tell us where you were."

"A witch?"

Sen shrugged. "Well, she's probably no more a witch than the rest of us. My father always called her a witch, but he isn't magic. Is Halla alright?"

"Yes, she's taking a bath and hopefully resting."

"Where's Dree?"

Tal shrugged. "We haven't seen her since we got back."

Sen frowned. "Navina doesn't know where she is. She said she hasn't seen her all day."

"I'm sure she's fine."

Sen moved his jaw back and forth. "I knocked on her door, and she wasn't there."

Mace shrugged. "She'll probably show up soon."

"No, we have to search," Sen said. "With Lenzo still out there, anything could happen. She should have someone with her at all times. There should be a guard at her door and following her everywhere. Why are you just staring at me? Go look for her!" Sen spun around and jogged away.

"I don't think it's going to be hard to get them together," Mace said. "We might not have to try at all."

Tal grinned. "I suspect you're right."

Chapter 19

Sen scurried through the castle asking anyone he saw if they had seen Dree. He was starting to panic. No one had seen her today. He sprinted up the stairs and ran down a hallway to her room. He pounded on the door. Still no answer. Reaching for the doorknob, he was surprised to find it unlocked.

The room was empty. He checked the closet and under the bed even though it was unlikely she was hiding. He ran his hands through his hair, his heart racing. Something was wrong. He ran back through the castle, telling everyone he passed to stop what they were doing and search for her.

"There is some smoke rising from the trees just south of the castle," Navina said when she saw Sen speed by. "Why don't you go see what the cause is?"

Sen nodded. She was wringing her hands and her brow was furrowed. If he didn't know any better he would think the former queen was nervous. As soon as he exited the castle, he saw the smoke. It had a purplish hue and was unlike any smoke he had ever seen before. He dashed into the trees and ran until he saw a ring of purple flames. They were burning high, but not catching fire to the surrounding forest.

He pulled his sword from its sheath and walked cautiously toward the flames. Two gray creatures leaped toward him, showing their large pointed teeth. Sen swung his sword at the nearest one and it broke into pieces. His eyes widened, and he took a step back. The second creature jumped at him and his sword connected with it. Like the first one, it broke.

Sen glanced around, then picked up one of the broken pieces and examined it. He turned it over in his hands. It looked like glass.

"Dree!" he yelled, his gut telling him she was near.

"Sen!" she called. "I'm in the middle of the fire!"

Sen teleported into the center of the flames. Before he could get his surroundings, Dree threw herself into his arms. His sword dropped to the earth.

She pressed her cheek to his. "As soon as we get out of here, you need to teach me to teleport."

He nodded. "I will, ready?"

She nodded.

Sen tried to teleport and failed. He tried again with the same result. Nothing like this had ever happened before. "I can't do it."

Her mouth turned down. "You mean we're stuck?"

"For now. I have the entire castle searching for you. I'm sure someone will come soon."

She looked up at him, still clinging to his neck. "Is the castle still standing?"

"The castle is fine."

"They put the fire out?"

Sen scrunched his forehead. "This is the only fire."

Dree tilted her head. "My room was on fire."

"I was just in there. It didn't seem scorched."

"It was a purple fire like this, and it went all the way around my bed. It must have been some kind of magic."

"This is a strange fire. It should be hot in here, but it isn't."

"It's hot if you get close to it. I jumped over it when it was surrounding my bed, but it wasn't as tall as this."

"Your mother knows I was coming to check out the smoke. It shouldn't be long before she sends people out here."

Dree's lip trembled. "What if she doesn't? What if we can't get out?"

Sen rubbed his finger over her cheek. "We will. Lenzo can't win."

Dree let out a slow breath. "Why wouldn't you marry me?" she asked.

Sen let out a slow breath. "Is now really the time?"

"We might die, and I want to know. Tal didn't want to marry me, and I know Mace doesn't. I don't care about that, but I care that you don't. What's wrong with me?"

"Nothing is wrong with you," Sen said, pushing a stray curl behind her ear. "I love you."

Dree's eyes widened as he leaned in and kissed her. She clung to him and kissed him back. After a moment, she pulled away and looked up at him. "Then, why did you push me off on Mace?"

"Because I'm an idiot," Sen admitted. "I've been in love with you for so long, but I didn't want to marry you if you didn't love me. I regretted involving Mace from the moment it happened."

"I do love you," she said, staring into his eyes. "You have been through everything with me. It took me time to realize it because I've never had anyone to love before. Kiss me again and then let's get out of here."

Sen smiled as he leaned in and kissed her. He didn't know what they were going to tell Mace, but he was pretty sure he wouldn't mind.

"The crown," Dree said, stepping back and pulling the crown from her head. "It has magic. Maybe we can use it to get out."

"How?"

"I don't know. It's supposed to be incredibly powerful. Hopefully, more than whatever is keeping us here. Let's both hold on to it, and perhaps it will combine our magic with it to burst through whatever this is."

Dree held the crown out with both hands, and Sen grabbed the other side. They stared into each other's eyes.

"Concentrate on breaking the barrier," he said. He wasn't sure what they should be doing, but that was what he focused on. Dree scrunched her eyes shut and her hold on the crown tightened. The ground rumbled, and a bright flash came from the crown, throwing them to the earth. The purple flames disappeared, and the ground wasn't scorched.

Sen jumped to his feet and pulled Dree up. "Are you alright?"

"Fine," she said, scooping up her crown. "Let's go before Lenzo comes back."

A billow of red smoke appeared in front of them, and Lenzo stepped out, pulling a struggling Halla with him. "Too late for that," he said.

"Let her go," Dree said.

He glared at her. "I will. Once you marry me, she can go free."

Sen clenched his teeth and wondered if he could throw a fireball without hitting Halla.

"I will not marry you," Dree said, placing the crown on her head. "Let her go, and you might not spend the rest of your life in prison."

"You seem to believe you are in charge here," Lenzo said, his grip tight on Halla's arm. "I will kill her if you don't agree, and then I will still get what I want. I've planned this too long to fail."

"You killed the king," Sen said, narrowing his eyes.

Lenzo smiled through his beard. "Not personally."

"Even if I were to marry you, I would hold the power," Dree said.

"Perhaps for a short time."

Dree pointed a finger at him. "Even if you married me and killed me off, you wouldn't be king. I have cousins that would succeed me."

"None of them are any more fit to rule than you are. I have my ways of manipulating my way into power. How do you think I became the captain of the guard?"

Dree's eyes shot daggers at Lenzo. "You would spend the rest of your life fighting to stay in power. If you manipulate your way into the crown, you never get peace. There will always be someone trying to overthrow you."

Lenzo jerked Halla in front of him. "Yes, and that is one reason I will have your cooperation."

"Never."

Lenzo turned as Tal and Mace came running toward them. Halla took advantage of the situation and bit Lenzo's arm. He yelled out in surprise and released her. She quickly shoved her palm into his nose, causing him to fall back a step. She ran toward Sen and Dree and got partially behind them.

From the silly grin on Mace's face, Sen was sure he wouldn't have any trouble convincing him to break the marriage contract. Not that he had been worried. Mace had already offered.

Lenzo waved his arms through the air and chanted something in an unfamiliar language. Sen was stuck to the ground and couldn't move his body. His eyes fluttered around to the others. None of them were moving. His heart sped up as Lenzo began laughing. Sen had seen magic hold a person in place, but usually, the person doing it could only do it to one or two people.

Sen tried to teleport, even though it wasn't likely to work. He had no plan for something like this.

Dree glared at Lenzo as he casually walked toward her. Her crown had fallen to the earth. Sen was worried she might break her teeth. She had them clenched so tight.

"It appears you will all be listening to me."

"Only because we can't plug our ears," Sen said, trying to draw Lenzo's attention to him.

Lenzo ran a finger over Dree's cheek, and she flinched. "It would be in your best interest to agree to marry me. We could be powerful. You've decided to marry a man you don't love, so it might as well be me."

"Don't touch her," Sen growled.

"Ah, yes. The one she loves but isn't marrying. You are all a very odd group of friends. All entwined with the wrong people."

"I know what you really want," Dree said. "You want the crown. You're just trying to trick us."

"Why would I want the crown? I tried to dispose of it if you remember."

"Yes, but your man Garin tried to steal it. I bet you wanted him to bring it back to you. Sen, we can't let him put it on!"

Sen frowned. Why was Dree giving the man ideas?

Lenzo picked up the crown and studied it. "I believe only a woman can use the crown."

"Oh, right," Dree said with a nervous laugh. "No reason for you to try."

Lenzo placed the crown on his head. A flash of light burst from the crown, causing everyone to close their eyes. When Sen opened his eyes, Lenzo was convulsing on the ground, and the crown had fallen from his head. Sen could move again.

Tal raced forward and pulled a metal cuff from his pocket. He kneeled beside Lenzo and slapped it on his wrist.

Sen tilted his head. "He's been putting those on people. He might know how to take them off."

Lenzo stopped convulsing and took several deep breaths. Sen was ready to throw a fireball if he tried to remove the cuff.

"He shouldn't be able to take them off," Tal said. "He stole them, but there are only a handful of people who know how to remove them, and I trust them all."

"You haven't won," Lenzo wheezed. He sat up and placed a hand on his chest. Getting up to his unsteady feet, he pointed a hand at them. He must not have noticed the cuff. "What have you done?"

"It's not so great when it happens to you, is it?" Mace said, crossing his arms.

Lenzo ground his teeth. "No matter. I am skilled in more than magic." He pulled his sword from its sheath and took a step forward.

Sen held a ball of fire in his hand and held it in Lenzo's view. "Really? You want to fight us with a sword?"

"I've got this!" Oscar said, running into view, a sword in his hand.

"No, Oscar!" Dree protested. "We can use magic."

"I was a pirate, remember?" Oscar said, smashing his sword into Lenzo's as the two began exchanging blows.

Dree wrapped her hands around Sen's free arm. "Throw it! He might kill Oscar."

He shook his head. "I can't. I could hit Oscar. He's jumping around too much."

"I say let him fight," Tal said. "He looks like he knows what he's doing."

"Are you alright?" Mace asked Halla. She nodded.

The clanging of swords filled Sen's ears, and he wondered if he should interfere. Oscar was holding his own, but Lenzo hadn't become the captain of the guard for being a poor swordsman.

"Lesandri!" Navina called, running up to Dree. "Are you alright? Why is Oscar fighting Captain Lenzo?"

"I'm fine," Dree said, her arm wrapped around Sen's. "Lenzo is no longer the captain of the guards."

Navina watched the two men fight, her forehead scrunched in worry.

Lenzo cut Oscar's arm, causing him to take a few steps back. Both men held their swords and stood glaring at one another.

"Give up, pirate," Lenzo growled. "I haven't been defeated at swords in over twenty years."

"And I've never been defeated," Oscar boasted. "Not even as a little boy." Oscar blocked when Lenzo took a swing at him. The clanking began again.

"Would it be unethical to hit Lenzo in the head with a rock?" Dree asked.

Tal nodded. "Completely."

"I disagree," Halla said. Everyone turned to her in surprise. "Lenzo is evil and unethical. That means we don't have to fight nicely."

"Maybe not," Tal agreed, "But Oscar is doing fine. It's strange. His moves are unconventional, but it seems to be working."

Navina had her fan out, waving it dramatically in her face. "I can't believe Captain Lenzo deceived us for so many years."

Dree glanced at Sen and rolled her eyes, but didn't say anything to her mother. He just smiled.

"Does it feel strange that we are just watching them fight and not helping?" Halla asked.

Sen was thinking the same thing, but there wasn't a lot they could do without endangering Oscar. If there was an opening to use magic, he would take it.

Mace turned to Halla. "There isn't a lot we can do when they are jumping around like that. We might just be a hazardous distraction."

Oscar took a step back and tripped, his sword falling to the ground. Lenzo smiled as he raised his sword. Sen lifted his hand and levitated Lenzo's sword into the air. Lenzo looked at the sword in surprise and failed to see Navina charging toward him. She plowed into him with enough force to knock him to the ground.

Dree took a step forward as her mother stood up, a bloody dagger in her hand. She pushed a curl from her eyes and held her hand out to Oscar, who was staring at her with his mouth hanging open. Lenzo lay unmoving on the ground. Sen let the man's sword drop gently to the earth as Oscar let Navina help him up.

"That was the most amazing thing I've ever seen," Oscar said.

Navina blushed. "Yes, well, you should have seen me when I was younger."

Dree's eyes were wide. "I never would have believed it if I hadn't seen it."

Navina smirked. "There is a side to me you've never seen. I was quite wild before I married your father."

"Nice sword fighting," Mace told Oscar. "And you've never been defeated?"

Oscar scratched his chin. "Well, I've never been in a real sword fight, and the only person I've ever sparred with is Ernesto. He's a little too slow to beat me. I learned everything I know from TV shows when I was a kid."

"What are TV shows?" Navina asked.

"Well, if you would allow a mangy old pirate to escort you back to the palace, I would be happy to tell you."

Navina linked her arm with Oscar's. "Of course." The two walked away, and everyone else stared at them in silence.

Tal moved closer to Lenzo's still form and nudged him with his boot. "He's definitely dead. I've been neglecting a lot of things back home, so I'm going to take off. If you ever need me again, let me know."

"Same," Sen said, bumping his knuckles against Tal's. Everyone said their goodbyes and then Tal left in search of Sheba.

"What do we do with him?" Sen asked, gesturing at Lenzo.

"Leave him," Dree said. "We can send someone for him."

"What a pleasant job that person will have," Sen said.

Dree grinned slightly. "There are some advantages to being the queen."

"Whoa, what's happening?" Mace asked, pointing at Lenzo. "Is he sinking into the ground?"

Dree's eyes widened as she watched Lenzo vanish beneath the dirt. She walked over to the spot. "The ground is packed tight. What does that mean?"

"Maybe it's something that happens when sorcerers die," Sen said. He remembered hearing something like that once.

Halla shuddered. "I hope he doesn't come back."

Mace shrugged. "I guess it's less clean up."

Dree linked her arm with Sen's, and they made their way toward the castle. Mace and Halla followed behind.

Sen glanced sideways at her. "There is more to your mother than I would have suspected."

"That was surprising. Well, I'm not surprised she would stab someone, but I'm surprised she did it to save a pirate."

"I'm glad she did. I didn't want to be the one to do it."

"Can we stop for a moment?" Mace asked. They turned and faced him. "Does nothing seem a little wrong here?"

"With Lenzo?" Dree asked.

"No. With you two," he said, pointing to their linked arms.

Dree pulled away and looked at the ground. Sen just shook his head as he watched Mace try not to smile.

"Can you pull up another ball of fire?" Mace asked.

Sen held out his hand, and a bright ball of fire jumped into his palm. Mace took a folded piece of paper from his pocket and unfolded it. He placed it on the ground and winked at Sen. Sen threw the ball of fire at the paper, leaving a small crater where it had been.

"What was the paper?" Dree asked.

Sen shrugged. "Hopefully, your marriage contract."

Mace's mouth turned up as Dree peered guiltily up at him. "I wouldn't mind a place on the Queen's Council."

Dree beamed. "It would be an honor to have you."

"So, go on. Kiss her," Mace said, nudging Sen with his shoulder.

Sen scowled. "Not in front of you."

Mace laughed, and Halla smiled shyly. Dree grabbed the front of Sen's shirt in her fists and pulled him toward her. He smiled as she pressed her lips to his.

Halla sat on the ground outside the castle. She mindlessly arranged some weeds into a bird nest like she used to do as a young girl. Her insides were a mess of emotions. It took little to make Halla content. She hadn't enjoyed her time at Vetta's, but she had been alright. Now, she was full of unfamiliar emotions that she did not know how to deal with. She wasn't a social person, but she had enjoyed talking with Mace in the pit.

Now, Mace would be on Dree's council, Dree was queen, and Sen was—whatever the person who's in love with the queen was, and Halla was the maid. Mace, Dree, and Sen's lives had changed for the better, and hers had stayed the same. She scolded herself for being ungrateful.

Working at the castle was a lot better than working for Vetta.

Halla felt like she had finally been part of a group, and now, she would go back to being their servant. She knew she was being ridiculous. She hadn't become their friend. Even when she was with them, she was more of an observer. Still, it had been nice to feel like a part of something for once in her life.

She tried to push thoughts of Mace from her mind. Being stuck in the pit with him had been frightening and amazing. It was the first time since her mother died that someone had forced her into conversation. Talking to people wasn't easy, but she enjoyed it more than she should. Now that he wasn't tied to Dree, he would probably end up finding someone else, and that was going to be difficult to watch.

"Nice nest," Mace said from behind her.

She squealed and jumped to her feet. "You scared me," she said, placing a hand to her heart.

He grinned. "Sorry."

"Do you need something?"

"Um, I just wanted to, uh, talk."

Halla narrowed her eyes. He stuffed his hands in his pockets and blew out a slow breath. What could have happened?

"I was talking to Dree. I guess I should start calling her Queen Lesandri, but anyway, I was talking to her, and she said something interesting. Well, not interesting, but something I didn't know. Well, it makes sense, but I never thought about it because I never thought I would be in this type of situation.”

Halla raised her eyebrows. “Alright?”

He ran his hand through his hair. “Sorry, I’m babbling. I rarely do that.”

She nodded. This was the only time she’s ever seen him flustered. Something must be eating at him.

Mace peered into her eyes. “I want you to be honest with me.”

“I’m always honest.” Halla felt like she swallowed a rock. Was he angry at her for something?

“Well, first off, back to Dree. Queen Lesandri. She said that members of the Queen’s Council can’t spend their free time with the staff. It causes all sorts of problems apparently.”

Halla looked at her hands. “I understand.” It was good of him to tell her so she wasn’t hurt if he ignored her if they ever crossed paths.

“No, you don’t because I’m acting like a fool. Halla? I really like you.”

She gazed up at him and then away. What was he saying?

“You caught my eye a long time ago, but I ignored it because I wasn’t looking for a relationship.”

Halla’s heart was pounding, and she felt faint. He couldn’t be saying what it sounded like he was saying. Perhaps, she was hallucinating.

“I admire the way you are kind to people, and you don’t get angry even when you probably should. I saw you sneaking apples to the alicorns more than once. Spending time with you this week has made me like you even more.”

Halla forced herself to peek at him to see if he was joking. He appeared serious. "But I'm a maid."

"Dree said that she was planning on offering you something else even before I went and spoke with her. She said the council could use a person to take notes during their meetings. It isn't the same as being a member of the staff. It is a part of the council."

It was hard to concentrate on her thoughts because there were so many happening at once. "I'm not sure I would be much help to the council. It's hard for me to talk to people."

"You wouldn't have to talk. I want to spend more time with you. Get to know you better. If you don't want to do it, I suppose I could ask Dree to make me a maid."

Halla smiled and shook her head. "I'm not sure how well I will do, but I would like to try."

Mace smiled. "And what about the other? Do you think you could ever be interested in spending time with me?"

Halla took a deep breath and ignored the heat in her cheeks. "I would like that."

"Really?"

She nodded.

"Wonderful." He held out his hand, and Halla took it. Things were looking up.

Chapter 20

Dree sat on the throne and arranged her dress neatly around herself. She forced herself to remain calm and not fidget. Sen stood by her side. Almost as soon as they had returned to the castle, a servant informed her that a woman was there to see Lenzo. From the description, she was almost positive it was Vetta.

"Why am I so nervous?" she said, glancing up at Sen. "I never liked Vetta, but I'm not scared of her."

Sen squeezed her shoulder. "Maybe it's because you've had a hard day already. You're going to do fine."

The door opened, and a guard led Vetta into the room. She had pulled her blonde, frizzy hair back into a tight braid. She was wearing a fancy pink dress, and she frowned when she saw Dree. The guard ordered her to stand facing Dree, and then he moved back to the door.

"I requested a meeting with Captain Lenzo," Vetta said, not bothering to bow.

"I am sure you did," Dree said, her eyes fixed on Vetta. "I'm afraid you cannot meet with him."

"Why?" Vetta asked, crossing her arms. "Is he away?"

"He is dead."

Vetta sucked in a breath and blinked rapidly. "Oh. Well, I guess I will be on my way." She turned to leave.

"Wait," Dree commanded. "I have been meaning to speak with you."

Vetta turned back, her jaw clenched tight. "Yes?"

"You have one of the most prosperous farms in the kingdom. Many people depend on your crops."

Vetta's face relaxed. "They do."

"You are not the nicest person to work for, and I am assuming most of your servants will want to come here. That will leave you in quite the predicament."

Fire flashed in Vetta's eyes, but she only nodded.

"We can't let your farm fail. I will talk to your employees and let them know they are still welcome to come here, but I will encourage them to stay on with you."

Dree really wanted to take the farm from Vetta and let her see what it was like to work for what you have. She knew that would be vengeful, and she didn't want to be her father. She would give Vetta another chance.

"You won't have a hard time convincing new people to work for you. I want you to treat them better. I will send some of my own servants to work for you, and they will report back to me. Don't let me hear of you mistreating any of your staff. Do you understand me?"

Vetta nodded and studied the ground. The tension was back in her face.

"And another thing. When I was told you were here, Mace told me about Halla."

Vetta's head shot up. "What about her?"

"He said that she is your sister?"

"Half-sister."

"I cannot believe you would treat your own sister the way you have. Halla is a good person, and you could have benefitted from a family relationship with her."

"I am not having a half-sister waltz into my life and try taking over," Vetta growled.

"Halla would never do that. I bet you even know that."

"So, what about her? I don't have time to sit and talk all day. I have things to do."

"I doubt your father meant to leave everything to you and nothing to Halla. Mace is checking on your father's will."

"He didn't have a will."

"Halla said he did. He told her about it. I would assume he would have split everything between the two of you. Halla is too shy to contest you on anything. I will see that she gets anything your father meant for her. Halla doesn't want to return to the farm, and she wants nothing that belongs to the farm. She will keep her alicorn and a percentage of your profit every year. I'm sure that the will probably states that anyway."

Dree wished she'd had more time to talk to Mace and Halla about everything. She hoped she had understood everything Mace had told her before she came in. She glanced up at Sen, and he winked.

Vetta's eyes narrowed. "I don't care if you are queen. I will not lose any of my hard earned money to that little beggar!"

"You don't work hard, and Halla is not a beggar. We all know that."

Vetta suddenly grinned. "I think you should forget about all of this, or I might have to tell Mace about that little wink. I'm sure he doesn't want Sen winking at his fiancé."

Sen laughed, and Dree smiled. She loved hearing him laugh.

Dree tapped her chin. "I don't believe Mace has a fiancé, although I wouldn't be surprised if he and Halla end up together. You may leave now. I will send you a copy of the will, if it exists, and I will expect you to surrender anything to Halla that your father wished her to have. If a will isn't found, I will decide on the percentage she will receive."

Vetta stomped toward the door as the guard held it open. She looked over her shoulder. "I hope you are a better queen than you were a maid."

Dree smiled. "So do I."

As soon as the door to the throne room closed, Dree deflated. "Was I too hard?" She slumped back against the throne and peered up at Sen.

"Not at all," he assured her. "I think you gave her more than she deserves."

"I don't want to get vengeful and turn into my father."

"That's a wonderful goal to have. I only met your father once, and I'd prefer you didn't turn into him." Sen ran his hand over the golden arm of the throne.

"Do you want to sit here?" Dree asked, raising her brow.

"No." Sen would feel ridiculous on the overly ornate throne.

Dree stood up. "You know you want to."

"I'm good."

"Just do it."

"Nope."

Dree grinned and grabbed Sen's arm. She pulled him forward and gently pushed him back.

He sighed and sat on the throne. "Happy? I'm pretty sure this is illegal or something."

She laughed. "Not if I tell you to. Do you feel powerful now?"

"No, I feel stupid. It is more comfortable than it looks, though."

"It has to be comfortable. My father spent hours a day sitting there bossing people around. You look really awkward. Just relax."

Sen slumped back. "Is that better?"

She grinned. "A little. You love competition. Sitting on a throne should make you feel like a winner."

Sen grabbed her hand and pulled her forward.

She stumbled and fell onto him. "If you're worried about doing something illegal, I don't think you are supposed to pull over royalty," she said, shifting so she was sitting on his lap.

"Now I feel like I won."

Dree smiled and put her arms around his neck. "Why didn't we fall in love two years ago?"

"I did," Sen said, pushing a lock of hair behind her ear. "I was just waiting for you."

"I think I fell in love with you, and I just didn't know it," Dree said. "I needed you to refuse to marry me before I realized my own feelings."

"Well, I'm glad you figured it out before I let you marry Mace."

"Me too."

Sen stared into her eyes. "You make me want to smile. That isn't easy, you know."

She grinned. "I know. So, what do I need to do to make you want to kiss me?"

Sen smiled and leaned toward her. "Exist."

Dree forced herself to stop watching for Sen. It had been a week since Lenzo was killed, and Sen had been gone for almost as long. He had gone to invite his family to visit. Dree was nervous. She knew Rosendo and Kraya, but now, things were different. Would they be happy to hear that Dree and Sen were in love? They had always been kind when Dree visited, but that might just be because they were polite. That didn't mean they liked her.

Sen wasn't going to tell them until they came. He wanted them to do it together, and he assured her they would be thrilled. She made sure the best rooms were ready for them, and she had the chef preparing something special.

Dree paced back and forth across the courtyard. She should have had Sen give her a time. He had been gone for four days. Four days she should have spent learning her duties instead of daydreaming. He would be back sometime today, with or without his family. She hoped they came.

"Are you wearing a hole in the grass?" Sen asked, walking into the courtyard. His family wasn't with him, but he could have shown them to their rooms already. She gathered up her shimmering green dress and ran toward him. She jumped into his arms, and he laughed as he spun her around.

"That was a long three days," she said, as he placed her on her feet. He leaned down and kissed her.

"Gross! Mom, tell him to stop!"

Dree pulled away and looked at Sen's entire family standing in the castle's archway. Some of his brothers were snickering, and his mother was smiling. His father's mouth was hanging open, and his youngest brother appeared disgusted.

Sen placed his arm around her. "You look good in red," he said in her ear.

"My dress is green," she muttered.

"Yes, but your face isn't."

She pressed her face into his shoulder. "This is so embarrassing."

"Don't worry about it. Everything my family does is embarrassing." He led her to them.

Kraya opened her arms and gave Dree a hug. "It's good to see you again, Dree. I'm guessing there are a few things Sendo left out when he visited."

Sen shrugged. "I told you almost everything."

"So, what did you leave out?"

"Just the part where Dree and I realized we were in love and burned up her marriage contract."

Kraya playfully slugged him. "That is the kind of thing I want to hear, not about evil sorcerers."

"Does that mean you're getting married?" his brother Pablo asked. "Because that means you'll be kissing all the time like Mom and Papá, and kissing is nasty."

"It's probably not nasty if you get to kiss Dree," Juan argued.

Javier nodded. "I would kiss Dree."

Rosendo and Kraya burst into laughter, and Sen pulled Dree to his side. "You better stay away from my brothers."

Dree giggled. It must have been great growing up with Sen's family.

"So, if you marry Dree, does that make you the king?" Javier asked.

"Who said anything about getting married?" Sen asked. Dree smiled at Javier's frown.

"You have to marry Dree," he said. "We all voted the first time you brought her to our house. It was almost unanimous."

Dree tilted her head. "Almost?"

"Miguel was against it, but that was because he was jealous. The only girl that ever liked him was Meera, and she eats bugs."

Mateo rolled his eyes. "She was only four. I'm sure she doesn't do that anymore."

"So, you aren't going to get married?"

"I didn't say that, either."

Javier glared at his brother. "Well, you better decide. Dree isn't going to wait on you forever."

Dree laughed. "Are you all hungry? The chef has been cooking wonderful things all day. I'm pretty sure I smelled cake baking earlier."

"But no one answered me," Javier said. "If you get married, will you be king, Sen?"

"No. Dree is the one ruling, so there can't be a king."

"He would be a prince," Dree said. "And he would control the guards."

"Like the one that Sen told us about? The guy who stole your crown?"

"No. That would be the captain of the guard. Whoever that person is will report to Sen." Dree felt her face turn red again. "That is, if we were to get married."

Sen winked at her. "Dree, did you ask Oscar?" He turned to his father. "We thought maybe Oscar could take Lenzo's place."

"I asked him, but he doesn't want to. He's going to get a new ship and take people around to the different islands. I believe he called it a cruise ship."

Rosendo laughed. "That sounds like Oscar. He would probably love having a bunch of people stuck on a ship. That way he can talk their ear off and they can't get away."

"So, who does the captain of the guard report to when you aren't married?" Javier asked.

"I haven't had time to think about it," Dree said. "I guess me. That won't work for long, though. I have too much to do."

"Well, I'm hungry," said Rosendo. "And I'm curious about the type of food they serve in a castle."

Mateo studied his boots. "Can Sen take everyone to eat so I can talk to Dree for a minute?"

Dree glanced at Sen, and he shrugged.

"That would be fine," Dree said. She watched Sen lead his family away and then turned to Mateo.

He shifted from one foot to the other and let out a slow breath. "Since you are the queen, that means you can make people do anything, right?"

"Within reason. If a ruler takes advantage of their power, the people will revolt. It's important to be kind and fair."

"What I want would be both of those things."

Dree hid a smile. "Oh?"

"Let me stay here. I hate it on Earth, but my mom and Sen think I'm too young to leave home. I'm not that much younger than Sen was. I'll be thirteen soon. It isn't fair to leave me in a place where I'm not allowed to be who I want to be. I'm not allowed to do magic, so I think I'm being held back."

Dree watched him fidget. "I can't force your parents to leave you here," she said carefully. She didn't want to upset him, but he was frowning. She understood what it was like to grow up feeling like you didn't belong. "How about we make a deal?"

"What kind?"

"I can talk to your mother, and if she agrees, you can come stay with us when you don't have school."

Mateo's eyes moved around like he was thinking. "I guess that would be fair. I get a few months off in the summer."

"I'm sure Sen would love to have one of his brothers around."

"And he could teach me more magic. I never get to practice."

"I need to let Sen teach me more magic as well."

"Sen's a pretty good teacher. He's a lot more patient than my other brothers."

"So, should we go eat?"

"Sure. Just don't forget to talk to my mom."

"I promise."

"You realize what you've done, right?" Sen asked Dree later that night, as they walked around the castle grounds.

"Are you talking about Mateo?" she asked, as he took her hand.

"Yes. I've tried to stop being so competitive, but my brothers bring it out in me."

She smiled. "So, you're saying every time Mateo comes, you are going to start climbing things and eating stupidly hot peppers?"

"Probably. And then Mateo's going to be in a constant bad mood because I won't let him win."

"Perhaps, I'll join in the competitions."

Sen grinned. "Why? So, he won't lose completely?"

"No, so you won't win every time."

He laughed softly. "Oh, I see."

"I think I won the pepper eating contest."

"I'm sure I won."

"Maybe in your view. You ended up rolling around groaning, which makes me feel like you lost."

"What about your eye?"

"I admit that was pathetic. I haven't eaten a pepper since."

"Let's just say we had a tie."

"Alright. I'm sure I've beat you at something, though. I did beat you to proposing that first time. You did say no, so that might not have been a win."

He stopped and turned to face her. "You've forgiven me, right?" He hated reliving that moment.

She went on her toes and kissed his cheek. "I have."

"Good." He cleared his throat. "Dree, you know I'm not good at saying things." His mind jumped around as he tried to decide what he wanted to convey. "You know I love you, right?"

"I do. And I love you."

He took a deep breath. "I would follow you across the world and do anything to be at your side. If you are willing, I'm ready to sign a marriage contract."

Her eyes filled with tears. "Really?"

"Really. And then when we feel ready, we can get married. So, will you marry me?"

"Yes." She jumped into his arms, and he wrapped her in a hug. Sen closed his eyes and hoped this feeling would last forever. He was sure it would. He had been in love with her for so long already.

Before the Amethyst Crown there was The Silver Eclipse.
Read the first chapter now.

Akkron (The Silver Eclipse)

Wren closed the door to Professor Dovin's office, being careful to make as little noise as possible. She left it unlatched and slightly ajar to ensure no one could enter the connecting classroom without her knowledge. If she got caught, it would not be pleasant. As a precaution, her friend Ming Li was keeping watch outside the classroom and was ready to alert her if anyone came close. The office was a mess. Papers blanketed the desk, and the floor was littered with garbage that hadn't quite reached the bin. Wren inched to the desk as quietly as she could and pulled open a drawer. It was full of smudged old papers. She reached for one, but froze when she heard the creak of the classroom door.

"We can talk in here," came Professor Dovin's smooth voice from the connecting room. Wren shuddered at the familiar oily tone. He was many students' favorite professor, but something about him always reminded her of a pre-owned alicorn salesman.

"Are you sure?" An unfamiliar woman's voice asked. "A school doesn't seem like a private place."

"No one comes into my room at lunch. I don't allow it." Arrogance dripped from his lips, as if he was the only teacher to carry out such a basic feat.

Wren squeezed her eyes shut and tried to stay focused. She could get suspended for coming into his office without permission. She looked around desperately for an escape. There was a window to the outside, but they were on the fourth floor. Levitating wasn't one of her strong points, so if she tried to lower herself down, she would probably break her head. Fortunately for her, the windows between the office and the classroom were clouded. Since she couldn't see out, she hoped that meant they couldn't see in.

"I'm getting tired of not being told things," the woman complained. "I've done everything you asked, and I've gotten nothing in return! Do I get to meet the leader of the organization? When do I get to meet the other Dark Cl–"

"Shhh," Professor Dovin interrupted. "You have to be patient, Melly." Wren could imagine him smiling in the annoying, superior way he always did. "We will tell you more when we come to trust you. Trust takes time."

Wren sucked in sharply. *The Dark Cloud*. That must have been what the woman was about to say. Sweat trickled down her back. Professor Dovin and Melly continued to talk quietly, but Wren wasn't listening anymore. She was too busy panicking. The Dark Cloud was dangerous. If she was discovered now, it would be worse than being expelled.

She could open a portal, but that was forbidden, not to mention dangerous. Unpredictable and uncontrollable, there was no way to know where the portal would open, and one could find oneself in another world entirely. Returning home from a different world was easy. You could always return to the place where you made your first portal. Nothing else about them could be controlled.

Where was Ming Li? She should have been keeping watch. Wren shouldn't have gone along with her friend's scheme to sneak into the office. They had suspected that Professor Dovin was up to something, but had never imagined this.

"The paper is in my office," Professor Dovin said, breaking Wren out of her anxious stupor. Quick, heavy footsteps moved across the floor in the direction of the office. Wren decided. It would be better to fall into the ocean than to be caught by The Dark Cloud. Putting her pointer fingers and thumbs together, she quickly pulled them apart, opening a shimmering silver portal. The door to the office squeaked, and she jumped through without looking back.

Wren fell out of the portal and landed hard. Her hands and knees scraped as they barely stopped her from smacking her face against the cement surface. She inhaled deeply through her nose, ignoring the pain in her hands and the way her arms were shaking. Going through a portal was draining, and she wasn't sure she could stand yet. The wind blew long strands of red hair into her face, obscuring her vision. Thunder rumbled above, but thankfully, there was no rain. Wren had hoped to make a new portal to return home as soon as she landed, but her magic felt exhausted.

A rhythmic, pounding sound, like something smacking against the earth at an even pace, rang in her ears. Once she realized the pounding wasn't only in her head, Wren pushed herself into a kneeling position and took a moment to get her bearings. She was in a park. The houses across the road were crammed together, and in various stages of falling apart. Weathered fences with red words painted across them were surrounded by yards that were green, but overtaken by weeds.

After a few false starts, she managed to get to her feet. Now that she was standing, she could locate the source of the pounding. A boy, a little older than her at fifteen or sixteen, was bouncing a ball up and down and throwing it through a suspended net. Behind him was what appeared to be a children's play area, also covered in red writing, and behind that a grove of trees.

The houses didn't look inviting, so Wren walked carefully across the untended grass towards the boy. In a practiced motion, she pulled a handful of dust from her pocket and sprinkled it over her head. It only took a small amount to make her invisible. She silently thanked her father for always insisting she carry it in case of an emergency. The boy wouldn't be able to see her, but if she made too much noise, he would hear her. She stopped when she reached the cement rectangle he was playing on and observed him.

He was wearing a strange blue shirt. It was silky and hung loose on his tall frame. The shirt was sleeveless, and on the back it had the number 12 with the word *"Dryson"* printed across it. Wren had never seen clothing with writing on it. She had also never seen a shirt with no sleeves or britches that only went to the knee. She wondered if he was trying to show off his muscles.

Wren watched as the boy threw the ball in the net over and over. He never missed. Sweat beaded on his warm brown skin, but he didn't seem to mind. Wren shivered. She hated sweating worse than anything. Being smelly and sticky were things she avoided. The boy was extremely good looking, and if it wasn't for the fact he couldn't see her, she would be embarrassed by her staring. Another wave of exhaustion hit her. It would be awhile before she could go back home. It couldn't hurt to stay here observing the handsome boy. There were definite advantages to being invisible.

Graham sighed. The girl was still hovering nearby, watching him. The air was getting heavier, and the wind had picked up. Any second it might rain, and he wanted to go home. Going home would mean passing her. He threw his basketball into the hoop and snuck a glance over his shoulder. What was she wearing? She looked like someone out of a movie. Her long green dress and black cape blew dramatically in the wind, and her tangled red hair flew wildly around her face. If he didn't get home soon, Aunt Temperance would be fuming, if she wasn't already.

Graham retrieved his ball and sighed again. Tucking the ball under his arm, he walked in the girl's direction. When she saw him coming nearer, she fidgeted with a long, thin gold necklace. She looked like she was younger than him, but not by much. She was pretty, but definitely not Graham's type. People in capes were probably a little odd, in his opinion.

"Hey," Graham said, stopping approximately five feet in front of her. He held out the ball, not sure what to do. "Do you wanna play?"

She looked around, eyes wide, as if he wasn't staring right at her. "Ummm ... me?"

Graham wondered why he didn't just walk around her and go home. "Yes?"

"You can see me?" she whispered, taking a step back.

"I can see you," he said, raising an eyebrow. There were always crazy people in this park. "You should probably go home. It's going to rain soon."

She looked at the dark sky and shivered. "I can't go home right now." She gave her necklace another little tug. "I'm kind of lost."

Graham followed her gaze up to the sky and wondered how this peculiar girl had suddenly become his responsibility. "You're bleeding." He pointed to one of her scraped hands. She dropped the gold chain and looked down, assessing the damage. She quickly folded her arms, hiding her hands in her cape.

"I fell. They're fine."

"Do you live around here? What's your address? I can help you." He pulled his phone out and brought up maps. She shrugged and looked at the ground.

"You might want to wash your hands. There's a restroom over there." Graham pointed to the small brick park bathroom covered in graffiti. "It's probably not very sanitary, though." The girl didn't look up.

"Graham!" a familiar voice yelled. "You are in T-R-O-B-L-E!" Graham's ten-year-old cousin Kaylee was hurtling towards them at full speed, black braids flying.

"You missed the U," Graham said, wishing the little busy body would leave him alone for once. The mysterious girl took a few small steps back.

"I never know what the heck you're talking about," Kaylee growled, putting her hands on her hips in the universal gesture of annoying ten-year-olds everywhere. She looked like her mom, right down to the thin-lipped sneer. "Mom said you were supposed to get home an hour ago to wash Walter."

"She never told me," Graham protested, as he continued to watch the caped girl out of the corner of his eye. She had taken another step back, and she was nervously chewing on her bottom lip.

"Well, how could she?" Kaylee said with a smirk. "Mom didn't know he was gonna go roll around in the mud. And you didn't do the dishes. You're so lazy. Mom's gonna take away all your dumb books if you don't straighten up. You ain't ever gonna go to doctor school, anyway. You are too D-U-M. Mom said you better come home right now. I hope you don't though, cause then I get your lunch."

Graham wondered if Kaylee would ever pass out from talking so fast. He bent over, resting his hands on his knees so he would be at her level. "Tell Aunt Temperance I'll be home after I help this girl."

"What girl?" Kaylee asked, looking around suspiciously. Each turn of her head sent her braids whipping through the air, nearly catching Graham in the face.

Graham held up his hands protectively and rolled his eyes. "The only girl here besides you." Despite getting along with her most days, when Kaylee channeled her mom, she could be one of the most annoying people on the planet.

"I'm Graham Dryson," he said, turning his attention back to the girl. "What's your name?" A raindrop hit Graham's nose and ran onto his cheek.

"I'm Wren," she muttered, looking at Kaylee and stepping back again. She was making distance and was now a good nine feet away from them. Wren inclined her chin at Kaylee. "I don't think she can see me."

"She's just being annoying. It's her favorite thing to do."

"Stop trying to trick me," Kaylee said, crossing her arms. "How did you make that girly voice? You better come home. Mom's already thinking of your punishment for not cleaning Walter."

Graham was sure she was. Aunt Temper, as he liked to call her, liked nothing better than punishing him. They had the cleanest house in the city because of how often she had him clean it.

"I should go," Wren said, her eyes focused on Kaylee.

Graham pointed at her hand. "You need to put something on that to stop the bleeding." A small line of blood was dripping down the side of her dress. She clasped her bloody hands together and nodded. She walked forward at an angle to move around Graham without passing too close to him and moved towards the trees. "Do you have a phone? Should I call someone for you?" he called after her, holding up his cell phone.

"Why are you such a freak?" Kaylee said, baring her teeth. "I'm telling mom you were trying to scare me." She grabbed a stick and chucked it at him. It whizzed past his head and barely missed Wren. She looked back with wide eyes and started running.

"Nice," he said, side-eyeing Kaylee. "You scared her. She's lost; we should help her."

"There is nobody there and I AM TELLING!" Kaylee yelled, as she ran across the park. Graham ran after Wren.

"Wren, wait!" he called. "Let me help you!" Wren looked over her shoulder and ran faster, cape billowing behind her.

Graham should let her go, but there was something wrong about her. Maybe she was on drugs, or maybe she hurt her head when she fell. Graham couldn't help it. After being raised by Aunt Temper, it was hard to see someone in trouble and not help. That was one reason he wanted to be a doctor. Doctors could help people in a way a normal person couldn't.

Wren ran into the trees. Thanks to years of running laps for basketball, Graham had almost caught up to her when she shouted something he couldn't understand and flung her arms out wide. A bright, silvery light flashed, and she disappeared into it. Graham tried to stop, but he was going too fast and plowed through after her. He felt himself falling, and before he had time to wonder what had happened, he slammed into the ground.

About the Author

Kristy Dixon received a degree in English from the University of Utah. She started writing stories when she was seven and never stopped. She enjoys writing fantasy books for middle grade and teens. At home, she spends her time playing board games with her husband and kids and writing. Occasionally she takes part in a Super Mario marathon. She has six chickens and a cat that help keep life amusing. If she isn't playing with her kids or writing, she is usually eating cookies, or wishing she was eating cookies.

Also By Kristy Dixon

<u>The Silver Eclipse Series</u>
Akkron
Boztoll
The Other Continent

<u>Upon a Time</u>
More Than Once Upon a Time

<u>Coming Soon</u>
Trapped Upon a Time